SUMAN'S WALL

A Novel

Dano Vukicevich

☼

"Drink your tea slowly and reverently, as if it is the axis on which the world earth revolves - slowly, evenly, without rushing toward the future."

- Thich Nhat Hanh

I: Suman

The slow procession of morning sunlight began its descent into the valley on Chatima's southern ridge line. Cooled from a long night under the stars, the peak's scattering of prehistoric rock started to glow like embers in an old fire. On these mornings, when Suman basked in the first blue-pink colors of dawn, the silent explosion of the orange sun inching through the snow above could warm his face better than a cup of tea.

Slowly and methodically, he began to hammer one more character into a piece of rock shale with his father's chisel. This one was the character, 'Pad,' the fourth of six characters he carved into stone each of the mornings that he climbed the steep hillside above the village. These simple six syllables, all representing thousands of the Awakened One's observations, had brought Suman patience, love, and peace for nearly two decades.

On his hillside, Suman could hear all the sounds of the valley. The noises reverberated upwards, traversing ancient terraces, trees, and crops before finding their way inside his ears. He loved the river's constant, frothing melodies of crashing water on stone. On that day, the chirping of birds sounded an alarm, as a charcoal-colored cat hunched behind a stack of old timber. Pausing with his chisel, Suman's thoughts drifted into his past.

Suman first remembered his father bringing him on the hour-long walk up the hillside soon after he turned eight years old.

"This is my favorite time of the day," his father, Chetan, had told him then. "After I look at you of course." A smile brighter than the midday sun shone in Chetan's eyes. But Suman couldn't help but laugh at the man. He had always felt his father's love but had never been spoken to so directly about it. His father sat, almost three times the height of Suman, always donning his favorite green and red dhaka topi hat. Normally one would save the traditional hat for special occasions, but Chetan preached to his neighbors that every day was a celebration.

With one arm over his son's shoulder, Chetan reached towards the earth and lifted up a palm-sized stone. His hands caressed the stone as if it was a piece of gold or a glittering diamond. His hands were well-scarred from almost a lifetime of working in the earth and stained a darker shade of brown than the rest of Chetan's body. The recessed lines on his hands would forever be pronounced by an earth-colored hue.

Suman took the stone with both of his hands. He had thought his little, bony fingers looked pathetic next to the fat, muscled digits of his father.

"I want to teach you something."

It was the clearest memory Suman had of his father. Another lifetime later, he can't help but laugh again, as he begins the next character in the stone. When he finished, he placed the stone with the others and sighed, content and calm in the first moments of the day. He looked at his finished work. The stones were nothing more than a reminder of some kind of truth of the world; an explanation of what is inside and its reflection on the outside. It wasn't all the truth, he knew - this is what he loved about his world - just a piece of an ever-changing puzzle.

Suman looked out toward the valley below. When his vision adjusted to the view beyond the stones, their presence was somewhat miniaturized by the vast valley, itself unknowing to a tiny etching in its endless flock of stone.

Hands linked together behind his back, Suman walked down the hillside, pausing briefly to watch the sunlight wash over the thatched roofs of his sleepy village. The sounds of the river below lessened as he descended lower and a tranquil stillness returned. Somewhere below, a yak interrupted the silence. *Probably looking for a female*, Suman guessed. The spring mating would start soon, and the yak herders would begin the arduous journey to the summer pastures. Suman always missed the voices of the yaks in the summer, but the growing season occupied his mind enough that it was only just before and after the journey of the nomadic creatures that he really understood this longing.

When Suman stepped onto the dirt road from the hillside path, a small cloud of dust swirled around his ankles. It had been two weeks since the last snow and already the roads had absorbed the drying effects of the spring sun.

As he rounded the final bend in the road before the prayer wheel-lined entrance to the village, he saw his neighbor, Tauko, coming up the road. With a deep bow, Tauko greeted Suman, then held his hands towards the mountains.

"Have you been welcoming our spring?" Tauko inquired.

"It'll be a fine year. How's your land?" Asked Suman.

"The ground is still thawing."

"You are always welcome to share my garden," Suman responded, gesturing towards his small, cleared patch of earth on the edge of the village.

"You're a good man, my friend, but you know that my family's land always begins late."

"Which is why you're always late for our card games."

Both men smiled wide enough to show their teeth. Tauko bowed and continued walking towards his own plot. Tauko and Suman's fathers were close friends, and since their childhood, the two farmers have always shared an innate, deep bond.

Suman spun the prayer wheels as he entered the village; simple wooden cylinders with intricate carvings, hung under a tiled roof, greeting anyone who entered the village in either direction. He paused before the last wheel. Flags snapped against the wind, their sound mixing with the distinct yet subtle presence of the river below. He breathed in deeply. As he exhaled, he felt calm, yet possessed a new energy for the busy season ahead.

The houses in the village began to wake up. Smoke began rising from the kitchens inside, and then Suman heard his stomach start to stir as well. His mouth watered as he imagined the *dal* bubbling in his wife's pot, and already he could smell a room full of newly-cooked *bhat*. The staple daily meal of mainly rice and lentils had sustained villagers here for generations. His steps began to quicken and lighten as if his feet hardly touched the ground anymore.

His own thatched roof came into view after the next bend in the road. The light brown of the mud walls in the morning sunlight contrasted with the background of green hillsides so dramatically on spring mornings. The deodar cedars proudly showed their fiercely dark green color, seemingly satisfied to watch the snow melt on the slopes around them. Next to the hand-carved front door, Suman's outdoor table, still wearing the red and yellow cloth from the night before, looked particularly inviting.

But before he could reach the door to his home, his daughter, Maya, burst outside, and the wooden door flung against the wall behind it. Maya was giggling mischievously. He scooped her off her feet before she could duck under his legs and spun her through the air. She broke out into a laugh as the warm sun found them on the steps outside.

"What are you up to?" He asked while rubbing his cold nose on her cheeks. She responded with another giggle.

"She thinks she can play without eating first."

Suman turned to face the door and saw his wife, Sanjana, standing with her arms crossed but a smile hidden in her eyes.

"Oh really? Think you can survive only on cuteness?" Suman asked. Maya gave a quick nod and giggled uncontrollably. "Come inside and help your mother spoon out the *bhat*," he said as he scooted her towards the door with a pat on the butt.

"I think I know where she found her beauty," Suman said to Sanjana, and she shook her head.

"Come inside, we have a busy day coming." She ducked under the door frame, hiding her lips, which had started lifting at the corners.

Suman stole one more glance at Chatima Mountain. It was completely blanketed in the morning light, its glaciers reflecting the blue sky above it. This slowly growing giant towered over the other mountains at its flanks and appeared to puff up the chest of a bulking mass. There was no questioning the strength and free will of this upward thrust of earth. Everything in the valley had remained unquestionably obedient to the mountain, and in turn, generations of creatures have flourished during its watch.

The first day of spring planting always started with excited voices from inside the village's houses. Husbands and wives discuss the crops to be planted and yak herders argue about which route to take. The growing season lasted for about six months, and in that period the yak herders had plenty of time to graze their animals and trade for supplies along the valleys south of the village. Like a leopard kitten introduced to the world from its mother's den, the villagers were thrust into the newly warmed atmosphere of the day with bright eyes, full of high hopes for a good season.

Following the first day of planting, there had always been a celebration at the end of the day, and each villager showed off their best clothes, even the farmers who didn't have time to bathe before the festivities. Farmers gathered to discuss soil conditions and predict crop yields, placing exaggerated bets with each other. Typically, the yak herders drank more apple brandy than normal as it was their last big social event until they returned in the fall.

Suman spent his day planting potatoes, eggplant, squash, lentils, tomatoes, corn, and chili peppers in his half-acre plot on the western slope, just behind the apple orchard. He moved slowly with each planting of a seed or quarter of sprouted potato, and he gave the soil above just enough pressure afterward, like tucking a child into bed. His friends had laughed when they watched him planting since many used their feet to cover a seed, but somehow, he always returned to the village at the same time of day as the rest.

Suman accredited this to his rhythm. There was hardly a moment, especially not a long one, when Suman had thoughts outside of his work. Each seed that passed from his bag to his hand to the ground never experienced a delay or uncertainty. He lifted, bent, and stepped in an unconscious rhythm, like a man shuffling to an Earthly beating of drums. But if one could write chords to his planting symphony, it would be excruciatingly repetitive. While he was shuffling, time stretched into irrelevance, and he never noticed the bags of seeds becoming empty until he reached inside to find them empty.

His friends have told him he gets 'lost in his work,' but Suman didn't feel lost at all, if anything, it was a pleasant meander. Everything within his field of vision was vividly clear. He saw each grain of dirt as his fingertips spread them away from a small, thumb-sized hole in the ground. He noticed each chunk of manure, frosted with light-colored soil, as it refused to balance on the edge of the hole. He saw the lines, crisscrossing his knuckles, as his middle three fingers gently flicked some manure further away from the hole. He saw the worms, wiggling in the sudden exposure to daylight, trying to dive deeper into their warm, terrestrial beds. He felt the delicate seeds roll off the tips of a finger and land without a sound in the bottom of each hole.

When he returned to each row of freshly planted seeds, he saw each drop of water, momentarily-suspended midair, before fusing together with the soil, changing the color to a moist, dark brown. He saw each speck of dried dirt on his hand, even after brushing away excess soil on his already dirtied pants.

Dirty. The word always perplexed Suman. Surely the word for being covered with soil, with earth, should be called 'earthy.' He remembered the first time the word 'dirty' was spoken to him in vain. His father had pointed to a trash-filled, concrete drain in the city, telling Suman that he was ashamed at the condition the local population left their streets.

"I can't believe that people can get used to these dirty ditches."

Surely that dirtiness and the dirt that now covered his clothes were not one and the same. The earth, from which Suman watched beautiful, life-giving plants hatch, couldn't be dirty like a trash-filled ditch. If anything, the earth's topsoil was the cleanest surface around. From working year after year in the earth, he knew that the most decomposed organisms were further below the surface, and the top soil was fresh and saw the newest form of interaction with other species.

He once corrected Maya, when she came home crying. She was completely covered in dirt, her face an ink splatter test of the Earth's crust.

"I'm so dirty, Dad, I'll never be clean again."

"You aren't dirty, my beautiful girl, the Earth has just given you a big hug."

When he bathed her, they both watched as the brown-colored water ran downhill into a patch of soil.

"See, the Earth has returned to itself, as it always will. That's just how we will return. Back to the Earth, exactly where we came from."

"But I came from mommy," she retorted.

Suman laughed as he dried her cheeks with a towel. He was content to wait a bit longer to expand on that particular conversation.

Standing up from his now wet rows of fresh seeding, Suman eyed his plot with great satisfaction. He bowed his head towards the Earth, and silently thanked it for providing the gift of food for his family. He looked at his hands, covered in fresh soil.

Walking down from his plot, he spotted several other farmers brushing soil from their clothes, a similar look of happiness shone brightly on their faces.

A bird chirped from a nearby apple tree, quickly darting its head from the empty branches back to him. It maneuvered its head to the side, eyeing Suman from every angle as if to ask where the apples were.

You're a bit early, he thought. *Have patience, my friend.*

When the village-wide celebration began, Suman joined his closest friends in a level pasture that usually served as the site of communal events. His hands still covered with the cool earth, he lifted his cup of tea to Chatima and then to his friends. Once again, he had arrived to the village before sundown and like many, refused to wash off the day's work from his hands.

"For another good year and the soil-covered hands that come with it," he toasted.

"And the warm beds that come with it?" Another farmer suggested.

The men exploded with laughter and touched their cups of tea and glasses of brandy together while exchanging brief eye contact with each man in the circle. Suman sipped his tea and looked across the festivities towards Sanjana. Her eyes glowed from the reflection of a bonfire, and she still looked as beautiful as the day he met her. Her black hair, tied with a red cloth at her neck, hung long until the small of her back. A red and turquoise necklace rested loosely on her tan wool shirt, while the colorful, striped front of her dress slowly danced in the wind. Her cheeks and chin, although soft to the touch, were strongly chiseled, adding to the intensity of her look.

As always, when he held his eyes long enough in her direction, she caught him. It didn't take long before she smoothly lifted her head, noticing his staring, and returned a smile.

Originally from a yak herding family, she had met him in another village, several-days trek away. It was a cold day, but she was walking without a hat, and her hair flew effortlessly in the wind. While his nose was red from the piercing wind, her soft skin appeared immune to the freezing air. She smiled shyly when she noticed him watching her. When he realized his mouth was hanging open, he shut it so fast that his teeth banged together. Embarrassed, he spun around and rubbed his jaw, turning even more red. He heard her giggle, just as his daughter now giggled. It was the most beautiful sound he'd ever heard.

When he told his father that he wanted to stay in that village for a few more days, his father knew why immediately. He had watched the awkward exchange earlier that day and saw how Sanjana was looking at his son. He nodded to his son's request and without a word, left their tent to find Sanjana's family.

That night, Suman waited by their fire for what felt like hours. He wondered what his father might be saying to Sanjana's parents. He knew that his grandfather had asked his grandmother's parents for her hand once, long ago. The tradition in his part of the world required a formal meeting of families before children ever began courting each other.

When his father returned, he walked slowly towards their camp, head forward, and hands loosely entwined behind his back. When he neared the fire, Suman stood up, eyeing his father with a questioning look. His father, seeing his son's look of anxiety, smiled wide.

"She wants to talk to you," he said.

A loud, collective gasp broke Suman from his memory. It was followed by more laughter from the group of men. Suman turned to see a yak herder picking himself up after tripping over a rock near a bonfire. The herder brushed off his coat and waved his arms at the amused neighbors. Tauko laughed and shook his head.

"If spring came more than once a year, the yaks would go mad."

Another villager stumbled into the circle and sat down

heavily as a drunk man does. He belched and several of the farmers chuckled.

"Time fo' cards friends, an' I hope ya brought 'nuff money fo' me to win!" The drunk man announced.

"And what will you buy with your fortune, Ukali? Tauko asked.

"A moto' cycle first, the best you e'er seen. The same tha' movie stars drive," Ukali declared.

A trader had driven a motorcycle into the village two months earlier, during a break in the snowfall, and ever since, Ukali had told everyone he was going to buy one. The roar of the engine had woken Suman that night, and when he left his house to find the noise, he found Ukali and the trader revving the engine on the road.

"My family is asleep Ukali, my friend, can you wait until morning to drive this?" he asked.

Before Ukali spoke, Suman smelled the brandy steaming off the two men. "T'is a ma las' chance ta hear it," Ukali slurred. "He leav' ta 'morra." Since that night, Ukali mentioned the motorcycle at every opportunity, but the other farmers just laughed and shook their heads. Ukali always wanted something it seemed. He was the first to have a radio in his house, and there was a running joke among the farmers that if you put a stone on your roof, Ukali would put two on his own, just to be the one with the highest roof.

The group of farmers played cards the rest of the

evening but kept their money safe from Ukali's hands. Instead, they played with uncooked dal beans. Suman's pile of dal shrunk slowly, as Tauko won several hands. Ukali cornered Suman into a large pot, smiling wide. The drunken smile looked too forced to be true, and Suman followed the supposed bluff. When their cards were revealed, Ukali slapped his knee happily and reached for the pile.

"T'is why ya won't play me fo' real! I almos' took ya outta ta game, Suman." Ukali tossed his cards on the table for the next shuffle.

The game carried on as the festivities around them started to quiet down. Eventually, the women of the village gathered up the children and wished each other a warm night before retiring into the dimly lit houses. The yak herders slept nosily around the fires, and somewhere in the distance, a glacier broke off into a high alpine lake.

One by one, each farmer left the card game to join their families. Walking uphill, back to the village, each family faded into the clear night.

Eventually, only Suman, Tauko, and a snoring Ukali remained in their circle. Ukali's winning pieces of dal were in a pile under his arms.

"I think the sun will be even more kind tomorrow, Suman, and my fields will be ready," Tauko said.

"I hope your corn is taller than Chatima."

"What should we do with our liquor sponge of a neighbor?" Tauko pointed to Ukali, who slept at their feet, with a rock for a pillow. Suman stood up to find an unused blanket from the mess of yak herders and placed it over Ukali.

"One day, that rock will give him a large enough headache that he'll switch to tea."

The two friends chuckled, then sat in the silent memory of the shared sound. "We have two beautiful wives, some crazy children, enough pickles to make our dal bhat spicy for a lifetime..." A tired yawn broke Suman's words.

"What else do we need?" Tauko finished the thought.

II: Jiang

Jiang straddled the metal frame of his red Flying Pigeon bicycle as he watched the black sedan turn onto the gravel road leading to his family's house. With his left foot on the pedal, he leaned onto his right, straining his ankle just enough so the toe of his shoe balanced on the ground. The bicycle, although it was the most beautiful thing he'd ever seen, was far too big for him.

He still hadn't grown like the other boys in his class, but his father told him that as soon as he did, the Flying Pigeon would fit him perfectly. He didn't mind, after all, he was ultimately waiting until he was old enough to buy his own motorbike. That was the order of life, as he saw it. The faster you grew, the more speed you were allowed to manage.

The road to his family's house was bumpy and full of holes, despite how often his father tried to smooth it with shovel-loads of earth and rock. Between the holes, patches of grass grew, kept short by each passing animal. It wasn't a perfect road but it could still be easily negotiated by a careful motorbike rider. Jiang knew from the first time a car attempted the road, that too much speed could snap a very important piece of metal under the front of the car, just as easily as a tree branch snapped under his feet.

The glossy black sedan appeared to be in no hurry, or at least the driver must have been warned about the dangers of driving too quickly here. It slowly edged towards the front of the wooden house, barely emitting any of the brownish-gray road dust from under the wheels. He heard the cranky sounds of his house's front door as it swung open on rusty hinges, and he turned to see his father approaching with crossed arms.

Standing just over five and a half feet, his father was not a large man, but his muscles sprung out from his sleeves and his hands bore the deep, recessed lines of a man who worked outside for a living. He had an intense line of eyebrows above his steady gaze that made some men unable to hold his eye contact for long. The intensity and determination of his posture made him appear taller than he was. A humble but proud man from a long line of farmers, he made his home on Jiang's grandparent's land, about 600 kilometers south of Beijing, in the Shandong Province. Their house rested near a tranquil village, along a gently-flowing river that moved east until it emptied into a large reservoir. Jiang's father had liked to boast that he spent nearly his entire life within a one-hour radius of his home, declaring that their wide valley was the only place worth visiting.

On that morning, his sleeves were rolled up, as they usually were, and the front of his shirt had several strands of loose tobacco from a morning rolling cigarettes on his stomach. While other men who didn't grow much facial hair, trimmed theirs away, Jiang's father kept the small patch below his lips. It formed a half circle and seemed to maintain a one-inch length his entire life. Jiang thought this particular sprouting of hair somehow showed more about his innate ability as a farmer than anything else his father grew.

As the sedan came to an unimpressive, metallic shrug of a stop, Jiang shifted his weight to the left, in order to rest his right foot. The driver of the car slid out of the car, in an almost robotic fashion. His dark sunglasses shielded the ray of sunlight that shone on a lightly wrinkled forehead. He shuffled to each of the rear doors, opening them in a single, smooth motion. The legs of the driver's black suit moved with a barely audible whooshing sound, as he moved around the sedan's trunk.

Jiang didn't recognize the two, sharply-dressed men who stepped out of the rear car doors. They wore suits as well, but the coats had hints of color. It could have been a blue tint. Jiang remembered that the last men in suits who arrived at the house unexpectedly had been old military pals of his father. But this time, his father stood standing, watching the group approach the house without a hint of a smile on his face.

The small amount of dust that rose from the gravel and followed the men seemed to annoy them, and they swatted their pants aggressively to prevent any from settling. With all the calm and flowing movement of the driver, the passengers' awkward movements were almost comical in comparison. They slowly made their way to the house by connecting each patch of grass into a path. Jiang remembered a similar game he used to play when he was younger.

He could have stayed to listen to what this unusual meeting was all about; he knew that the small crawlspace from the outdoor hatch for trash to the indoor kitchen was still unknown to his parents as the perfect place to eavesdrop. But he was already on his way to the creek to meet his classmates. He glanced at the silent driver, who stood guard at the bumper of the vehicle, apparently looking nowhere behind his thick, dark shades.

Jiang looked at his father, trying to catch his eye between the movements of the approaching men. His father, seeing this, waved him onward, before turning his attention forward again. His father gave a shallow bow and opened the door without a word spoken. The men brushed at their pants once more at the top of the porch's steps, then slithered into the house with a whisper of words that Jiang couldn't hear from his distance. Jiang shrugged, kicked off the ground, turned his handlebars, and began to pedal.

The ride over to the creek was only a great distance if the rider was unfamiliar with the local shortcuts. As a fourteen-year-old, Jiang had been an expert in cyclical navigation for over four years. Rather than taking the easy, predictable road around the orchards, with enough speed and courage, a rider could cut the distance in half by taking the rice field route. It was no easy task, and it took nearly an entire summer to master the narrow banks alongside the flooded fields.

The most important factor that determined a successful rice field crossing was traffic. Just one old lady or a lazy water buffalo blocking the path could send even an expert such as Jiang careening into the shallow, murky water. Luckily at this time of day, most women were at the market, surely complaining or bragging about their children, and he hadn't seen any buffalo moving in that direction all morning.

After ten minutes of precision rice berm riding, Jiang was almost to the popular swimming hole at the creek, and he could already hear splashing and the sharp, playful screams of the younger students.

He crossed a single-planked bridge over a drainage ditch from a rice patch and caught several small birds by surprise. The birds, in a panic, shot out of the shade of their hiding place in a small bush, and into the late morning sun. The sound of the flapping wings nearly made Jiang lose his balance, but he recovered in time to come to a skidding stop along the creek's upper bank.

"Well, here he is, finished picking your nose already, Jiang?"

It was Li Jie, his best friend, and also the friend most likely to tease him in front of the other students.

"As soon as you're finished eating what I find." The other students exploded in laughter as Jiang leaned his bicycle on a nearby tree. Li Jie turned to splash water at another student, just as Jiang took two quick strides towards a tree root, which served the kids as a natural diving board. His jump into the water was well-aimed and he landed right next to Li Jie, covering him with a Jiang-sized tidal wave. The action suddenly enticed the group into an all-out water war.

Although Li Jie was Jiang's primary target and he expected swift retaliation, he began taking fire from all sides. He knew the best option was to maneuver around his opponents. First, he dragged his hand quickly in a semi-circle in front of his body, making a wall of water. Then, before the others could regain their sight, he ducked beneath the surface, and slowly, expertly, swam between the mess of splashes and legs in the murky water.

When he reemerged from his underwater hiding place, he was directly behind the group, and he watched, as they continued the war, naive to his disappearance. Without much more hesitation, he propelled thrusts of liquid with both hands at his opponents, giving at least one student a mouthful of creek water. It was Jiang's signature move, but somehow, they still didn't expect it.

The aquatic explosions finally subsided the way they usually did: with one student, near tears, yelling for peace, as he coughed and waded away from the mayhem. In this group of students, they never teased the first to give up, since they were all equally happy to stop and recover from such an intense splash battle.

Under the shade of a row of juniper trees, the wide section of the creek was perhaps the coolest place in the summer. Even though it was just becoming spring, the students, perhaps eager for the warm weather, insisted on starting their weekly meetings at the creek. It was Sunday afternoon and the most important topic of discussion was the next day's classes.

A small breeze blew down the creek from the west, prompting the students to begin searching for their clothes and towels. As the classmates discussed their homework assignments, Li Jie motioned for Jiang to come sit with him on the opposite bank of the creek.

The breeze became stronger as he approached the pebbled bank. The branches of the trees creaked and moaned under the pressure, waving their limbs down river.

"Hey egghead, what are you doing?" Li Jie only smirked at Jiang's playful jab.

"There's something serious happening Jiang," he said quietly. "My father told me about it this morning, and I think your parents might already know. But if they don't, you'll need to tell them."

"Some businessmen came to my house this morning…" Jiang's face lost its smile as he realized his friend was not teasing him. Li Jie was almost a year older, and Jiang had always idolized his knowledge about the world. Somehow Li Jie knew what happened before everyone else did. He had a way of always making the best of situations, as if he could see the future and it wasn't as bad as it seemed.

"Then they know too." Li Jie let out a slow sigh and looked towards their classmates, who were already ridiculing incorrect homework answers. "A lot is going to change around here," he said.

☼☼☼

Jiang could hear his heart pounding against his chest. It was almost as loud as his mother's voice on the other side of the door. He wondered if his parents could hear his heart beating as well as he could hear them talking. His mother was clearly upset. His father's voice rolled through the conversation, while his mother's pitched higher and higher. Then a cupboard slammed shut, half-concealing a shrill curse from his mother.

Jiang had pedaled as fast as he could back home, still soaking wet from the swim. He would have arrived sooner but was delayed after the second turn on the rice berm trail when he forgot to lift his front tire over an old tree stump. His tire pivoted sideways on the root, sending his thin body over the handlebars, then he splashed down, among the flooded rice sprouts.

Now, with mud-laced water dripping off his chin, Jiang decided this wasn't the best moment to approach his parents. The black sedan had already disappeared and his father must have just brought his mother up to speed. Between the slamming cupboards and the rustle of a shopping bag, Jiang figured his mother had just returned home from the market. He took a slow step backward, but the old, wooden planks gave him away. The wood moaned under the pressure of his muddy shoe.

Inside, his mother's voice cut off mid-sentence, and he could feel her listening.

"Jiang?" She called from the kitchen. He stayed motionless and hoped that if he held his breath his heart would also hold its beating.

"I can hear you outside, come in here." She was no fool. "Take off your shoes if they're dirty too."

There were several days that Jiang considered the worst days of his fourteen-year-long life, The first, undoubtedly, was when Zhang Fei pulled down his trousers in primary school. It was also the last time he dared look his primary school crush in the eyes. Pant-less, in front of the entire third-year class. His crush's name was Hui Yin and he always seemed to be paired up with her in groups. He thought she was the prettiest girl he'd ever seen, but he never told her or any friends that. She was staring at him, wide-eyed, with a look of horror because she wasn't staring up at his face.

He tried to take a swing at Zhang but his fallen pants gripped his ankles tightly as he stepped forward and he fell clumsily on his stomach and let out an audible "oomph."

The entire class seemed like they would wet themselves with how uncontrollably they laughed. Jiang was frozen, rigid, and blushing, as he sprawled out, naked butt in the air. The teacher, trying not to break character and laugh too, grabbed Jiang by his shirt and carried him towards the door. Once outside the classroom, the teacher told Jiang he had two minutes to stop crying, then had to rejoin the class. He hadn't even realized he had been crying.

Because of this outburst, the class had apparently fallen behind on the day's work, and the teacher had lost her patience with all of them. She told him they were here to learn, not mess around. He remembered hearing the teacher clapping her hands in the classroom and telling the students it was time to study. He waited until the classroom was quiet, and started to wipe his tears with his shaking hands.

But this particular day, after the first creek day of the year with his friends, may have even topped that as the worst day, at least that's how he felt, standing in muddy socks, just inside the door frame. After his mother explained why the black sedan had shown up at the house, Jiang shook his head in disbelief. Even though his best friend had already warned him this was happening, hearing the words from his mother's mouth suddenly made it all too real.

It wasn't just sadness that he would have to leave his childhood home. Of course, it was the only house he had ever lived in, but also the awful feeling deep in Jiang's stomach must have been sympathetic pain. He felt the sadness on the faces of his parents also. He felt pain for the distraught, empty looks in front of him. He felt sick inside, and he felt increasingly small. He wanted to melt into the floorboards, and like spilled butter, dissolve and disappear under the old, cracked wood.

The two men had been real estate developers and had arranged with the local government to purchase the family farm, along with the land of their neighbors. The deal had already been made, contracts signed, planning commission meetings concluded, sketches drawn up, and even a new town name was being discussed. Even though Jiang's family had always worked the land, it technically belonged to the government, and it was their position that a new development would be better for the region and the country as a whole.

The developers quoted the Premier, telling Jiang's father that 'urbanization was driving the economy into the future. They needed to stay ahead of the trend of the country's population moving into cities, where they could work and become a modern family. If a region could compress its agricultural space into productive and efficient zones by using more mechanical automation, the villagers could be free to enjoy the comfort of modernization, without slaving away in their fields. It would be a big change for the farming community indeed, but a noble progression. As the region demonstrated its ability to expand and increase productivity, more funds would be allocated to the region from the central bureau, thus bettering the standards of living indefinitely.'

When Jiang's father asked if they had considered that a farmer might enjoy his lifestyle, the developers explained that the technicalities of the situation shouldn't concern the farmers, it was in the interest of all to move forward. They couldn't expect an uneducated class member to fully grasp the situation. It was the fate of the land and the farm would have to go. Cities were expanding, and their village, if they didn't modernize, would only hold the region back. The land to the north and the market, where Jiang's mother had just bought a week's worth of rice and eggs, was to be removed to make room for what the developers called a 'modern shopper's paradise.'

The developers envisioned a thriving metropolis on

what they saw as an antiquated agricultural scene. Plans were set to construct one of the many 30-floor apartment buildings in place of Jiang's house, accessed by wide boulevards, which ultimately would lead to the centralized shopping zone. The eyes of the developers lit up as they spoke as if the village was a canvas to paint their masterpiece. They further described fountains, glistening with thousands of LED lights by night, strutting out from the courtyards. The currently rudimentary creek would be widened, lined with comfortable footpaths, and straddled by an elegant bridge, complete with European-styled statues.

Jiang's father asked what the people in the buildings would eat if the crops disappeared. The two men looked at each other, smirking. They explained that there were several industrial farms overproducing nearby, and the community would have too much food. Before he could ask more questions, they told him not to worry about a factor that certainly didn't concern himself or his family.

The men's faces were not quite aggressive, but instead, as their explanations continued, had begun to look almost bored. It was as if they were annoyed that the farmer's family had been living on this space without once lending extra consideration towards economic expansion. Now here they were, with the degrading task of informing the locals. When asked how many people would be living here, the men told Jiang's father that they expected at least three hundred thousand within the first year, and many more after that. It was going to be the city of the future. Something other countries would envy. They told Jiang's father he should be proud to be the former resident of such an impressive statement to the world.

With the memory of the developer's words still hanging in the air of the house, Jiang's mother held her son closely. His father stood in the kitchen, gazing out at the green and brown fields beyond the window's uneven glass. The blue paint of the window frame was chipped around the handles and the handle screws needed tightening; a project he had intended to repair the following week. He saw the four wooden chairs on his terrace, one with a leg repaired with a piece of an old broom. His friend, Weng Fei, had broken it one night after too much rice wine. He tried to imagine 300,000 bodies in a space where he could only now see one buffalo and the man trailing it with a long stick.

"Where will we live?" Jiang looked at his father, who was now staring at the floor of the kitchen. He looked up at his mother, but she only tightened her hold. Her hug felt warm and strong, yet he could feel the distance of her aching heart.

"They've offered us...an apartment...and... a subsidy," his father slowly managed to reply.

"You know that won't be enough," Jiang's mother said. Her tone had lost its anger and instead was punctuated with a low sigh. "We'll have to find other work."

"I can work. I don't need to go to school." Jiang deepened his voice to try to sound brave, but it came out awkwardly. His young pipes cracked and raised his voice uncomfortably high.

"Nonsense," his mother retorted sharply, as she pushed him away from herself. Looking him in the eyes, she said plainly, "You are the future of this family. You will study as much as possible."

The sound of his father lighting a cigarette broke the brief silence his mother's words had left. His gaze found the window again.

"What's wrong with being antiquated?" He asked no one in particular. He took a slow pull from his cigarette. "My father was antiquated, and he was the strongest man I'd ever seen."

III

Suman was repairing the hose that connected his field's irrigation to the mountain spring above the village. Several springs passed under the snow above, percolating into the village on the way to the river below. The source flowed throughout the year and was a commodity the residents had relied upon for generations.

Earlier that day, a local flock of finches managed to find a weak point in the well-weathered irrigation line, and haphazardly peppered holes in it with their tiny beaks. The sun overhead baked Suman's body until he removed his shirt and sprayed his face with the icy water. Instantly cool, he fitted the damaged hose with plugs made from stick ends. It would suffice until a new length of hose could be found. When he finished, he descended to his field to check on the moisture of the soil, as he suspected it was feeling the heat from the sun as much as he was. His mind drifted as he picked at the grass growing around his chili plants, careful to just take enough that his plants would be the dominant species in the plot.

"Nature makes its own future." He heard the words of

his father. "We are allowed to borrow just what we need, but we must respect the need of nature first."

Then, sharp shouts from below cut through his reminiscing, reaching his ears, and snapped him to his feet. He couldn't quite hear the words, but he saw the figure of a man below, waving his arms excitedly, and motioning for Suman to come down. He dropped his tools and bounded downhill. As he got closer, he realized it was Khayo, a friend who tended the apple trees in the adjacent orchard.

"Come quickly Suman, there's a problem at the river!"

Both men sprinted down the road to the river, while flexing their toes to keep their sandals underfoot. They found a dozen villagers gathered at the rocky embankment near the water. A water buffalo had waded too far into the river and was now pinned against a broken tree limb just above a series of churning rapids.

Two men were tying ropes into lassos, while the others stood in the thigh-deep water along the shore, shouting with excitement and concern. Suman joined one of the men with a lasso, and reached for the end of the rope. The other farmer pulled the knot tight, then began to twirl the looped end over his head. He released the rope mid-spin and sent it flying towards the buffalo. It landed an arm's distance from the head of the animal and sank into the water. They pulled the rope out of the river, as another man tossed the other rope. That missed too, landing flat and limply even farther away. Tauko yelled something inaudible from behind them. Tauko moved to Suman's side, relaying a better technique to the farmer with the lasso. The man nodded and tossed the end to Tauko, who carried the loop into the shallow part of the river. He edged closer to the current, while Khayo and another man took hold of Tauko's shirt to keep him in place. Then Suman and another held the following shirts, creating a link to less turbulent water. Tauko spun the lasso high over his head and thrust it forward with a grunt.

The rope sailed high in the air. For a moment, the circle of the lasso paused in the air, and the sound of the river too seemed to disappear within the brief lapse of motion. The rope found its target, falling directly onto the buffalo's head. Suman pulled at his end, the rope cinching around the neck. The other men dropped the second rope and rushed to Suman's side. The veins in his neck looked ready to burst as the first man grabbed a piece of the rope. They each lined up behind Suman, tugging towards land. Their muscles strained through their shirts as they clenched their teeth against the weight.

The water flowed against their efforts and their feet sank in the soft river bottom. Suman couldn't tell if they were sliding further into the river or if the buffalo was getting nearer. The buffalo began to bellow, its neck already strained upwards, away from a bubbling mess of water under the branch. Then, in some sort of foreboding outcry, the buffalo screamed. It was a loud, frightened yell that clung to life, but one that knew fate before it was delivered. The rope snapped. The release of the massive tension sent the five men backward into the shallow water.

Frantically, the men jumped to their feet, as another

farmer joined the group with the second rope. Suman sat, up to his neck in the cold water, watching the man attempt a new toss of rope. He felt it coming. He knew the opportunity was lost. The man cranked his arms to his chest, pulling in the rope, but before he managed another throw, the tree limb cracked. Time paused again. The buffalo locked the gaze of its one visible eye into each of the watching eyes on shore. It didn't scream. It must have also felt it. Then it went under.

Seconds passed, which could have easily been an eternity each, while each man looked helplessly into the rapids. Downriver, they saw the head bobbing between exposed boulders, before disappearing again in the rushing, white-capped torrent.

It was the middle of spring, and the river was alive with intensity and strength from the melting snow. The men collapsed on the beach and watched as the futility of their efforts manifested in a depressing cloud around them. After a long silence, each slowly rose to their feet. Suman asked the group whose buffalo it was.

"It was Ukali's," a man named Resham responded, keeping his eyes on the ground.

"Where is he?" Suman asked, searching the faces around him.

"His herd may be upriver, but it doesn't mean he is," came another reply.

The men were silent. They all shared a moment of pity, for both Ukali and his lost buffalo.

As they walked back to the village, someone found Ukali. Fast asleep under a rock shelter with an empty bottle at his feet. The remaining buffalo, seemingly indifferent to their caretaker's snoring, grazed on the hillside behind the shelter.

Tauko approached, gently tapping on Ukali's shoulder. Ukali didn't move, until Tauko yelled, sharply, inches from his face. "Ukali!"

Ukali opened his eyes achingly, the red, haziness in them obvious and painful-looking in the still-fierce afternoon sun.

"One of your herd fell into the river. We couldn't save it," reported Tauko with his head bowed, holding the torn part of the rope outstretched in his hands.

Ukali squinted towards the group, shifting his gaze across a few of the faces. Then he shut his eyes and turned towards the stone wall. Tauko glanced back at the group, then reached out to shake Ukali awake again, but Khayo took his arm at the elbow. Tauko turned to meet Khayo's eyes and nodded. There wasn't anything left to say. Ukali's ways were known to the whole village. He did great damage to himself and his livelihood. But he had been lost a long time before the loss of the buffalo. Still, the men had known Ukali for a long time, and with the anger and disappointment they may have felt, there was also pity. Pity and perhaps apathy. Many had tried to save their lost neighbor, and most had given up years ago.

The men walked back uphill and without any words began to return to their fields or homes. Suman trailed slightly behind the group as they neared the village.

The constant, low humming sound of the river was occasionally broken by a brief gust of wind, fiercely trying to hold onto the high branches of nearby trees. Suman noticed the trees, on the other hand, seemed to dance gracefully around the air. Suman's mind drifted toward nature's graceful display of juxtaposition. Would he know the sound of wind without the existence of trees, without bells hanging outside a house, without something to disrupt the path of the wind? Suman decided he needed the trees to further understand the wind, and just as necessary, the wind to become more intimately aware of trees.

His thoughts returned to the lost buffalo. There was never one angle to view life through. Why else was humankind given two eyes to see through? He knew that a scene of tragedy could only be realized as a tragedy if one already was familiar with joy. When something was funny, it was only because Suman knew something else that had been sad or serious. These contrasting events never needed to happen separately as well, he knew, because he had seen countless displays of comedy that were not considered funny to someone else involved. The drowning of a buffalo as a comedic act was surely a stretch too far and sinister for his imagination, but he could identify a comparably positive scene that simultaneously occurred. The incident had brought a large group of men together, quickly acting on behalf of another being. Difficult times can make the witnesses stronger and more united.

When a tragedy falls on us, we can respond in an infinite number *of ways. Overall, they can be positive or negative. Is the response improving our ability to live through struggle or hinder it? We tried to help the buffalo. Ultimately, we failed, but if it happens again, would that experience better prepare us? Was this a good experience to have or a bad experience? Can any experience be bad if I am still living? If life is a gift, then what is my mind...*Suman saw ahead, the impending spiral of philosophy waiting for his already busy mind, and decided to bring them to a halt with an inward chuckle. He knew his mind well enough to know there was no end to introspection and this dissection of nature, and he still had work to do.

He walked behind his neighbors, up the path, his hands comfortably stretched behind his back, and watched a good moment unfolding, as the trees again started their graceful dance in the howling wind.

In the evening, Tauko and Suman were drinking tea outside Khayo's house, as their children ran around his small front yard. Maya and Khayo's daughter, Rakshya, had always been inseparable. They were born only a month apart, and were constantly inventing games and creating their own worlds inside the world their parents resided in.

"Here, uncle," Maya said to Tauko, offering a handful of mud from the garden. "It's magic dal."

"Oh, how nice of you. So, what can I do with it?" Tauko humored the two girls, who responded with giggles. "It's not really magic," Rakshya offered. Maya bumped her roughly on the shoulder with her own and shushed her friend.

"You know, I think I'm already quite full from your mother's dinner, how about I have some for breakfast?" Tauko said, looking towards the table with a grin. The girls laughed and ran into the house, where the men could hear them let their mothers in on the joke. Then they burst, full speed from the house as Sanjana yelled through the window, "…and wash your hands when you're done!"

Shifting his weight on his seat, Khayo interrupted the distant sound of their daughters laughing on the street. "What should we do about Ukali?"

"What can we do?" Tauko replied. "Someday he'll just have to learn to pace himself or he'll lose his whole herd. But we've each tried. Suman knows better than anyone that the solution is within Ukali alone."

"But it's not only the buffalo that concerns me," Khayo said as he reached for the pot of tea, offering it around the table before pouring his cup full again. "Someday he will bring his mess to our doors."

"He hasn't yet," Suman responded. "We've seen this behavior for years already, and this is the first buffalo that succumbed to his *mess.*" He lifted his eyebrows with the emphasis on the last word.

They sat still, appearing to be deep in thought, but each man's mind as blank as the high blankets of snow looking down on them.

"He needs a good woman. Maybe then he will find something more important to spend his money on." Khayo offered. The men chuckled at the idea.

"Perhaps you're right," says Suman. He remembered that Ukali had an unfortunate experience with women in his earlier years, but felt it wasn't information he needed to share. Long ago, Ukali would confide in him more than the other villagers. While Suman felt he could never save the lost man, at least he felt it was appropriate to keep certain aspects of Ukali's life private.

"Well, until Ukali's actions disrupts our own lives, what can be done…" Suman began.

"But then what was today?" Khayo interjected. "I'll never forget the last look the buffalo gave us."

"But Khayo," Tauko began. "It was showing us peace. It was showing us what we would want to show. Acceptance. It let go as the tree let it go. "

"A humble buffalo," Khayo agreed. "Although still a horrible scene to watch…"

Suman was about to lend his own thoughts when the girls returned with a handful of flowers and began passing them out to the adults.

"Well, this certainly is an improvement. Is it a magic flower, Maya?" joked Tauko.

"Flowers are always magic," Maya responded quickly.

Sanjana exited the house and joined her husband at the table. Her hand on his shoulder signified the closing of the evening, and Suman gave his friends a nod before picking up a yawning Maya.

They gave their warm wishes to their hosts, each putting their hand over their hearts to express their thanks. Then, husband and wife started down the road to their house. Tilting his head out from behind Maya's head, Suman snuck a glance at Sanjana.

"Is everything alright?" She asked.

"When we're together, everything is perfect." She rolled her eyes, which reflected the moon above them. She nudged him lightly with her shoulder and looked forward, smiling brightly.

The night was lit by a waxing moon, and the thundering river below reminded the couple not of the day's sad events, but of the humbling effect that their place in the valley presented. Without having to say it, they both knew what a powerful world they lived in, and they both looked at their daughter, and back at each other. Suman stopped Sanjana on the road and kissed her. As soon as their lips touched, Maya began to snore loudly. They had to hold back laughter out of fear of waking the tiny, energetic girl. The rage of the river quieted down as they overtook the last hill before their house. Once inside, Suman laid Maya on her bed and fastened a mosquito net under her mattress.

"Goodnight my magic girl."

As he slowly walked towards his room, the familiar creaking on floorboards gave sound to his careful steps. He drifted into his room, floating through the dream-like lighting of the moon that shone through the small windows. He noticed Sanjana changing into the long gown she usually wore in bed. He stood at the threshold of the doorway and watched her move towards the bed. As she climbed in, he turned off the oil lamp above to door with a silent twist of his fingers. The glow from the moon replaced the lost light, casting a thin veil of blue tones across the bed. His eyes found Sanjana's hair shining delicately above her face. He used the light and memory to guide himself into the bed next to her and felt her arms searching for him beneath a yak-hair blanket. *What else do we possibly need*, he considered quietly, afraid that if his thought was too loud, it might disrupt the fragile moment.

☼☼☼

The spring planting brought a full crop for Suman and his village, and by the end of summer, they prepared for a large harvest. The summer had passed by with ease. Each day the farmers tended their fields, the buffaloes splashed about lazily in the springs, children sprinted around the village, back and forth from their homes and school, the women in the village kept the air alive with laughter and calls after their children. Occasionally a trader would pass through, impressing everyone with something new brought from the city far away. One day, a television was plugged into one of the generators, and everyone gathered to watch a series of music videos. Although the entire village was mesmerized by the device, only Ukali and one other family bought a television set, for which Ukali sold off a buffalo. The summer passed by like most before it, without incident, but with many blue-skied days and the occasional breaking apart of a nearby glacier under the melting heat of the sun.

One day, Suman stood triumphantly on the edge of his garden and looked at his stocks of corn, tomato plants as tall as his daughter, chilies pointing towards the sky, and the potatoes growing happily under the rich earth. It was going to be a big harvest. He began to salivate thinking about the fresh-tasting meals his crop would soon bring. He smiled contently as he watched the flight of a group of birds overhead, maneuvering in disorienting circles above the apple orchard. That particular variety of apple was used to ferment into a strong brandy. He never drank much alcohol, but preferred the energy that raw apples gave him. On the other side of the valley grew several other varieties that were eaten seasonally or cooked down into spiced chutney. Remembering that he had traded a bag of chilies for apples that morning, he reached into his pocket and pulled out a fist-sized, golden apple.

The initial crunch broke the silent air of the afternoon, as he squatted, chewing noisily next to a chili plant. He finished the apple, core and all, then collected a handful of chili peppers to dry on a shallow wicker basket that rested on the roof of the family bath hut. Once below, after he laid out the chilies, he entered the doorless hut to bathe. He had purposely put the door of the bath facing the river for added privacy, and looking out towards the silent guideline, he started to wakefully dream about the first time he and Sanjana tested the bath. A cool breeze drifted into the open frame, his toes feeling the freshness of the mountain air as he poured a ladle of warm water over his head. His harvest would be sufficient to fill the needs of his family once again. His mind was calm. After his last ladle of water, he joined his hands in front of his chest in silent prayer, gently resting his chin on his fingertips. He thanked the earth, its soil, and the mountains for the abundant water and its omniscient protection.

The next day, he was walking up the road to his garden and found Ukali coming down towards him with a sly grin thick on his lips.

"Namaste Ukali, you look happy!"

"Namaste my friend," Ukali said. His voice was so coherent that Suman was sure his eyebrows gave away his surprise. "And goodbye to you as well. I traded the last of my buffalo and am on my way to Kathmandu!" Suman looked into Ukali's eyes, searching for the drunken eyes that often looked through a person rather than at a person, though he couldn't smell any beer or brandy.

"I didn't know you were moving back to the big city," Suman said.

"I just decided today. It's been a long time coming. It is time to finally do something great with my life." Suman smiled genuinely at his neighbor. "Do not fear, my friend, I will return soon, with enough money to buy televisions for the whole village!" Ukali declared.

"Well, don't worry about one for me, I don't see the appeal to be honest."

"Oh, my simple friend. There is a whole world out there."

"Indeed." Suman smiled. "But, forgive my intrusion, how will you find money?"

"There is always money in the city. I should know. So today, I got rid of the rest of my herd to Tauko's brother, and am going to find my fortune, since you scoundrels won't let me gamble with money here," he said with a chuckle. "Be well my friend, and remember that there is more to life than farming."

"Alright my dear Ukali, be safe in your travels, but remember that there is more to life than money"

"Oh, my poor Suman, someday we'll all need money. Chili peppers cannot buy motorcycles after all."

Suman forced a grin and gave Ukali a deep bow. Ukali spun around on his feet, readjusted the pack on his back, and began to whistle happily as he walked down the dusty road toward the edge of the village. It was a long walk to the next village that had buses to the capital, Kathmandu, almost a full day's march. Suman shook his head but wished the buffalo herder a happy journey.

Farther along, Tauko met Suman on the road.

"Did you see him?" Tauko asked. Suman nodded and

then shook his head again.

"Ukali the businessman," Tauko laughed. "My brother said he'd happily return the buffalo back to Ukali if he returns. He said they're impossible to control." Both laughed hard and joined in a deep sigh. Whatever the outcome, they were glad to see Ukali clear-eyed, and with a goal in his mind that wasn't the bottom of a bottle.

That night, Sanjana and several other women made a special dal bhat for Suman and his friends to celebrate the first big harvest. The food tasted incredible. Fresh chilies, potato and cauliflower curries, stacks of warm bhat, the local word for rice, and a thick buffalo yogurt to counter the spices that made them sweat through the delicious meal. After dinner, each farmer had to lay horizontally to stretch out their stomachs.

"I'm so full, I couldn't look at grain of bhat," Khayo said letting out a belch that sent a wave of giggles through the smaller, kid's table.

"I'm so full I don't want to ever eat again!" Maya added.

"I'm so full, I...I..." Suman began to mock snore mid-sentence, sending the children into hysterical laughter.

The night was clear and peacefully still. The small lamps around the tables allowed the stars to dominate the sky, and the farmers took turns talking about the wealth of food they were harvesting and what meals their wives were going to make for the other men. A friendly competition usually followed these types of discussions, with each man arguing who was married to the best cook in the village.

The next morning, the men met each other outside Suman's house. They decided to spend the morning making an enormous swing for the children of the village, from huge bamboo poles bought the week earlier from a trader. They dug four holes, buying a quarter of each pole, then used rope to tie pairs together, bending the flexible wood together. The tension on each corner stabilized the knots enough until they used an additional pole as a crossbeam, on which the rope for the swing would be tied. It took them most of the day, and after the swing was tied securely, they all collapsed in laughter and exhaustion.

They looked up at their creation.

"Who has energy to yell for the children?" asked Suman. He didn't notice Sanjana standing over them, barefooted, a red sari flowing at her ankles. She laughed loudly; her head tilted up towards the swing. She shook her head, thin silver earrings bouncing gently on her upper jawbone.

"Maya! Come quickly!" she yelled towards the house. The group heard muffled shouts of joy from inside the house, and Maya and several friends burst outside and shrieked as they bound down the grassy slope to the swing.

Sipping afternoon tea behind the swing, many of the villagers laughed and offered commentary as the children took turns swaying up and down. Their tiny bodies looked like dolls, as they dared each other to push the wooden seat of the swing higher. Two of the mothers took turns to make sure each child shared time with the new toy. The makeshift line of children squirmed while they waited. A few kids even broke out in spontaneous dance moves as their excitement grew. A general happiness floated among the villagers, and silences were broken by gasps as some older children jumped from the swing, kicking their feet to their sides.

"What are you building tomorrow?" A small boy looked up inquisitively at Khayo and a group of farmers.

"A new school," Khayo replied with a smirk. The boy imitated vomiting, holding his belly and turning an open mouth to the ground. He spun around and ran to deliver the terrible news to his friends.

The sounds of the rope creaking against the bamboo and children playing were heard until the sun dipped beneath the rocky, still snow-covered peaks. When it was time to collect their little ones, some parents had to physically pry them from the ropes of the swing. Other children negotiated their positions in line for the following day.

The summer's warmth faded within a few weeks, and the colors of autumn began to show proudly throughout the valley. Rounds of autumn harvesting occupied the farmers for weeks, to the same fervor and determination as the swing occupied the lives of their children. As the harvest progressed, the village began making preparations for the winter months. Extra buffalo dung was stored for fuel for kitchens and heating. Food was moved into store rooms, yak hair blankets brought out of storage and cleaned, and parents knitted new sweaters for the children that grew taller over the warm season. And so, the days became shorter and the pace of life grew more hurried. Calm, confident movement, but daily tasks accelerated in preparation.

Maya was helping Suman pick the last squash from his crop one day when Tauko approached their farm from below.

"Namaste neighbors!" he called out as he stepped carefully around Suman's irrigation lines.

"Hi uncle!" Maya said. "Are you hungry?"

Suspecting another handful of mud, Tauko replied, "I just ate my fill of magic dal my son cooked this morning."

"Alright, well you know where to find me," she said, before skipping towards the other end of the field.

"How are you, Tauko?" Suman looked up with his shirt full of corn.

"Well, thanks. I've just finished in my field, and wanted to help if I can."

"This is the last of the squash, and Maya has a pocket full of chilies." They sat on the ground and watched Maya chase a bird through the field. Tauko opened up his bag to reveal a bottle of beer and two glasses.

"Is it that time of year already?" Suman shook his head as he spoke. "How the years drift by faster with every year we gain."

"Indeed, my friend, or is each year just a smaller fraction of your long life?"

"Or are my bones moving slower while the world continues full speed?"

"Hah! And you are the younger of us. But tell me, how is it that even though I plant later than you, I'm always the first to finish harvesting?"

"You're the hungriest?"

"Said the man with the biggest belly," Tauko said, grinning and patting his stomach. They touched their glasses together and tasted the beer. It was more bitter than Suman remembered.

"What type of beer is that?" he asked Tauko.

"It's all they had. It's Chinese. Imported something or other."

"They should stick to building motorcycles." Despite the taste, the men took their time on the hill, sipping the beer, and marveling at the mountains in front of them. Slowly, Tauko began searching through his bag for something.

"I'll drink this out of tradition, but one's enough," Suman said, holding up his glass. Tauko looked up confused, then chuckled brightly.

"This is better than a stale beer," he said before unwrapping a stone from a scarf. It was shaped precisely like Chatima Mountain. The resemblance was unmistakable. "For your mantras, my friend."

With his left hand on his heart, Suman took the gift. He was happy he came to the field prepared that day. He was someone that couldn't bear receiving a gift without returning one as soon as possible. He reached into his pocket, outstretching one leg to dig in deeper, then pulled out a deck of cards. Each card was illustrated with a different picture, showing scenes of mountains and forests.

"An appropriate theme with such a view," Tauko said, pointing at the snow-capped peaks. They played a few hands of cards, each winning once, then Tauko winning the third. After finishing their glasses, they descended the hill back to the village with Maya in tow. It was a quiet evening, the silence scattered only with Maya's sporadic whistling.

Lying in bed that night, Suman couldn't sleep. He shifted his long legs, feeling not quite aching but a restless annoyance within his tired kneecaps. He looked over at his sleeping Sanjana, her chest rising and falling without a sliver of sound. A tinge of jealousy draped over his chest. He shifted the lenses of his brown eyes at the ceiling. He wholeheartedly knew he was happy. He was content. His mind felt empty yet busy. He tried to will his body to tiredness by feigning a yawn. He forced his eyelids to shutter but they lurched open on invisible springs.

After what felt like hours, he stood up and walked out of the room to make tea. Sitting at the table outside, feeling the cold winds of an approaching winter drift down the valley, he watched a faint light downriver. It looked larger than a person, and the distance made it impossible to hear any noise. He watched the light climb farther up the road. His eyes anticipated each turn the light had to take; he knew the road up the valley well enough that he could walk it blindfolded.

The light moved faster than any man or animal could run. *A trader perhaps? Only a motorcycle could move like that.* Then as the light rounded a curve, it split from itself and one light became three. As the distance between the lights grew, he understood that one must be a motorcycle, but the other might be a vehicle since those two beams remained a fixed distance apart. He'd never seen a car that far up the valley before; no bus had ever attempted the road. Eventually, the lights stopped in the last village before his own, and they were silently extinguished. His eyes adjusted their focus and the entire valley stood silent, hints of trees and rocky outcrops barely exposed under a half-moon lamp. The mountains and Suman waited, watching the darkness. They watched until Suman's eyelids finally became heavy and pulled him inside.

IV

Jiang woke to someone screaming. At first, he imagined he was hearing things - that it was a scream within a dream that had woken him - then he heard it again. Short, piercing shouts came from the front of the house. He quickly pulled on his pants, flung a shirt over his head, and threw open his bedroom door. He followed the sound to the front door where he finally recognized the voice as his mother's. He realized he had never heard her scream before.

"You're mad! They'll throw you all in prison!" His mother yelled from outside.

"*Hien*, come with me or stay and pack your things, but I won't leave without trying!" His father shouted back. The emphasis put on his mother's name was acute and serious. "Wake up our son at least!" his voice sounding farther away.

Jiang swung open the front door faster than he intended, sending the outer doorknob crashing into the side paneling of the porch. Hien spun around, briefly locking eyes with Jiang, then turned back towards her husband.

Her husband was walking down their driveway with several other men. He continued on, head bent forward, ignoring the next words. as if no sound hurled at his back could catch up to his ears.

"What are we going to do when they arrest you?" Hien reached one arm back towards the house, stretching a finger out towards Jiang. "Tell me! Jianyu! You'll leave your son! Damn you, Jianyu!" She cried out, her voice cracking into a higher pitch.

In her frustration, she bent over and grabbed a small stone, standing up and throwing it at the group of men. The stone bounced several times in the dirt, far behind them. Jianyu and the others took no notice of the stone, walking until they were out of sight.

"What's going on?" Jiang put a hand on his mother's shoulder, letting her turn into him, as she reached over his neck with her own hands. She hugged him tightly, then taking his shoulders, pushed him half an arm's length away.

"I love your father, Jiang, but he is a fool. A big, fool. He and his friends are going to block the road into town. They want to stop the bulldozers from entering the town." Tears freely streaked down her face; her mouth trembled slightly as she spoke.

"But I thought we had a few more days before we leave?"

"Our neighbors came over this morning and said they had just heard that bulldozers were heading this way. A dozen of them, strapped to giant trucks. They want to clear us out early."

"But that's not fair…what can we do?"

"We can't do anything, my son. They have decided, whatever they want, will happen to us." Hien turned, squinting her eyes toward the road, with a look that was altogether angry, tired, and sad. Jiang watched the lines on the corners of her eyes bunch together and moved as she spoke. "There's certainly nothing a few old fools can do to stop the trucks."

Jiang peered past his mother, seeing the bend in the road where the group of men disappeared; then glanced back towards the house. His bicycle leaned against the side of the house.

"I'm going to talk to him," Jiang said, pulling his shoulders up and chest out. He ran to his bicycle, with Hien following close behind.

"Ok, good…that's good Jiang, maybe you can reason with him." She stood at the front steps of the house, wiping her eyes with her sleeve. "I'll finish packing our things. But stay out of the truck's way, Jiang. I don't want both of my boys trying to be heroes."

Jiang mounted his bicycle, looking at his mother's face. "Everything will be fine," he said, hoping his voice was as brave as he tried to make it.

He pedaled away from the house as fast as he could, kicking up clouds of dust as he bounced over each bump in the road. Before rounding the corner, he glanced back, seeing his mother open the front door of the house.

When he finally skidded to a stop at the main road into town, a small crowd had already gathered near the bus depot. Beyond the onlookers, Jiang spotted his father and eight other men sitting farther down the road. They sat, cross-legged, with their arms locked together, their bodies stretching across the width of the asphalt. Jianyu had his head pointed directly down the road, his chin a hair higher than the rest.

Jiang let his bike fall onto the ground, hopped over the frame, and took off in a sprint towards the sitting men. Before he could get more than a few strides, a strong hand snatched his right arm, almost pulling his shoulder socket out as the hand kept him in place.

"Where the hell are you going, Jiang?" He spun back towards the voice, meeting the eyes of his school teacher. She was a large woman, with wide shoulders. Jiang had always imagined that she could hold a student in the air with the palm of one hand. She towered over most of the parents of the children she taught and had been a boxer in her early years before settling into the countryside. Now she watched Jiang with furrowed brows, waiting for an answer; a look Jiang remembered well from class.

"That's my dad on the road," he replied.

"Of course, it is," she said, slightly annoyed. "He's a brave man. My husband is out there too. Brave or complete idiots, I actually don't know."

"I'm going to tell him that my mom…" Jiang began.

"You'll stay right here with the other children. Let the adults make their own choices, Jiang." She motioned to a group of his classmates, standing off to the side of the crowd. Li Jie met Jiang's gaze and motioned him over. Jiang pulled free from his teacher's grip and jogged over to his friend.

"Is your...dad...out there too?" Jiang said, trying to breathe between his words.

"Nope. He's packing up our house. But the neighbors are in there. Man, your dad is crazy - shit, here come the trucks!"

Jiang turned back to the road, following the line of Li Jie's pointed finger, to see a line of enormous trucks cresting over the last hill on the road. The caravan of vehicles was flanked by black SUVs with two military motorcycles leading them.

The line of vehicles didn't slow down until just before the line of sitting men. The two motorcycles swerved to a stop at the opposite ends of the men, while the SUVs parked with quick, tire-screeching motions, in a semi-circle directly in front of them. The line of men stayed put, but the boys could see some of the men adjust their weight and look among themselves with quick turning heads.

Some people in green, military uniforms, stepped out of the vehicles, a look of annoyance on each of their faces. Several of them opened the rear doors of the SUVs, and then a few men in black suits stepped out. They wore black ties and sunglasses, and seemed

55

almost identical to one another. One man in a suit carried a bullhorn and slowly walked to the middle of the ordered lines of vehicles and stiff uniforms. He looked at the flanking motorcycles, then raised the horn to his mouth.

"You are interfering with government action. It has been decided that this town will be removed. Unlock your arms and leave the area immediately or face arrest and criminal charges!"

The line of men stayed still. Quietly at first, Jiang heard the men begin to sing. He couldn't hear the words, but the melody floated back towards the crowd, barely audible over the idling of the truck's engines.

"This is your last warning. Citizens, return to your homes and prepare for eviction!" The man roared into the horn, gesturing his arms towards the crowd, and then pointed back towards the town. He looked around the crowd, making sure his contempt was felt as the echo of the bullhorn wafted down the road. He lifted the horn again. "That is all."

The soldiers in military fatigues pulled black-handled wood batons from their belts and formed a line along the front of the cross-legged men. The line paused long enough to take no more than one breath. Then slowly, they walked towards those sitting, as the singing became louder.

The first soldier stepped forward, to the middle of the group blocking the road. "You have no - !" One of the sitting villagers began to yell as a baton whipped across his cheekbone. The cracking sound of the wood on skin made Jiang jump. He watched in horror as the man's face turned with the blow, the one sitting next to him getting sprayed with spit and blood. The man's head fell limp to the side, while his arms remained locked with the two men next to him.

Immediately, the rest of the soldiers stepped towards those on the ground, swinging wildly, connecting with arms and heads. Jiang felt sick, his knees felt heavy. He needed to stop it. He needed to be in that mess and put his hands in front of the flying sticks and scream. He tried to lift his feet forward, but they only dragged below. Gravity suddenly became such an overwhelmingly strong force on his feet, almost like the road and his shoes were full of magnets. The cracking of the batons echoed through the screams of the crowd. Some villagers turned to run from the scene, several ran towards the violence, and others dropped to their knees, hitting the hard asphalt with their hands in agony.

Jianyu's body slumped into the man next to him, as a soldier grabbed his legs and pulled him away from the others. An officer followed suit and began to drag the line away, pulling at limbs and breaking the chain of arms in the twisted mess. Jiang could see blood streaking down the faces ahead, and he then heard himself scream.

"Leave the area immediately!" The bullhorn bellowed. "Return to your homes and pack your belongings, or you will face the consequences!"

The group along the road began to run back to the town. Someone pulled at Jiang, tearing him away from his unsteady stance. He kept his eyes on the road, as Jianyu was carried and shoved through the backdoor of one SUV. A strong arm pulled him farther away until the madness disappeared behind the fleeing crowd.

Jiang's leg muscles burned as he pedaled with fury up his driveway. He dismounted the bike while still in motion, letting it crash away from him, and running through his landing, kept his momentum up until he could jump over the steps on the porch. He threw open the front door to find his mother sitting behind a pile of bags and suitcases, staring at a framed photograph.

Jiang stood in the doorway, breathing hard, feeling like his heart might leap out of his chest. His knees shook like tiny jackhammers. A strand of his slick black hair fell over his forehead, covering one eye.

"I'm not sure we'll be able to carry all the photographs, Jiang." Hien didn't look up as she spoke. Jiang could feel his heartbeat in his ears and began to feel dizzy. He braced himself against the wall until his knees started to calm. Then, pushing himself forward, he stood with his arms hanging at his waist, fists clenched together.

"Dad's…"

"I know, Jiang. Such a fool…such a fool…" Her words became more quiet as she spoke until the last word was more of a murmur to herself.

Jiang's shock let up enough that he could walk forward steadily, looking over the bags on the floor. His mother had packed a suitcase for each of them, then a bag of kitchenware, a bag of books, one of photographs, another of old clothes he'd never seen before, and several bags of food. He looked at her and the frame in her hand. Walking over to her, he peered over her lap and saw a photo of the three of them standing outside the house. His father stood on the left, hands in his pockets, as he stood in front, his mother's hands resting on his shoulders.

He walked over to the bag full of books. His mother looked up as he pulled several books out and tossed them to the floor. As one book snapped loudly on the floor, he looked up, meeting her eyes.

"We can find more books, mom." Taking the photograph from her hands, he gently placed it on the top of the open bag. "We have to hurry. They're coming here soon."

Taking both of her hands, Jiang pulled his mother out of her chair. Silently, she walked into the kitchen, turned on the tap, and splashed cold water on her face. Wiping the water from her eyes with the ends of her fingers, she exhaled loudly. She heard her son rummaging around in his room, adding toys to his suitcase of clothes.

Hien had lived in that old house long before Jiang was born. Unbeknownst to him, she was pregnant three years before he was born, but they had lost the baby prematurely. It took her a long time to risk trying again. Jianyu was patient, loving, and understanding. He worked long hours in the fields alone while she rested the first year. He took over cooking and all orders of the household. She joked that when she finally had all her strength back, what got her moving was her husband's inability to spice a meal properly. But they both knew the ordeal had delivered a heavy blow. When they finally conceived Jiang, she was more nervous than any time before. Jianyu reassured her every night and every morning that a baby was on its way, and that it was finally time for them to be tested as parents. She continued to be nervous, yes, but something had indeed changed over the years. The space inside the house became linked to the space inside her heart. It had become a place of comfort and love, where once had been misfortune. It contained every sweet word that Jianyu had spoken for more than two years. More than two years of pure, loving energy between two people. She soon began to believe a child was coming.

Hien looked through the walls from where she stood in the kitchen, seeing every happy moment they all shared in the house. She began to smile. When her son emerged, he had a suitcase in one hand and two bags in the other. Looking out the window, she saw clouds of dust over treetops. To the left, she saw a bulldozer inching closer to a neighbor's house. Shaking her head and blinking her eyes twice, she arched her eyebrows upwards, feeling the air on her eyes bring her back into the moment. She faced her son.

"Let's go."

Their bags bounced down the front steps of the house after them, as the front door slammed behind. Jiang turned his head towards a sudden outburst of noise coming from the neighbor's house to the left. He saw a man sitting in front of a yellow bulldozer. Two girls and a woman stood behind the bulldozer, struggling to pull away from uniformed arms. The man in front of the bulldozer was holding something above his head. A can or bottle of something. He was shaking it up and down. Liquid fell from the bottle onto his head, soaking his hair and shoulders. Jiang could see the excess liquid bouncing off the man's shoulders, creating a puddle around his bent legs. The woman behind the bulldozer screamed, and Jiang saw the man take something out of his pocket. Then a long pause.

Hien had started to pull at her son's sleeve, but then she noticed what he was staring at. She looked on as her neighbor of 20 years struck a match in front of his body. In a burst of orange light, he was on fire. Flames danced above him, oily black smoke swirling back towards the bulldozer. The man's wife fell to her knees just as he bent forward to the ground. Neither Hien nor Jiang heard either of their neighbors make a sound.

Jiang felt his mother's grip resume as she pulled at his arm. He didn't realize he had stopped moving. Up ahead, another bulldozer was coming down their driveway. They moved to the side, stopping along the edge of the road, and watched as the bulldozer passed them. A middle-aged man in an orange plastic hat sat at the wheel, and he kept his eyes forward as he passed the mother and son below. The metal tracks of the bulldozer crunched and buckled, sounding like rusty pipes breaking apart. They slowly spit out dirt behind them, leaving a messy rut in the road. Another tug on his arm, and they were both moving again.

"Come on, Jiang. Don't look back."

☼☼☼

Standing at the bus stop, Jiang tried to shake away the images of the last half hour. He needed to distract himself. Everything had happened so fast. Standing on the balls of his feet, he straightened his back slightly. Despite the effort, he felt the length of his body compressing and the landscape around him grew upwards. He had never felt so small in his life.

He looked around at the other villagers. Some stared up the road in silence, some cried, and others sat on their pile of bags, watching beads of sweat fall from the tips of their noses onto the hot ground. He recognized most of them, but there were strangers too. A girl stood behind a woman, whom Jiang assumed to be her mother, grasping at the woman's brown skirt, and peaking just one eye out from the bunched-up fabric. It was the first time he had seen the girl. *Where had that family been all his life? Was the girl in Jiang's school?*

A man, much older than his father, leaned against a crooked walking stick and kicked at a cluster of stones. Jiang failed to recognize this villager too, and somewhere in his chest, Jiang felt a tinge of tightness, of worry, that he may never know who that man was. Without trying, his thoughts conjured up images of his father. Jiang knew his father was a brave man - his action against the destruction of their village didn't work - but he had tried, when all Jiang did was watch. Jiang imagined himself at the scene again, flinging his tiny body in front of the batons. Shouting and clawing at the man with the bullhorn. In his head, Jiang would have been a hero, maybe a martyr, but in reality, Jiang had a notion that he could never be that brave. Jiang lifted his weight up onto his toes, seeing how tall he could make himself. The old man with the stick tilted his head and Jiang quickly let his feet return evenly on the ground. Jiang kept his eyes low, unsure if the old man had understood his thoughts.

He wondered what was happening to his father now. He was an intelligent man, and people usually liked him. Surely, he could reason with the police and talk his way out of trouble. When they let him go, Jiang could organize a big party. He'd decorate the new apartment and invite all their neighbors over. His father would be pleased and perhaps in the evening, Jiang could ask his father for tips on how to grow faster.

He tried to imagine their new apartment. He'd seen plenty on TV before. Box-shaped houses balanced hundreds of feet above the earth. Some were enormous, with walls completely made of windows. His new bedroom would perhaps be the size of his entire old house. Their apartment so big that he could ride a new bicycle from his room to the kitchen. His mother would chase after him as he left black streaks across the polished, wood floor. The furniture would probably be new. There would be no gaps between the wood planks on the floor, and even if he stomped on them, they wouldn't make a sound.

Jiang figured that all of his friends would likely be living in the same apartment high rise, and they could find a new place to gather. Maybe the rooftop would be their new meeting grounds, a playground high above the earth, or maybe there would be a swimming pool in the apartment building. *Anything was possible*, he remembered a narrator saying during a TV program they watched in school. Modern science was making living completely different. Everything was clean, the paint never peeled, and houses always smelled brand new. Paths were lined with perfect, square bushes, and flowers bloomed year-round.

Jiang was watching the vivid scenes of his future life play out when a van honked its horn at the end of their road. The van twisted and swerved around potholes, as it outran its own dust cloud. As it came to an abrupt skidding stop in from of him, Jiang was still picturing white walls and floors so shiny that he would have to re-learn how to walk, in order to keep from slipping and embarrassing himself.

As he passed his final bag to his mother, who was already seated on a torn, brown leather seat in the van, Jiang looked back towards the village. It was the only place he had ever known as home. He considered his father again, and of the man in the uniform, who stopped them at the end of their driveway, after they had passed the bulldozer.

He said they were taking his father to a jail not far from their new city. The man couldn't say how long he would stay in jail, but he handed them a slip of paper with the address of the district police station. He said to inquire about his father's sentencing there. Jiang had to take the paper from the man. His mother had only looked forward, shaking her head from side to side. So, his father was actually closer to where they were going than where Jiang was now. There was no sense in staying any longer. Suddenly, it didn't feel like his village anymore.

Someone slid the rusted, noisy door of the van shut.

The bang of the door snapped Jiang away from his thoughts. The driver yelled behind him that they needed to shut the door with more force. A man slid the door open again, bringing rays of sunlight across Jiang's face, before slamming it closed. This time the loud, metal bang was followed by the sound of automatic locks engaging inside the left side of the door. The van sped off immediately, swinging wide to miss a buffalo, napping in the middle of the country lane. As the van accelerated, Jiang felt his stomach start to turn over a little, and a small wave of nausea rose towards his throat.

V

The morning after his restless night, Suman was woken up by the roar of engines. He looked next to him. Sanjana had already left the bed. He stood up and walked to the window, and from his room, he could see a few neighbors walking towards the sound. When he stepped outside, he found Sanjana eating with Maya.

"Motorcycle trader?" He asked, remembering the lights the night before.

"Not sure. Tauko said to meet him there when you woke up. You feeling alright? You slept a long time."

"I'm fine, but going to need a lot more sleep if we're going to hear that engine tonight," Suman said, missing the usual morning chorus of birds or Maya bouncing around the garden.

"I'm ready to swing," Maya interrupted. "Dad, can we swing now?"

"Not until you finish eating, Maya," Sanjana responded calmly. Maya folded her arms and stared at her food.

Suman leaned into the table. "Eating makes you swing better. All the older children eat well before a long day swinging," He watched Maya consider the idea. Then to Sanjana, "I'll go see what's going on down there."

He walked down the road as the engine finally went silent. In the middle of town, some villagers stood around a large vehicle and a man on a motorcycle. Suman approached slowly and soon realized who was sitting on the motorcycle.

"It's called a Jeep, and it can drive anywhere, even over the mountains!" Exclaimed Ukali, who was wearing a leather jacket and new, black laced boots. Three men climbed out of the Jeep and gave brief bows to the crowd gathered around them. They were wearing matching brown jackets, and tan slacks, and the cleanliness of their shoes suggested that it could have been the first time they left the Jeep. Ukali smiled and waved when he saw Suman joining the crowd, then he faced the crowd again.

"These are my friends, and they want to make us all rich," he said swinging his arms in the air, in a gesture that expected a great applause. When met by silence, he turned to speak to the two strangers.

Suman found Tauko, who gave him a silent look of annoyance and motioned him over.

"They're from China. They want to invest money in our village," Tauko said in a soft tone. Ukali turned to face the crowd again, as Tauko pulled Suman outside the gathering.

"We'll have more televisions than buffaloes!" They heard Ukali exclaim over their backs. The two farmers simultaneously rolled their eyes as they leaned on a neighbor's stone wall.

"What's going on?" Suman asked.

"Apparently, Ukali met some businessmen in the city, and they learned about our village. They told him that they have building projects all over the mountains, and each village becomes very wealthy, they bring in electricity, new roads, and everything. So, he led them up here, and by the looks of it, he made some money on the deal," Tauko said, pointing at the motorcycle.

"Indeed, so they want to buy our village?" Suman asked his friend.

"Not quite. I guess they only need some grazing fields just up the river," Tauko responded, hearing a sigh from Suman. They both felt their heads becoming busy with thought.

"But, it's not ours to sell," Suman said, squeezing his eyebrows together.

"Don't tell them that."

"You're right. We just have to convince the farmers and herders that they're not to sell anything. The last thing we need is more mouths to feed around here. We had a great crop this year, but who knows about the future, and selling valuable land certainly won't put more food on our plates."

"We need to talk to Ukali alone," Tauko said, as Suman nodded in agreement. A gasp from the crowd diverted their attention, and as the men spun around, they saw Ukali hold up a stack of paper money. Tauko and Suman hurried back to the crowd.

"I'm going to show my friends around our beautiful town but think about this. This is just a piece of what we can be earning on our land. Land that we don't even need. Let's keep what we need for food and houses, and make this with the rest. And imagine more to come, with their construction workers buying food from us. We can have motorcycles, lights that stay lit all night, televisions, stories from the world, exotic food, everything we want!" Ukali handed the money to one of the brown jackets and stepped off the motorcycle with a big grin.

"But most importantly, remember that these men don't want to bother us, they will leave us in peace to go about our lives. They will be kind to all of us like they have been with me, and even give us jobs if we want. It's the deal of a lifetime, I promise you," he said as he turned to lead the men up the hill out of town. The crowd began chattering about what they just witnessed, slowly dispersing from the side of the Jeep. Whispers about money and reminders of Ukali's drunken behavior of the past floated through the street.

Tauko looked at Suman with wide eyes and shook his head once as if to shake away a bad image. The two men quickly stepped in line behind Ukali and the two strangers. As they approached, Ukali appeared to hear them and stopped mid-stride.

"Hey, my friends, exciting day, isn't it?" Ukali asked, pulling out a flask from his jacket.

"We need to talk with you," Suman said. Ukali smiled and nodded in agreement.

"Of course, of course," Ukali replied, pausing to sip the flask. "But later, I need to show them the land."

"Hey!" Tauko yelled so loud that Suman and Ukali both jumped. One of the strangers stepped forward, waiting for a confrontation.

"Easy, my friend, we'll talk soon," Ukali said quickly before motioning his business partners forward. His eyes darted quickly between Tauko and Suman, turning with a pleading glint.

As the three continued uphill, Suman put his hand on Tauko's shoulder. "We'll wait," he whispered.

"I don't trust that drunk," Tauko said, loud enough for the other men to hear.

"It might be nothing. At least they are looking upriver for land, and we can still talk to the men who graze their animals there," Suman said, trying to calm his friend.

"A new motorcycle, a handful of cash? Ukali sold the land already," replied Tauko, and Suman swallowed some air.

The two friends decided to wait on a rock wall near the

entrance of the village. Hours passed and Ukali still hadn't returned.

"Let go home," Tauko said, sounding defeated. "We can talk to him tomorrow." Suman let out a long breath and agreed.

"Tomorrow," he said, standing up and walking down the road with Tauko.

He gave Tauko a pat on the back before wishing him a peaceful night.

At home, Sanjana was waiting for Suman at the front door. Maya must have been asleep already, whisked away by her dreams.

"What happened up there?"

Suman looked at Sanjana, the bottom of her nightgown gently fluttering in the night air. He explained about Ukali, the cash and motorcycle, and the sudden rise of anger from his friend.

"All people have a different form of happiness," Sanjana began. "For you, I know, it is your hilltop, your garden, and us. You are happy with the simple things. Ukali has never been someone who appreciates the little things we have. We've known that for a long time. He wants things, and here, the things he wants can't grow from the land."

"Sanjana, you're right. But what if he is trading the happiness of his neighbors for his things?"

"Then we will have to prove to each other that we still have heart, despite the decisions of one person. When I was young, I traveled with my family, from valley to valley, always searching for greener grass for our herds, and I thought there must be something more for me. Then you came to me. You showed me the beauty in remaining still, the beauty of family. My greener grass became your village and my questions faded away with the river. But I could never foresee what my wanting would lead to, and we'll never know what Ukali's wanting will lead to. Like the river, we are always changing and moving. If we try to force the changing to stop, it would go against the flow of nature we know so well. We can't stop the river."

Sanjana's words floated around Suman's mind, and he found himself sitting next to her, unaware of how they moved from the doorway.

"So let these changes come, and we'll face them together." Sanjana's last words seemed to drift away with the wind, down the valley and were carried off by the churning of the river below.

☼☼☼

The next morning, Suman woke up before sunrise. He peered out of his window to see the village still asleep. This time the air was silent. He had even beat the birds to the morning. He stepped into his sandals and walked up the road, slowing his step to spin the prayer wheels, softly murmuring: Om Mani Padme Hum. His fingers interlocked behind his back, he walked up the path to his father's collection of chiseled stone. He sat on a rock and reached into his pocket. He pulled out the mountain-shaped stone that Tauko gave him. He worked slowly, making sure each character was perfect. When he finished, he found a place on the top of the collection, with the carving facing the mountain it represents.

"That mountain is more powerful than any of us, my son. When the sun first touches its face, you can witness its strength. It will shine gold with the morning light, and you will understand what is truly valuable in life." His father's words seemed to echo down the valley with a cold breeze, as Suman pulled his jacket closer to his body. He looked out towards Chatima as the sun began to push powerful rays over an eastern ridge. But the mountain didn't glow gold. Soon the entire peak was glowing an intense crimson red.

"Is that strength?" Suman asked into the wind.

When he returned to the village, Suman found Tauko outside his house pacing. "There you are, I found Ukali. He hasn't slept, he's drinking in his old house with his new buddies."

They approached the house from the grassy field behind it. They could hear the clinking of glasses inside and muffled laughter. They peered through the window and saw Ukali pouring a round of beer for his partners.

"It was well worth staying up all night," one of the

businessmen said with a strong accent. "Those buffalo herders took some convincing, but I think the cell phones and whiskey sealed the deal."

"Indeed, me frens," said Ukali, looking across the table as he took another gulp of beer. "But, when d'aye get my cut?"

Tauko looked at Suman, and Suman saw fire in his friend's eyes.

"I'm going in there," Tauko whispered. He spoke with such intensity and anger that the whisper couldn't hide.

"Not now, they're drunk, and you're angry," Suman responded, holding onto his friend's arm. "There's nothing we can do if the herders sold already."

"Forget it, there's something I can do right now," Tauko said, balling up his fists and breathing heavily.

"Tauko, my brother, be calm. We'll wait until they sober up."

They heard a loud thump inside and peered back into the house. They saw Ukali with his head on the table and the other men grinning at each other. Ukali started to snore, having finally succumbed to the long night of drinking. The men began speaking in Mandarin, a sound familiar yet impossible to understand. After a pause, they snickered quietly in a rhythmic procession. They wrote something on a piece of paper and left it on the table, before standing up and walking towards the door. Tauko and Suman ducked out of view, and they crouched below the window, waiting until they heard an engine start up. They rushed around the side of the house to see the Jeep drive away in a cloud of dust, heading out of the village, and back down the valley.

"OK, now we-" Suman turned to see his friend had disappeared. He heard the house's front door kicked open. He rushed around to the entrance to find Tauko shaking Ukali awake.

"You drunk bastard! You sold out your own village for your filthy habits!" Tauko was yelling now, and pushing Ukali. As he woke up, Ukali fell from his chair onto the dirt floor, wide awake but groggy from the booze.

"Wuss goin' on?" Ukali slurred into the cold room. He looked up at his two neighbors, searching for their smiling faces but finding only annoyance and agitation. "Easy mah frens, everytin's fine. The land sold, and we gonna ben-fit." Suman grabbed Tauko's arm as his friend moved toward Ukali.

"I hope everything will be fine," Suman said, as he took a large step between the two. "You will finally be able to buy everything you want, but you better hope that the village will be safe."

"WE gonna buy everytin' WE wan'," replied Ukali, his voice shaky. "I'm not the on' one who's makin' dough."

"A couple of cell phones won't feed those herder's families," interrupted Tauko. "Who are they going to call anyway?"

Looking confused, Ukali defended himself. "I dunno where ya heard that, but them all...they nevuh gonna work again." Suman looked to Tauko, seeing the fight in his face, fists clenched white at his sides. Suman moved away from Ukali, pulling Tauko with him, out of the room.

"Go to sleep Ukali, and be happy," Suman said. "But if something happens, we know who to thank."

"And while you're showing off your motorcycle, go ahead and drive off a cliff," said Tauko as he was pulled through the doorway. They heard the door slam shut as they walked down the hill.

"What are we going to do?" Tauko asked Suman after a long period of silence.

"What is there to do?" Suman responded. "The land is good to us, and hopefully that will be enough. Come to my house for breakfast, my friend. Sanjana and Maya should be awake by now."

The morning had arrived and the village ahead was already stirring in the new daylight.

They passed Tauko's son, Ruku, on the road. He and his friends were dressed for school.

"Hi Dad. Hi uncle." Ruku said, with a level of energy fitting a young boy loathing a day of school.

"Study well my son," Tauko said, patting the boy on the head. When the boys were far enough away, Tauko wiped a tear from the corner of his eye and turned to face Suman.

"What will happen when they are our age? Will there still be land left that isn't sold off?" Suman looked at his friend, seeing the anger in his eyes replaced by fear.

"Don't worry, my friend. Don't let your mind concentrate on these thoughts. Their future is long. They'll have a full harvest if they want to farm, great wealth if that is what they desire, and us old men could never dream of the amazing things they will build for their families."

They were almost in sight of Suman's house, as a yak bellowed in the distance. "Yak cheese, my dear Tauko," said Suman. "That's all we need to think about this winter."

VI

After several hours in the van, humid and hot from all the bodies and bags piled so closely together, Jiang asked the question he was trying not to ask.

"Why are we driving so long?"

His mother looked at him but didn't open her mouth. Only tired eyes watched Jiang's quizzical face. There had been a long silence in the van. Heavy hearts beat against a few masked sobs. Finally, a neighbor sitting behind them tried to explain to the young boy, as gently as possible.

It turned out that neither his family nor any of his classmates would be relocated to new apartment buildings nearby. Even in the nearest city, construction was still ongoing, and they would need to live in established cities.

"Besides," explained the neighbor. "Even if the new buildings were ready, they are too expensive for our families. We are moving about 200 kilometers away, in a city called…"

Jiang couldn't listen anymore. His ears had already started ringing, and his gaze shifted slowly toward the window and the bouncing landscape outside. He had never heard of the new city, but that didn't matter. He already felt lost amid the millions of new neighbors they'd have. He started to feel depressed. At least that's what he thought he felt. He hadn't been depressed before. His head hurt. All he wanted to do was to go back home and lay in his bed. Shut his eyes, and dream about something else. Anything else.

The van continued along. The neighbor had ceased speaking. Everyone was quiet, sitting in their new grim reality. Time moved along, even as their moment seemed suspended in the air.

Without warning, the van jerked to a stop. No one moved. The driver shifted in his seat.

"Uh, er…We're here everyone."

Someone slid the metal door open. Outside, a cement sidewalk straddled a tired-looking, white building. Under each window, a streak of rust ran down the white walls. Jiang imagined it looked like the windows were crying. Along the walls were hedges with yellowing leaves, a few rose bush stumps, and some aluminum cans.

As the villagers piled out of the van, a woman in a blue, business suit strode up to the van. She presented herself as a representative from the District Relocation Committee. She shook a few hands, and then turned to Jiang's mother.

"I'll first show you and your family to your apartment. The others can wait here for my colleague. This is your son, I presume? And your husband?" She searched the other faces.

"My father is coming later." Jiang was surprised at how his voice sounded. It felt deeper than normal. He wasn't sure why he spoke up first, but when his mother squeezed his hand gently afterward, he felt he had done the right thing.

"Very well, shall we?" The woman had already slid over to the white building and was holding a large door open. A few villagers said goodbye, and one of their nearest neighbors said she'd come visit that evening.

Their apartment was on the fourth floor and Jiang noticed as they climbed up the staircase, that each entrance to a floor smelled like old cigarettes. When they reached their apartment door, a different smell greeted them as the woman turned the knob. It smelled wet, like the inside of a rain boot that hadn't been allowed to dry.

Jiang eyed the empty hallway; bare walls and a single bulb hung from the ceiling. He wanted to cry, but looking at the expression on his mother's face, he realized that he needed to be strong. His mother looked across their new home with sad eyes, studying each corner, as if she were searching for something through the walls. Jiang shuffled past the woman, who had begun explaining the appliances in a cheerful tone, dragged his bag of clothes to the smallest room, and laid down on a folding mattress that sat on the floor.

The voice in the hallway faded away. He thought about his father. He realized that the apartment didn't matter. It was not how he imagined it, true, but it didn't feel real enough to matter. His home in the village was real. He wanted to be there again. He started to think about what opening the front door of their house felt like. But he stopped himself. As his eyes began to water, he decided it wasn't worth thinking about. He felt small. He thought of his mother. He thought that he needed to be strong, like his father. But in those first moments in the apartment, he instead felt an overwhelming urge to sleep. His eyelids pulled his eyes away from the strange new world they landed in. No more sad little apartment. No missing father. No sad mother. Just a long yawn, closing eyes, and dreams about something else.

☼☼☼

Every morning of their first week in the new apartment, Jiang's mother, Hien, would leave the house early. She left a plate of fried eggs and rice under a second plate on the table, put on her nicest dress, and quietly slipped out the front door before Jiang woke up.

It took her nearly two hours to reach the police station. The guard at the entrance directed her to the officer on duty, who always looked hungover, or perhaps his face was permanently twisted into a sleepy, annoyed look. Hien couldn't decide which, as she hesitatingly shuffled her feet towards that heavyset man slouched behind an enormous mug of steaming coffee. The first day, he told her to wait on a bench in the front lobby while he looked into her husband's case. After an hour, she was told that the file had not yet arrived at the station, and she'd need to return the next day. She did so the following day.

Then, this order of events repeated almost exactly like each preceding day, until the sixth day, when the file arrived. Then, almost as if it was a test of her patience and sanity, she was informed the case would need 24 hours for review before they could reveal information to her.

On the final day of the first week, she dragged her sore feet through the station lobby, eyeing the guard with suspicious eyes, when he directed her forward, no recognition on his face as if she had never been in the building before. She sat on the bench, along the wall, directly across from the officer on duty. It was someone new this time. He was instead quite thin and looked angry rather than hungover. After some minutes, he looked up over a brown folder and asked for her case number. As she spoke, she promised herself she wouldn't lose her mind if this new officer told her to return the next day. She knew that throwing a fit in a police station would only make the process more tiresome and demeaning.

But instead of more delays, the new officer waved her over to the desk.

"Four months, perhaps less." He said, still looking at the brown folder.

"I'm sorry, but…" She began.

"Obstructing government business and resisting arrest. This is a light sentence. He'll spend four more months inside a holding facility. You can fill out an application for a visit. The forms are behind you, on the wall." He pointed back behind her, still keeping his eyes away from hers.

She wanted to scream. To rip the folder out of his hands, jump across the desk, and beat this stranger with her fists. She was a strong woman. She knew she could easily break his nose before anyone could pull her off of him. She could probably force half of the folder into his mouth before anyone came to stop her. But between the rage building, she saw Jiang. He was still young, and she needed to be with him. They hadn't spoken much about his father since they came to the city. What would it do to him if she was locked away too?

The flashes of violence disappeared and she bent her head forward in a slight bow and turned away from the officer. She stuffed several visiting applications in her purse, and walked out of the building, letting the door slam behind her.

✧✧✧

On his first day of school, Jiang recognized five

students from his village. They all were wearing similar looks of confusion and disappointment on their faces. It wasn't only him who felt completely duped by the situation. The other students lived all over the new city, and they gathered together to exchange addresses. The building and street names were disorienting. So many strange names. He remembered when directions used to involve trees and crop fields, such as, 'Go five minutes past the corn, until the giant tree with the swing, then left for another five minutes…'

Along with the new addresses, he learned that there were dozens of other districts around their own and that different buses had brought the others to school. He needed to find a map.

At least Li Jie still lived nearby. His family was assigned a slightly larger apartment, closer to the shops and the school. Jiang's mother told him that the Li family owned over twice the land and yielded a considerable amount of rice, therefore, their subsidized housing reflected the land's higher value.

Jiang quickly enjoyed hanging out at Li Jie's apartment more than his own. He noticed the brightness of the rooms as soon as he walked in. The windows in each room hardly needed help from light bulbs. It didn't smell as moldy either. The balcony, which served as a hallway along the front doors of each floor, had long views over a courtyard below and the city beyond. The courtyard lacked the basketball hoops that Jiang's building had, but its large, meticulously manicured space looked easier to breathe in.

Even if Jiang didn't prefer to visit Li Jie's room after

school rather than his own, it wouldn't have made sense to make Li Jie walk the extra distance to Jiang's place. So, the boys usually hung out for a couple of hours, talking and doing homework, after the day of classes.

One day, both backpacks spilled their innards onto the floor in Li Jie's room, and the boys sat against a wall, feet spread out, across a twin bed. They were still navigating the social scene of the new school halls and were working out where they fit in the fold.

The students from the city were nice enough in the classrooms, but during lunch or between classes, the new, rural children were avoided as if they were diseased. But eventually, they did notice a few of their friends from the village having success at making new friends. The students from the city seemed extremely interested in toys, rather than stories they tried to tell. Jiang and Li Jie discussed which type of toy would make a good impression on their new peers. They sat on his bed, comparing ideas, while lowering their voices whenever an adult passed by the bedroom door. They didn't need Li Jie's parents weighing in too.

During the brainstorming session, their minds began to sail back into their memories. Memories of the simplicity of classroom politics at their old school, and memories of their original homes. What both of the boys constantly agreed on, was the worst part about the move from their old homes: they were hundreds of kilometers from their old village and they couldn't watch the enormous buildings being built. They couldn't see how their homes were currently being transformed.

They wanted to watch the giant, yellow cranes, lift impossibly huge pieces of metal through the air. They wanted to hear the sounds of angry machines, digging away at what used to be their farms. At least, they wanted to make sure that the canal construction didn't remove the tree root diving board. Why make a larger river and take out the best platform to jump from?

The worst part, by far, was not knowing. Not knowing what was happening in the place that held most of their memories.

The boys had once overheard another parent say they were suspicious that the housing project was a cover-up to a far worse project. Perhaps a prison. Before they had left their farm, Jiang brought up that proposal during one dinner. When he heard the suggestion, Jiang's father laughed.

"If they wanted to build a prison, or a zoo for that matter, they would tell us: Here's a shitty apartment and some money for your entire life's work, we're building a prison."

Jiang's mother had clicked her tongue at the curse but didn't say anything more.

"They never need our permission, and they never need to hide." His father had finished his thought and spooned a large portion of rice into his mouth. Jiang knew the tactic all too well. A full mouth meant his father would and could say no more.

Jiang had looked at his bowl, furrowing his brow. He

felt that the whole deal wasn't fair at all. From his first school, he had learned that the government made its decisions in the interest of the people, but how would this be in the interest of his family?

The following day in his new city, a fierce wind met Jiang as he stepped outside the front entrance of his apartment. Sand flew into his face before he could close his eyes. Frustrated, he violently swung open the door to take shelter indoors. He mumbled curses to himself as he carefully wiped the sand from his eyes on the sleeve of his school uniform.

When he first arrived, Jiang had guessed that the worst part about apartment living was never knowing what weather was waiting for you outside. A quick hand out his bedroom window would only tell him if it was raining or not, and sometimes that didn't even work. Their only windows were views of the next apartment's walls, and the smallest amount of sunlight came down the shaft during midday.

His mother, upon hearing his grumblings, told him to keep his head up, and that it would be easier if he accepted the changes. She was usually correct, but instead, he started to avoid complaining in front of her. He would rather hold his frustration inside, rather than allow someone to make it seem petty.

He knew his mother had it rough too. Transported from the only place she had known; she was struggling to make new friends. Besides two other mothers from Jiang's class, most of her friends had been moved to different cities. Her pleasant strolls down dirt roads to the market had been replaced by concrete journeys among noisy cars and the ever-curious eyes of the idling taxi drivers. She spent each weekend at the jail, visiting his father, and the weekday anticipation of the visits seemed to absorb her completely.

Jiang usually went along with his mother. She would dress him up in his best clothes and added a tie that choked his throat. Jiang hated the jail. The guards were rude and the gray walls seemed to announce the true color of misery.

He remembered the last visit clearly. His father sat behind a thick barrier of glass, its transparency faded by age and painful-looking scratch marks. He could only speak to them through a phone, which made his voice sound like it was coming from a distant cave. Jiang could only hear half of his parent's conversation, on his mother's end, and waited until he could use the phone. Each time, his father's face changed when he spoke to Jiang. While his father looked upset and frustrated talking to his mother, he put on a thin smile when he asked Jiang about school. Jiang found it difficult to concentrate, unable to take his eyes off the stitches that pulled together part of his father's forehead.

Jiang felt nervous speaking to his father behind the foggy glass and kept his answers as brief as possible. He was reminded to do well in school and that his father would find work to help them as soon as he was released. Then his father's face grew more serious. Jiang watched him lean forward, placing his weathered hand onto the glass.

"I know that this time has been difficult for you, Jiang. It has been for all of us. But joy and sorrow are always linked together. When we feel happy and on top of the world, we should count our blessings, because we never know when things will change. And when we are feeling low, when life pushes us down, remember that eventually, you'll be on top again. The further down life pushes us, only shows how high our potential will be when fate changes again."

Back inside the entrance of his apartment building, Jiang was still hiding from the sandstorm. Remembering his recent visit to prison, he realized that if his father wasn't giving up, then neither should he. He felt a sudden rush of determination. He decided to make the most of his new situation, and his school day ahead. Blinking several times, to ensure all the sand had submitted to his sleeve, Jiang reached again for the handle of the door and closed his eyes. An immediate gust of angry wind slapped what must have been several handfuls of sand in his face, but Jiang turned with the wind, brushing his face with his right hand. He cupped his hand over the right side of his face while using his thumb to block his ear canal. With this technique, he was able to open his left eye just enough to stay on the sidewalk. He knew once he got to the next apartment building, he could walk alongside it for a good distance before facing the wind again.

By the next sand attack, he was better prepared. He had tied his school scarf to the front of his face, leaving only a small slit open to see out of. Another ten minutes of hurried walking, and he could take another rest at Li Jie's apartment building.

The weather was always changing in Jiang's new city, and it seemed more violent than the weather he was used to. Back home, when it was sunny, he could usually count on it being sunny after school as well. But here, a wind storm could be replaced by sunshine by the time he arrived to class, and transformed into a downpour of rain once the sun set.

Li Jie, having missed the worst of the sand storm, waved happily from the safety of his building's corridor. He talked excitedly after the two boys finished their morning high-five ritual.

"Maybe this summer, we can go back to our village, Jiang, and have a look inside the new buildings." Li Jie pushed open the final door in the corridor, which led them outside, only a couple blocks from their school.

"I wish," Jiang said. "My dad's going to be released by then, and my mom has a lot of plans for us when he comes home."

The boys made their way down the sidewalk, stepping around a young woman pushing a stroller. Sunlight started to peak through the clouds above them. Jiang's shadow reappeared under his feet as they walked.

"Do you think all adults really know what they're doing?" He asked his friend. Li Jie stopped walking, and put his hand on his chin. He pretended to stroke a long, wispy beard, before continuing down the path.

"I sure hope so," Li Jie said. "Parents are smart. Smarter than us anyway. But we are young, we don't need to worry all the time. I'm sure in a few years, we'll be really happy about all these changes."

With these words and a soft, brief hand on Jiang's shoulder, Li Jie brought a small smile to his friend's face. Then Li Jie burst into movement, throwing his arms at the sky and spinning in a circle, mimicking a hysterical laugh without making a sound.

"Hey Jiang, at least the wind has stopped!"

Jiang's first classes passed with a blur of motion. Lectures, notebooks, tapping of pencils on the wooden desks, pages accidentally ripped by over-eager hands turning them.

In his social studies class, a teacher asked students where the food they ate came from. Jiang snorted a little at such an obvious question.

"From the supermarket," a student answered. Several students, including Jiang, couldn't help but laugh.

"That's right, but how did the food come to the market," the teacher continued.

He began describing large farms in the countryside, far from the city, where noble farmers provided food for millions. Jiang was dumbfounded. He assumed everyone knew about farms and farmers. One student queried that wasn't it correct that farmers just drove tractors, and didn't work for the supermarkets. The teacher was far more patient and relaxed in his answers than Jiang would have been.

After school, Jiang stopped by a market on the way back to his apartment. His stomach had begun growling during his last class. He had a few coins, making noise in his pocket, and figured it would be enough for a snack.

The doors of the market thrust open to reveal a strong, lemon-scented gust of temperature-conditioned air inside. Jiang shivered and stopped to pull a thin, blue jacket from his school bag. The markets in his village were always outdoors, and the food tasted better, so why did they have to keep everything so abnormally cold in the city? The markets of the city felt like a science lab, where food was being created out of sterile test tubes.

He walked past the meat aisle, where a young boy pointed at some sliced meat, only to have his mother choose a different package.

"No, pork!" Shouted the boy. The mother rolled her eyes, and dragged the boy down the aisle, with a full shopping cart trailing behind in her other hand.

Jiang wondered if that boy understood that pork came from a pig. Did he think that pork came from a backroom in the market, grown every day in the bright, cold lights on the ceiling?

Jiang paused at an entire aisle of bottled water. He remembered the springs that he used to fill up water jugs in. The water was always cold, no matter the season, and he never had to pay anyone to drink it. Everything seemed to cost money in the city. If you want to sleep, you must pay rent. If you wanted to relieve yourself, two coins in a public toilet. If you wanted to drink water, exchange a coin for a bottle of water that was gone in a few gulps. He tried to think what Li Jie would say about this.

"At least it's not windy in the supermarket!" Or perhaps, "At least you don't have to wait for the plums to ripen, you can eat them anytime!"

If farmers were so crucial to the function of the city, why did his family have to leave their farm? Was their food not tasty enough for the city people? Could their trees not ripen fast enough? Jiang wondered what the farms his teacher spoke about must look like. He imagined huge warehouses, with bright lights, constant cold air, and farmers in lab coats, squeezing trunks of trees to make the fruit bigger and more juicy.

Jiang left the store without buying anything. A greeter at the door, who had originally bowed when he entered, looked at Jiang suspiciously, as if to ask how someone could walk away from all this food. Jiang had the strange impression that the man was wondering if he had stolen something.

Jiang no longer wanted any snacks for the walk home. Instead, he was content to think about the small, but delicious plums he used to gather in his neighbor's orchard. Someday, he decided, he would have a plum tree of his own, and nobody would have to pay him to taste the fruit.

The next day at school, he was sitting in the same class, and he had some questions for his teacher. But the topic changed, and focused on how the government enforced the laws it created. Jiang chewed on his bottom lip; his mind raced with questions he needed answers to. He wanted to know more about farming and what was the appropriate size of plum for human consumption.

But the teacher stayed on topic, and Jiang found it increasingly difficult to segue from law enforcement to fruit. Finally, Jiang heard a rise in the teacher's sentence towards the end. He hadn't heard what the teacher said, but he knew it was a question. Jiang's hand shot up, waving slightly back and forth, and the thrust of his hand pulled him out of his seat. His other elbow braced his body on his desk and he tried to bend the teacher's free will with mind control. *Pick me, come on, point to me*, he cried silently. But his over-eagerness must have spooked the teacher because he pointed to a female classmate, who had calmly raised her hand and still had her butt firmly planted in her seat.

"They'll be arrested?" The girl answered, and sort of asked simultaneously.

"That's correct," the teacher affirmed. But Jiang wouldn't quit, he kept his arm vertical, unwavering with his attempt at pupil-to-teacher hypnosis. He released a pitiful moan, which could have been mistaken for a toilet emergency.

"OK, Jiang, what do you want to add?"

"Thank you," he grunted, sounding exhausted. His arm dropped to his side, limp from the strain. "Yesterday we talked about farms. I wanted to know how food travels from farms to cities, and why don't we just grow food where we all live? And, and, why is fruit larger in cities than in the countryside?"

"Jiang, we are well past farming. Today, we are talking about law and order. Were you even listening to me?"

"But…" he began.

"Alright, since we've just started, I'll indulge you, but quickly, then we need to move on. Food from our largest farms travels by trucks or trains, or sometimes even boats to reach the cities. They fill the transports to the top with food, and then smaller trucks deliver them to supermarkets. We don't have space in cities to grow food, because people need space to work and sleep. And science has helped us create bigger fruit, that makes your stomach more full when you eat it, therefore, we need less fruit overall to satisfy people's needs."

"But it seems like a lot of driving for the trucks, and it would make sense to just have an orchard near our homes, then we can just go pick it and don't need to buy it all the time."

"That was the way the world worked at one time, yes, but today, it's far more efficient to have large farms to feed many people. People don't have time to farm, because they need to work, to make the money that buys food. OK, moving on…"

"But if we ate free food, we wouldn't need to work, right?"

"Well, you still need money to rent an apartment, to watch your movies, to drive a car."

"But when I was young…"

"You're still quite young, Jiang."

"Yes, but when I was young-er, I slept outside a lot, and I never paid anyone."

"Well, aren't you lucky?"

"What I mean is, it seems like money isn't really useful for sleeping and eating, and I can't even drive a car."

The other students laughed at this. The teacher's face began to turn red, as he felt himself losing control of his classroom.

"That isn't progress, Jiang. Don't encourage him, class. Without people doing other things besides farming, how could we go to space? How could we build the classrooms you learn in?"

"My father helped build my old classroom, and it only took him and his friends a week."

"Your father wasn't building skyscrapers, I'm sure, Jiang."

"Why would they need to build skyscrapers where I lived? We weren't hurting anyone."

"I know about your situation, Jiang, but we live in an

enormous country and we have a lot of people to care for. Therefore, we all need to share the land to work for the common good of society."

"But, we always shared…"

"That's enough, Jiang! Welcome to the modern world.! The past is gone. Wake up, and get with the program. Today, we need bigger farms and bigger cities because we have more people. It's called progress, and the sooner you join us in reality, the sooner you'll learn how to live here!" The teacher turned to the chalkboard to compose himself. "Now, back to the topic at hand, as I was saying…"

Jiang wanted to say more, but he bit his lip. He couldn't argue with this man. Maybe he was right, maybe the new ways were better, and maybe Jiang just didn't fit in yet. He could hear whispers and snickers from his classmates behind him. He vowed to sit in the back row the following day.

The next morning's walk to school was calm, and not even a small breeze blew across the sidewalk. What should have been a relief, instead left Jiang feeling claustrophobic in the still air. But weather was not the main concern that day. Li Jie had promised to bring their new toys to school and began a more proper integration with their urban pupils. They had decided to buy two action figures from a recent Hollywood film, with movable body parts and a button that made realistic, sword-fighting sounds.

At lunch, Li Jie unpacked the two figures, a blue and red man with a shield for Jiang, and a huge, green monster for Li Jie. They stood the two action figures on the table and began a mock fight scene. Neither of them had seen the movie, but they mimicked what they thought the heroes would say anyway. The plastic feet tapped on the surface of the wood table, just loud enough to be heard over the mass of voices, clamoring of metal spoons on metal trays, and one student's occasional coughing fits reverberating inside the cafeteria.

Out of the corner of his eye, Jiang noticed a few curious students from his class edging closer to their table. Suddenly Li Jie thrust his green monster's fist at Jiang's shield, sending the blue and red man flying backward, off the table. Jiang's hand stung from the blow, but he was too distracted by the visitors to dwell on the pain.

"Cool! My mom doesn't let me have any of the action ones," one student said.

"Me either, she only buys me soft characters from those Anime films," another added.

"Oh yeah? You can play with mine if you want," Jiang offered.

"Cool!"

Jiang and Li Jie handed the action figures to the two students, who quickly resumed the battle on the lunch table. *We're in,* Jiang thought. *We're cool, for sure.*

After school, the same two students, followed by

several others ran up to Jiang as he was taking out his school bag from his locker.

"We're all going to my apartment to watch a movie if you want to join, Jiang."

"Sounds cool," Jiang said, trying not to sound too excited. "Can I invite Li Jie?"

"Definitely. You can call me Bo, by the way"

The small group of kids, each weighed down by overloaded backpacks of textbooks, set off for Bo's place. Across the street from school they zig-zagged through a busy park, full of adults exercising, walking pet dogs, and occupying small benches along the footpaths. The park had a tiny pond between two grass mounds, where several geese waded just out of arm's reach of a curious German Shepard puppy. Once they left the small patch of greenery back onto squares of cement sidewalks and passing cars, the boys picked up their pace.

When Jiang first laid his eyes on Bo's apartment building, it was as if his early dreams of city life had manifested into Bo's reality. The building was made almost entirely of windows, and rather than a musty corridor inside the street-level entrance, heavy oak doors opened into a wide lobby, complete with a security desk and four elevators. The security guard directed a quick nod at Bo but kept his attention on the magazine in his hands. The elevators were covered in mirrors, and the gang of students waved their arms around, laughing hysterically at the endless reflection of arms within the mirrors, waving back at them.

The elevator brought them to the 20th floor in an instant and parted to reveal a brightly lit hallway, with a floor so polished that Jiang could see his reflection as he walked. Bo typed in a four-digit code above the handle on door number 205, and a small red light changed to green. Instead of the putrid mold scent wafting out of Jiang's apartment, a breeze of air-conditioning and freshly cooked meat smell drifted into their noses.

The group paused in the kitchen to greet Bo's mother, who was eating a bowl of pork and rice and watching the local news on a small television. Miniature shade lamps hung upside down from long cords above the sink and somehow the refrigerator appeared on but noiseless. Bo led them to his room, which Jiang figured to be at least three, perhaps four times as large as his own. Beneath the threshold of the door frame, Li Jie met Jiang's wide eyes and smiled. Then Li Jie softly slapped his friend on the back as they joined the group inside. Several students were already seated on Bo's bed, while Bo pulled two plastic crates of toys from under the bed. Jiang was amazed by the collection, but what really caught his eye, was a large television in the corner and a black, plastic box with different colored wires clustered under and around the television stand.

"Don't worry Jiang, we will watch a film later, and sometime you should come play video games too!"

Jiang blushed. He'd only recently heard about video games, but he shrugged and said that sounded like a great idea.

The group of boys spent the rest of the afternoon

having giant, mock battles with Bo's toys, while occasionally debating on which movie they would watch. A film about a giant dinosaur that attacked a city won out, and finally they settled around the room, while Bo hit 'play' on the VCR. Bo's mom appeared halfway through the movie, with a tray of snacks for the boys, who each mumbled a thanks while keeping their eyes glued to the screen. As he ate, Jiang looked around the room, finding it impossible not to smile. He and Li Jie had done it. They made a new group of friends and ones who seemed to have access to an endless supply of toys. He imagined himself coming over again, watching another movie, playing video games, and eating more crispy snacks.

Jiang raised his arms behind his neck and twisted his hips comfortably in his chair. He finally considered that city life might be tolerable after all.

VII: Ukali

On the day he turned six years old, for the first time, Ukali was permitted to accompany his father as he watched over the family's water buffaloes. They were the primary source of income for their family, and nothing was as precious in the world to them. Often, it seemed, not even Ukali was tended to and fussed over as intently. His mother was a well-respected seamstress in the village, and while she did usually find it funny when infant Ukali rolled over piles of clothes while she worked, she was indeed grateful for the day her husband took the young boy with him, to lead the buffaloes to their pastures along the river's shore.

The large, black creatures walked slowly downhill until, like a bell going off in their heads, they began to sense the nearness of the mud. In unison, they broke into a run, with their heavy bellies swaying side to side, and their legs wobbled to keep up with the top-heavy motion. One by one, they slowed as they approached a hole, and sampled a lick of the murky water. When it was deemed suitable for a bath, they took another confident step forward. Stumbling into the holes up to their chins, they kept their necks stretched upwards, so their nostrils at least had air to suck in.

Some snorted approvingly, and others, finding themselves in more shallow puddles, fell over sideways to cover their backs with the cool mud. They bellowed their ecstatic delight and breathed heavily through their noses. Ukali noticed that somehow their horns remained dry as if it was the one part of their bodies that didn't require cooling down.

Ukali let go of his father's hand and ventured nearer to the giants, which must have weighed at least twenty times his body weight.

"Not yet, Ukali," his father cautioned. "Wait until after their baths. They look relaxed but are helpless in the mud. You'll be a threat. Wait until they are grazing to go near them."

He and his father watched the herd sitting still in the cool mud. Overhead, a group of tiny birds darted back and forth, casting quick shadows around the animals below. When this morning bath was finished, the buffaloes balanced on their front knees, up to the hooves, and began climbing out of the water.

As they set about eating the patches of green grass around the mud, Ukali mustered up enough courage to go near one and touch its belly. He placed his tiny hand on the giant patch of skin, feeling incredibly small. Its skin was cool and rough, like a thick layer of living armor.

It grunted, and Ukali stepped back, searching for his father's eyes. His father nodded and motioned him forward again. Ukali put his hand on the belly again, and this time, the buffalo didn't make a sound, except for the repeated crunching of grass between his teeth. Ukali laughed, and the water buffalo glanced briefly at the strange, little boy touching her stomach, before returning to the grass.

"I like them," Ukali told his father, as they sat in the shade of a large boulder near the herd.

"They are powerful creatures, but gentle and kind once they get to know you."

"Do you have a favorite one?"

"They're all my favorite, son. Each one puts food on our plates, in one way or another."

"Will I be a buffalo farmer?"

"Herder," his father corrected, softly. "You can if you want to, but I think your future lies somewhere else. I hope selling these gentle beasts someday will give you more chances. More chances to choose your path than I had."

He didn't exactly understand what his father was saying, but without wanting to sound confused, Ukali replied, "Oh."

Ukali spent his adolescent years going to school, playing with his friends, and occasionally joining his father with the herd. He loved running around the grazing fields with his friends, making up games to play. The boys eventually included the herd in their games, first encouraging each other to crawl under an eating buffalo. Then one day, the boys were found throwing rocks at the buffalo. The buffalo, unaffected by the small pebbles, continued chewing their grass. Ukali's father arrived on the scene quickly and shouted at the kids. He ran to the group and grabbed Ukali by the arm, squeezing the thin muscles in his hand.

When asked why he was mistreating the animals, Ukali began to cry. "I...I don't know why." He didn't look up at his father's face, but kept looking at the buffaloes, feeling somehow that it was their fault he was in trouble.

It took months before he was allowed to join his father with the herd again, and it was two years before his father trusted him to be alone with them. His father would have Ukali watch the herd after classes, using the extra time to share afternoon glasses of brandy with the neighbors. Afterward, he would join Ukali, but always first observing the boy from a distance. Ukali could sense his father's presence, but pretended not to know, and kept his face forward, watching the herd with a concentrated stare. Eventually, a hand on his shoulder arrived with his father's shadow and both watched the buffaloes quietly.

One day during spring, Ukali was leaving the pasture and returning to his home. His father had just relieved him of duty and told him to check a buffalo and a new born calf in their stable. As his father stood by the bank of the river, watching the might of the raging river pass before him, a male buffalo charged him. When he spun around, the crazed creature was only steps away from him. He shouted at the buffalo and waved his arms. The huge careening body of the buffalo suddenly slid to a stop, realizing the man had called his bluff.

But the rock the herder stood on was wet from the splashing water, and as he flailed his arms, trying to regain his balance, he fell backward into the whitewater. He clawed at the water's surface, trying to keep his mouth out of the torrent. Ukali's father, like many in his generation, had never learned to swim. He clawed upwards and kicked at the water below him, but the struggle was in vain. He tried to yell above the current, but there was nobody near the grazing fields to hear. His body was never recovered.

The village had a ceremony next to the river, after the traditional four days of mourning, while the water buffalo grazed, seemingly unknowing of the loss. Ukali left the ceremony and walked up to the herd. He picked up the largest stone he believed he could throw and hurled it at the nearest animal. It bounced loudly off the buffalo's shoulder and that time the animal noticed. It bellowed in pain and sent the rest of the herd into a frenzy that took them further upstream, away from the mad child.

The proceeding years were not easy for young Ukali. In and outside of school, he grew more distant from his peers, and constantly told everyone that he was leaving the valley forever. But for a young teenager, deep in the mountains, there wasn't far he could go.

When he turned sixteen, the path into the village was widened, and motorcycles could be driven up the valley for the first time. News from the city started to reach the villagers, and new information about city life, the political changes in the government, stories about a new wave of tourism, and the availability of jobs began to flood the community.

Most people didn't think to travel that far south to see the city, but several did, and when they returned, their stories turned into legends about life in a metropolis. Ukali was always part of the crowd that surrounded each tale of city life. He was enthralled by the recounting of enormous buildings, motorcycles whizzing around every corner, and especially, the lack of buffaloes.

On his next birthday, Ukali informed his mother that he wanted to make the journey to the city, find work, and live a new life. Realizing that she would be alone in the village, she begged Ukali to stay with her. But he was insistent and eventually, she relented, if he promised to apply for a university, at least then she wouldn't have to worry that he was unemployable.

He found a motorcycle trader who had just unloaded crates of beer and had space for one more on the journey back down the valley. Ukali's mother sold off one buffalo and used the money for the ride plus a month's worth of money to help Ukali start his new life.

The ride to the city lasted two long days, on the back of a 50cc motorbike, which crunched painfully over each bump. Ukali feared that every bump would be the last for the rear tire, as he heard his seat scrape over the grooves on the tire, making a rubber buzzing sound. It was a slow and arduous journey, yet his excitement rose each hour the rear tire still survived and as the distance from his home grew.

When they first came into sight of the city, Ukali was surprised at how big it was. A thick cluster of tall buildings covered a central point, and the city stretched out in all directions, thinning with buildings up along the ridges of the wide, bowl-like valley. On the top of the hills above town, he could see temples, yellow and red, glistening in the sunlight, almost shining like gold. The other buildings were less stylish, with flat roofs that were sometimes topped with improvised shade made from fabric or bamboo. The walls seemed to be each painted a different color from the neighboring building, expressing some individuality of the painter, with hues he'd never seen before. Sometimes entire walls were just left with their brick skeleton showing, and he could make out little signs of life within the unfinished walls.

He could hear the sounds of the city, horns from thousands of cars, and a static buzzing sound as the underlining tone, which was as strange to his ears as the landscape was to his eyes. Dust seemed to rise from beneath the giant structures, and as it poured upwards to the roofs, it dissipated in a thick, brown tint of air above the city. He had never seen such air before. He had known only blue skies or cloud-covered skies. He didn't mind, the color was not something unclean for him, just the colors of a new life, and he breathed in a chest full of the new air, exhaling into a feeling of motivation and excitement.

A mass organism stretched out before him, seething with noise…life, movement, chaos, and surely new, wonderful experiences. He watched as the buildings grew and grew, as the motorbike chugged steadily into the strange new abyss. Soon, they clunked to a halt, bouncing up a steep curb.

"Welcome to Kathmandu, young man. This is as far as we go together."

The rider dropped Ukali off at a hotel on the outskirts of the city. The building was far less impressive up close. It looked older than his family's own stone house. Clusters of black wire ran from wall to wall, creating a bird's nest of tangles on the corners of the buildings. The dust from the road painted the lower third of the building brown from years of speeding drivers. He counted three windows without broken glass, and the sounds from horns almost deafened him as he tried to thank the driver.

Ukali wasn't deterred from the first steps in the city, he knew the outskirts were where he had to begin, although he felt an urge to venture into the center of the mass of buildings, to see what bizarre worlds he could find. But after two days of travel, he was exhausted and decided he needed some rest before finding his place in this environment. First, the outskirts, soon the center of it all. The man at the lobby desk asked how long he would be staying with them.

"Not long," he answered.

✧✧✧

The next morning, with a handful of school report cards and letters from teachers in his village, he set off to find a university. He had no idea what he would study, but from books he had read, he knew he wanted to do something with business. Business. Companies. They seemed to possess the most power, make the most money, and have the most variety. It seemed like the most opposing idea to sitting around watching buffaloes eat that he could imagine.

He walked most of the morning, stopping to ask strangers if they knew where the university was. Surprisingly, most people ignored him completely. They shrugged, without missing a forward step, and kept walking past him. He couldn't help but shrug back at them. Fine, he thought, if strangers don't care here, then I don't care either.

Finally, a group of boys, around his age, pointed him to the nearest one. They asked him where he was from.

"A village two days north."

"Another lost cog for the machine city."

The remark from one of the boys made the others laugh, and one boy slapped the speaker on the back. They continued walking past Ukali, who stood, staring at them, trying to figure out if the joke was at his expense or the city's.

He found the building that housed "Imperial University,

East Campus." It was several times bigger than his hotel, and none of its windows were broken. It looked impressive. Smooth, tan, concrete walls, stretching several stories above him, and to the sides, covered an entire block.

Inside the doors were pictures of students busy studying, and a tan, rectangular board on the wall was covered with pieces of colorful paper, each exclaiming something in bold print.

'Have you signed up for Autumn classes?' 'Study more for a better future' and 'Entrepreneurs Club meeting Tuesdays at 4 pm.' Each flyer chose a brighter shade than those underneath.

He wondered out loud, "Now, where can I speak to someone?" He glanced around the room again and noticed that to his left were a pair of doors, one with a stick figure of a man and one of a woman. He walked to the door with the man, opened it, and found just a row of toilets. He left the bathroom, shaking his head at himself. Across the foyer, he approached another door.

The color of the wood door shone off the overhead light as if it were just polished. Just next to the door, about eye-level, was a gold plaque on the door, spelling out: 'Admissions.'

He turned the round knob and pushed the surprisingly heavy door open, revealing several desks, with nicely-dressed adults busily writing in notebooks or talking into phones. A woman about his mother's age in the middle of the room looked up from her papers and watched Ukali curiously. He immediately felt nervous under her gaze and he could feel his hands gather moisture.

"Can I help you?"

"Yes...um...I want to be a student here...My names Ukali, I...."

"OK, Ukali, come have a seat." She motioned to the wooden chair in front of her desk.

From the chair, her desk and position looked even more intimidating to Ukali.

"We are still accepting for this Autumn, lucky for you. Do you have transcripts, or recommendations from your secondary school?"

He fumbled with his collection of papers and handed them over. She watched him, and he suspected that she knew something was different about this boy who wandered into her office.

"I see, I see."

He waited. He heard the clock behind him, clicking off each second that passed. He felt glances from the other staff members around the office.

"I see. Well, first, welcome to our city. Is it your first time here?"

He nodded quickly, then noticing this, slowed his head

into a single, affirmative nod.

"Well, honey…"

"Ukali…"

"That's right. Well, it looks like you are a good student, but the curriculum today is a little more…advanced…than where you come from. You see, we need transcripts from secondary schools that are accredited, or at the very least, you need to take an equivalency exam…or two. You will, most likely, need a state sponsorship to go to school here. It isn't too much, and we have many types of sponsorships. You can try the other universities in the area, but I would suspect they'll just about say the same thing…"

Her words fused into a confusing jumble of syllables and sounds, rising and lowering in tone, amassing together in what sounded like an alien tongue. Ukali couldn't help staring at the wall behind her as she spoke.

He blinked his eyes a few times to readjust his attention, and her voice faded back in.

"…So, we can certainly help you, but it's going to take some time. You're not the first. I've seen wide-eyed villagers come in before, all ready to make it in the big world, but not knowing where to start. I would recommend getting to work by studying for the equivalency exams. After that, maybe sometime next year at the soonest, we can talk further."

"But…uh…I promised my mother."

"I'm sure you did. I'm not saying don't give up, honey. Just work and study a bit on your own first. You can take secondary school classes easily, we have them every quarter. Then come and see us after you pass the exams."

He was lightheaded. So many new words bounced around his head. He stood up, mumbled a thanks, and walked out of the office. He felt a bit nauseous in the entryway, and realizing he might be sick, rushed to the door with the man on it.

Leaning over the toilet, he felt the wave of sickness pass in a tremor through his leg, his knees shaking to remove the abnormal feeling until it evaporated through his feet. He splashed water on his face from a bucket in the corner.

When he emerged from the building, he was still confused about everything the woman had said. More tests. Equiv…something. More school before university? He needed a place to sit down.

Walking farther along the street, he found a row of rock-carved benches that some older men were sitting on. A line of rickshaws waited on the street in front of them. They were evidently waiting for customers and passed the time spitting reddish brown liquid from their mouths while talking in a rapid, strange dialect.

Ukali sat on one of the benches and watched the street in front of him. Dust flew up from tires of enormous buses passing by, and the city's citizens hurried from one side to the other, always seeming to know exactly where they were going. *Everyone was late for something*, he thought. Was there a festival happening he didn't know about? But people moved in all directions. They couldn't be all going to the same place, could they?

He put his head in his hands, leaning forward towards the dusty ground. The sounds of the city, which seemed so inviting the day before, began to overwhelm him. His musings were ousted by every honking of a horn, his words pushed out of his head from every shout from a passerby. He stayed in that position for several minutes, his mind busy with considerations of his mother, his valley, his friends that he stopped playing with. He started to feel regret creep through his chest like congestion.

"Hey, buddy!"

More shouts from strangers sunk Ukali deeper into himself.

"Hey, guys, that's him. Hey, my friend, what's up? You. Village boy!"

The words were directed at him. He brought his heavy head up, his neck straining at the effort. His hands parted from his eyes and they focused on the image in front of him.

It was the boys from earlier. There were three of them. He thought they were students at first, but now he realized they had no school bags, and looked slightly older than him.

"What's up, my friend? Bad news at the university, eh?"

Ukali didn't respond.

"Hey no worries, man. We come in peace. We came from the mountains too, and definitely know this can be a crazy place for first-timers."

They talked among themselves for a few seconds then a second boy spoke.

"Hey, my name's Rollie, this is Jet, and that crazy guy is Chimp, because he is crazier than any monkey you've ever seen!"

The gang laughed and pointed at Chimp.

"It's a longer story than that, man," Chimp said, brushing off his shoulders, in some proud gesture. "Say, you should come with us, we'll cheer you up. The first day here is shit, unless you know who to hang with."

Ukali wiped his hair backward with his hands, using the sweat from his forehead to slick the loose hair.

"I'm Ukali. Those aren't your real names, are they? That your parents chose?"

The gang laughed at Ukali and walked up to him, and each shook his hand.

"It's cooler to have a new name here man, first lesson

of city life."

"Alright, Professor Jet," Rollie said, reaching into his pocket and pulling out a crumpled piece of paper and loose pieces of dried tobacco. He rolled the tobacco inside the paper in one quick motion, and struck a match under the sole of his boots, lighting the paper cigarette in another fluid motion.

"Can I try one of those?"

"You ever smoked before, Ukali?"

"No, but plenty of people in my village do."

"You can have one puff, but take it slow," cautioned Rollie, passing Ukali the cigarette.

He took a quick drag and immediately began coughing. He bent over again, feeling nausea immediately rise again. His head began to feel light, and as quickly as the sickness came up, it started to recede. He looked up, let out one more cough, and spit out the taste on the ground.

"OK, that's a good start."

The gang laughed at Ukali, but not in a way that felt cruel to him.

"Now let's find you a beer, man," Chimp said, putting his arm around Ukali's shoulder.

The gang of boys led Ukali farther down the street

until they came to a low door in a weathered, old building. The man behind the bar grunted when they walked in, but Ukali could only hear the sound of the man; the room was completely dark.

Only a dim light shone over the bar, and it took a long minute for his eyes to adjust. Around the bar, were several groups of older men, drinking thirstily from large glasses. A yellow liquid, full of bubbles on the rim, sloshed in their glasses as they drank.

The boys sat down at a table in the far corner, underneath a large poster of a shepherd holding a beer bottle, smiling unnaturally wide. Jet went to the bar and asked for four of the coldest beers they had. The bartender filled four glasses and said it was beer and temperature was subjective.

"You ever had a beer before, Ukali?" Rollie asked, who was rolling another cigarette.

"No, they just started bringing them into town. But I tried apple brandy once when my father was out with the buffaloes."

"Apple brandy! I love this guy." Jet said, setting the glasses down. "That stuff is like gasoline, this is the real drink of the modern world."

The boys touched their glasses together and Ukali began to make eye contact with them, but the others pulled their glasses away before he could. They each took a large, audible gulp from the glass, followed by a long sigh.

"Never mind with village customs here, Ukali, enjoy it."

Ukali tipped the rim of the glass towards his mouth and felt the slightly bitter drink splash over his tongue. He swallowed. It was good. His chest warmed slightly, and he felt a pleasant buzzing in his arms.

He took another long gulp. His mind, busy with a fluster of worry, regret, disappointment, and confusion, seemed to relax. He started to take another gulp, but a hand caught his.

"Slowly, my friend. There's no hurry. It'll do the job, don't worry."

"This guy is thirsty, eh boys," Jet said.

"Thirsty, that's a nickname?" Rollie suggested but then reconsidered. "No, no, that's too forced, it'll come to me. No hurry, no worry."

The four of them finished their drinks, ordered another round, and downed it at a slightly slower speed. The effects of the alcohol shown in their red cheeks, and the boyish giggles that came from every joke. Chimp did several monkey impressions when asked, which seemed to be his specialty. With each passing moment in the dark bar, Ukali felt more included with this funny group, and his worries of the morning seemed like a distant, irrelevant memory.

"Are there really monkeys here?" Ukali asked, after mulling over the possibility of it being a silly question.

"Are there monkeys? Wait, wait…you ever seen a monkey, Thirsty?"

"Nope, the nickname's forced, man, I'm telling you," Rollie said, slightly slurring his speech.

The gang, Ukali included, emptied their glasses, and set back onto the street. The sun was getting lower and several lights in windows had turned on.

"How long have when been in there?" Ukali asked.

"Beauty of beer. You can forget time," Chimp said.

"Forget about time, and you'll be feeling fine!" Rollie and Jet sang in unison.

The gang made their way to what was explained to Ukali as the oldest temple in the city, perched up on a hill.

"Tourists love this place," announced Chimp, proudly. Then he proceeded to imitate a tour guide. "On your left is an ancient mural from the original settlers of this land, The North-side Crew." He pointed to a scribbling of black graffiti, written in English. "On your right is a big pile of dog shit, look out folks!"

The boys laughed hysterically and jumped over the pile.

They twisted through alleyways, past shops selling spinning prayer wheels and colorful flags. Loud music played through crackling speakers, trying to entice buyers to enter. Ukali heard a familiar mantra, sped up to the deep, repetitive beating of drums. The dusty streets turned to stone, and Ukali found himself walking on a much harder surface. It was like stone, but darker, and he could barely see the spaces between each piece of rock. Rickshaws continued to fly past him, barely missing his arm, a quick flutter of warm wind following the back wheels.

But now, none of the cars on the road kicked up dust into their faces but instead were happily rumbling along the smoother surface, the horn beeps sounding friendlier, and the clusters of speeding machines gently wove between one another. Men carrying baskets of food on their backs stepped around the gang, and Ukali spied the bright green ends of carrots and beetroots bouncing joyously from the top of the baskets.

Shops spilled out of doorways onto the sidewalks, open doors covered with hangers of fur-lined jackets and colorful shawls. A passing glance into a shop showed Ukali an endless expanse of stacks of clothing, stretching far away from the street under dim overhanging lights.

Ukali had never seen a tourist before, but the first group of them was obvious to recognize. Three light-skinned men, with full beards and sun-burnt cheeks walked towards them. They carried huge packs with steel poles secured to the outside of them. Their enormous shoes rose up past their ankles, and their clothes were clean and multicolored. They had thick jackets on, while the locals were still wearing t-shirts. The three men looked determined in their motion, obviously feeling much more certain about their surroundings and purpose than Ukali.

Then Ukali spotted another group, on the other side of the street, arguing with a shopkeeper in some strange language about the price of a sweater made of yak hair. The potential buyers and seller countered each other's fingers with less or more fingers in return. A half-mimed brokerage of apparel. Both the vendor and the tourists looked unhappy, and the gang passed before Ukali heard a settlement being reached.

Then a group of women passed. They had thick jackets as well, but also the shortest pair of pants he had ever seen. He could see their legs, all the way passed their knees. He stopped, slack-jawed.

Rollie nudged him forward.

"Careful lover boy, they hate when you stare."

"But, I…They…"

"I know, it's a crazy time in the tourist district. Wait until the weather is hot again, you wouldn't believe what people wear."

"No touchy, just looky," Jet said, laughing, the others joining in. The women passed the gang of boys, looking up and down the shops, oblivious to the country boy with confused eyes.

But Ukali didn't want to touch them. He wanted to study them. What world did these people come from? What world freed so much skin into the open air?

They finally arrived at the entrance of the temple.

Some people referred to it as the Monkey Temple, but it wasn't named after Hanuman, a half-monkeyed representation of unwavering loyalty in Hinduism. Instead, it was after the residents of the temple, as Chimp informed them. Through the open, metal gates, they saw hundreds of statues in the fading light. Statues of those who found clarity in silence, Buddhas who would inspire and dumbfound millions of lost egos. It was eerily quiet. All the tourists had left well before sundown, and only the boys and a pack of dogs roamed through the statues. They walked towards the rear of the statue area until they came to a large flight of stairs. At the top of the stairs were yellow lights, larger statues, and large temple structures. Near the top of the stairs were small objects moving in the shadows. Too fast and agile to be human.

They climbed the stairs and came closer to the light and the silhouetted creatures.

Dozens, if not a hundred monkeys lined the sides of the stairs at the top. Some slept on the steps, others hissed and jumped into nearby bushes when they neared. Others slept in groups on the edges of the stairs, families clustered together, and some picked through each other's fur, eating whatever they found.

Several monkeys stood at the top steps, seeming to guard the passage. One showed its teeth and hissed, and Ukali took a step back. Its teeth were yellow, and even in the dim light, Ukali could see the long fangs on either side of its mouth.

"Hold on, I know this one," Chimp said.

He flung himself at the guardians of the stairs, swinging his arms in the air, screeching and mimicking a crazed monkey. The guards yelped and jumped out of the larger primate's path, scattering several families into the bushes with them.

"Now you see, one crazy ass monkey boy," Jet said.

At the top, the temple was actually several smaller temples surrounding an enormous stupa: a large dome with a pointed crown. Strands of colorful flags flapped in the wind around the complex, and soft bells rang from inside one of the buildings. It was quiet otherwise and Ukali noticed that he could barely hear the noise of the city below.

Apparently, the pack of dogs had followed them up the stairs, waiting for a path to be cleared, and burst in front of them, racing each other around the temple. Some barked at annoyed monkeys, and others wrestled each other, spilling lit trays of incense on the ground.

Once the frenzy ended, the dogs ventured further into the temple complex and left the gang alone at the base of the stupa.

Rollie produced a quart-sized bottle of whiskey from his pocket and motioned silently to a large landing to the left of the stupa. From the vantage point, the boys could see the entire tourist district and down to a cloud of smoke at the river. The noise from the city below melted into a song of horns, wheels, and wind. It gently wafted, with the smoke, towards them.

"The smoke is from the burning ghats," Jet explained, meeting Ukali's gaze.

Rollie took a swig of the brown liquor, grimaced, then passed the bottle. "It's good." He coughed and wiped small tears from the corners of his eyes.

The boys passed the bottle around and it arrived at Ukali. He shrugged and took a hefty pull on the bottle. The alcohol stung, more akin to apple brandy than beer he reckoned. He tried to show satisfaction in the taste when he saw the others watching him. The alcohol warmed up his entire body and he felt his face go slightly numb. The bottle was passed around twice more, while each of the boys took turns offering advice and telling stories about their first days in the city.

"Every time I think I know this place, I find somewhere new," Jet said. "It's an industrial beast that keeps getting bigger and bigger. You can find anything you want here, man….anything."

The city lights below started to blur and the sounds of horns and cars grew more faint as more whiskey passed through Ukali. He remembered walking down the stairs, a faint hint that there were more strange monkey interactions, then darkness.

☼☼☼

He awoke on the bed of his hotel room. He was fully clothed with one sandal still dangling from a foot. His head hurt, tremendously. He reached his arms around the bed, fighting nausea with every motion. The room seemed to spin around him. He tried to shut his eyes to make it stop but then he was just lost in a spinning, dark void. On the bed next to him, he found a crumpled piece of paper and a few coins, evidently emptied from his pocket before he fell into his heavy sleep.

He unraveled the paper and read a note. It was written in messy handwriting: 'Don't pout! It's time to learn to tout! See you at the bar at 12 o'clock!'

VIII

The yak herders returned to Suman's valley with much more than cheese that winter. They arrived bearing a new energy that the villagers found themselves completely immersed inside. A large celebration welcomed them back, with Tauko and Suman nestled amid the joyous sounds, sipping tea with their neighbors, laughing, and talking about what mischief their children were causing.

The only different sight at that celebration was Ukali driving to the collection of bonfires and revving his engine for the children gathered around him. The farmers rolled their eyes at each other.

"It's pretty loud, but at least it makes him drive out of the village once in a while," one farmer said, igniting hearty laughter from the group. After he cut the engine, Ukali stumbled over to the group.

"Hello my friends, I have brought gifts for all of you," Ukali said as he revealed a large bag. He pulled out cell phones and began to pass them around the group of farmers. "One for each of you. They have lots of credits on them, and your number is written on the back. Now when you're bored in your fields, you can call each other. Just don't give your wife the number," he punctuated the joke with a slap on his leg and let out a deep laugh, just before emitting a burp. He then pulled out a bottle from his bag and saw the bewilderment on his neighbor's faces as its strange label appeared in the light of the campfire.

"It's whiskey. It's a type of alcohol made in a distant land. Except not from apples."

"What's it made from?" asked a farmer. In response, Ukali shrugged and took a big gulp before passing it to the man next to him.

Before the next man could drink, Tauko stood up and threw his cell phone into the fire. The small, plastic phone smashed in half on a smoldering log, breaking chunks of ember off the log. Sparks lifted out of the fire, as pieces of the phone's screen bubbled and sizzled on the sandy floor of the fire pit. The men were silent, some looking at the destruction in the fire, and some gazing up at Tauko's face, which narrowed in anger.

Tauko turned his back to the stunned group and headed out into the night. Suman smiles at his neighbors, before standing up to chase after Tauko.

When he caught up to his friend, Tauko was sitting on a stone wall looking down the valley.

"You alright?" Suman asked.

Tauko pulled a crooked cigarette from his pocket. He gently straightened it out with both hands before lighting it.

"Since when do you smoke?" Suman asked him. Tauko shrugged, blew out a large cloud from his lungs, and handed the cigarette to Suman, who politely declined. They heard Ukali talking and the other farmers laughing back at the campfire. Suman glanced over at his friend's weary face.

"Don't worry," he said and put his arm around Tauko. The two men looked down the valley. Tauko nodded his head toward a stream of lights, far away, which must have been almost in the next village. They are moving slowly, possibly herders, but both of the men know better. A person with a light was easy to identify because lamps usually swayed side to side when carried. These lights moved more quickly, and in a steady, unchanging direction. Pairs of lights remained at an equal distance apart, moving in unison.

The next day, Suman was woken up by more engines, and looking through his window, he saw a caravan of Jeeps, and even some larger vehicles, carrying enormous loads. The metallic sounds were abrupt and loud. Suman couldn't help but feel uneasy listening to the rough sound of the engines, far more brutish than any animal cry, he mused. They drove through town and up the valley towards the purchased land. After they climbed over the first hill, the village grew silent again.

It happened again the next day. Trucks drove through, some carrying large metal machines on the back, each full of men and tools, then returning back down the valley in the evening. Some people in the village stood in their doorways and waved at the trucks. Suman couldn't see if the truckers were waving back because the windows of the trucks were tinted and only the village's reflection looked back.

This procession of trucks and machinery seemed to continue without a pause for weeks on end. Peaceful mornings were lost to memory for Suman. Sanjana joined him, her hands resting on her hips, as truck after truck bounced passed their house. The couple tried to continue their days as normal, and eventually, an ebb of bewilderment relented into acceptance of the daily disturbance.

Eventually, the trucks stopped coming, reducing the noise to just an odd Jeep every now and then. Then one Jeep stopped on its journey through town, and the driver inquired at a nearby house about food for sale. There weren't many stores in town, as people primarily traded among themselves. But as the Jeeps continued this routine, an entrepreneurial idea swept through part of the village, and several farmers began arranging tables outside their homes and putting up signs declaring: "restaurant," "cafe", or "hot food."

Suman watched one new restaurant from across the road. Men in bright orange shirts eating dal bhat like it was their last meal before a long trek. One of the men locked eyes with Suman and smiled. Suman returned the smile, but couldn't help feeling odd about the swift changes developing so close to home.

As the first snow started to fall on the high peaks,

Sanjana asked Suman if he had visited his father's hill since the commotion had begun.

"I haven't…"

"We've watched these strangers toil past us in their overloaded cars for over a month now. But the only thing I find more odd is that you haven't investigated more deeply."

"What do you mean?" Suman asked.

"Have you seen what they're doing with all that equipment?"

It was a fair question, and it lit a new wick of energy in Suman's bones, and he realized that his routine had been skewed off-balance indeed.

The next morning, Suman woke up early and put on his sandals. He followed the road to his father's path and climbed steadily uphill. He sat down and reached into his pocket until the tips of his fingers gathered a small stone into his hand. He pulled it out, lifting it up to his eyes, trying to see the details of its flat face. As quick as he pulled it out, he suddenly dropped it. His jaw slacked open, his eyes fixed on something up the valley. He saw the grazing land that was sold to the Ukali's businessmen. There were two large concrete towers planted next to the river, and several buildings on the nearest side. Little white rectangular boxes, connected by electric cables at the roofs. Trucks and men moved constantly around them, and a large, metal crane was swinging heavy loads of rock toward the river. He left the stone where it fell on the ground, and took off down the narrow path, taking large strides over two or three steps. Sliding into the main road that passed through the village, he cut left and jogged up to the men and machinery. Soon after, he overtook the first hill above town, the first false summit on the way out of town, but instead of seeing an open road leading to the construction zone, he was met by a small, hastily built house and fence that stretched away from it as far as he could see. A sleepy, overweight man exited the building and approached him, holding gloved hands above his head.

"What's going on?" Asked Suman.

"Dam business," the man replied in a heavy accent. "Everything good, but too dangerous now. Please stay out."

"Can I please just have a closer look? I'm a local." Suman pleaded with a friendly smile.

"Please stay out," was the reply. "Dam business." The guard motioned back to the village. Suman walked back to the village but paused at the rounded top of the hill to witness it all again. He heard a sudden, splashing sound from where the crane towered over the river, followed by lots of shouting.

When he neared his house, he stopped and turned around, deciding to instead head to Tauko's house. He found his friend outside smoking a cigarette, watching Suman as if he already knew what was coming.

"I tried to go to the construction site," Suman said.

"I know," said Tauko. "Dam business."

"What's a..."

"A dam is a big wall in the river, they are going to use the wall to make electricity somehow. Suman, they are stopping the flow of the river."

"What can we do?" Suman asked his friend.

"What can we do?" repeated Tauko, a searching look on his face.

Late that afternoon, they joined again, wearing their warmest clothes, and climbed farther along the hillside, just out of sight from town, where they could see the construction more clearly. The wind was a bit stronger than in the village, and Suman pulled his coat across his chest so it fit a little tighter. Tauko sat, smoking a cigarette and Suman chewed a strand of long grass, their eyes stayed settled, intently, on the once buffalo-covered fields. The cranes were placing large, concrete blocks into the river now, and everything on the ground was moving very quickly.

"What will this mean?" Tauko asked, breaking a long silence, as he stamped out his cigarette, and then picked up the butt and placed it in his pocket. The weather was becoming colder, and it became clear that the only reason the construction was continuing during the winter was that the river was smaller than during the warmer months. The speed of the construction meant

133

that they must be trying to finish the project before the snow melted. Without saying anything, both men nodded in unison as they both came to the realization.

"The river might be too strong for the wall in the summer," Suman said, beating his friend to the thought while glancing up at Chatima Mountain.

"I hope it is," Tauko said, bringing a new cigarette to his mouth.

☼☼☼

That winter felt longer than any Suman had known before. When the wind blew, its icy touch sliced easily through his clothes. The darkness enveloped the night with a deeper tint, and the daylight hours seemed to disappear far too quickly. He made the journey to carve his stones only once during the first two months. The cold combined with the construction of the dam in sight made the hilltop retreat less appealing. He felt restless indoors, and unable to sleep through the night completely. He eagerly waited to start farming again. He wanted the sun to warm his back, and he wanted to hear the roar of the river far below.

Thankfully the nights were warm inside his house, and he mainly occupied himself by playing with Maya and staying as long as he could in bed with Sanjana. The bed, under the yak-hair blanket, was the warmest place in the house, and it was a struggle to leave the warmth each morning. He would wake up and try to smile. He stared first at the cracks in the ceilings above. He followed the lines of wood until they reached the place where a knot in one board had opened a crack, forming a larger gap from the next board. He practiced moving his mouth into a smile, but it fell back to his chin easily. The only hope to maintain a smile was to roll over to his side and face his wife. It seemed like she became more beautiful each time he saw her. When she first opened her eyes, she'd see his smiling face and feel his kiss on her cheek. He began to cherish her first returned smile each morning, and it became his final contemplation before drifting off to sleep.

Some nights before bed, he was quiet and appeared lost in introspection when Sanjana tried to speak to him. She knew the dam troubled him. She also knew from her long nights growing up in the tents of a yak herding family, that the darkness and cold of winter could only exacerbate any troubles on a person's mind. Before sleeping, she made sure to tell him that the future was bright for them; that he should not focus on such negative emotions, and concentrate on the beauty of their life and the joy of watching Maya grow up. He listened and agreed with everything she had told him. He did find plenty of moments within the house that made him smile naturally. But when alone, worry crept back into his mind. It was a worry that spun through his head without warning or introduction. It was without beginning or end, just a puzzle of frustration that didn't want to be solved.

When he was with Maya, his head was more quiet and less relentless. She would start school soon, and he had already been teaching her to read and write. He knew she was going to be more clever than her father. Her calmness and mental growth in that dark winter world impressed Suman, yet he failed to stop himself from wondering what world she would grow up in. Would she stay in the village, and would their village look the same by the time she had her own children? Times had certainly changed since he was a child. Now, many villagers sent their young ones south to the city, to study and to work. Although the prospect of that new life enticed plenty of families, Suman understood well that most children who left the village seldom returned to live again.

He had been to the city once when he was a teenager. He went with his father to visit a political rally. He couldn't remember what the politicians were talking about, but he remembered the city itself. It was busy, more dusty than the village, and there was noise constantly. He remembered not sleeping well, and his father trying to sing him songs so he'd finally fall asleep. His father didn't like the city, and after a few days, they were both ready to return to their high mountain home. On the walk home, he remembered what his father had said to him.

"You can do anything you want in this life, Suman. Personally I feel trapped in cities and can't breathe well. The mountains and river bring tears to my eyes every time I return home after a journey like this. If you grow up and want to visit the city again, I will support you, but remember that the village will always be here, waiting for you to return."

Suman never went back to the city, and the idea of the

noise and thick air made him nauseous. He remembered when he and his father reached the last hill before the village that day. He looked up at his father, who had stopped mid-stride. There were tears in his eyes, and when he felt his own face, Suman realized that he was also crying.

Later during that cold winter, Tauko and Khayo's families visited Suman's home for a long dinner of dal and yak cheese momos. It was a welcome change of pace for everyone. After the meal, the children drifted into the next room, coaxing each other into recently invented card games. The adults remained at their seats around a handmade wooden table. The same that a neighbor made for them in exchange for a few jars of Suman's own spicy, pickled turnips.

"They've been pulling down sides of the mountain, and using machines to break the rock into smaller pieces," Khayo was saying, while seated next to Tauko, and across from everyone else. "It's made the walls along the bank higher…every time I look, it's grown."

"It's strange that they stop us from walking up there," Added Sanjana, folding her hands softly onto the table.

"Why would they do that?" Khayo said, shaking his head.

"Because they are going to stop the river. That's their intention. And they know we will be upset." Tauko answered.

"I still don't understand how stopping the river would

be useful for them," Khayo said.

"Because this will give them electricity. A strong river means a lot of power."

"Right, but I still don't understand."

"We don't need to, but what will it do here? Just seeing what they've done to the mountain-"

"It can't be good."

"Yes…"

"Who do we know that takes water from the river?" Suman said, making his two friends turn their heads.

"I know some-" Khayo began.

"Suman, down the river…" Sanjana said. "…everyone downriver. Where the snow stops too…"

"The cities are there." Tauko looked past the table, at the rear window.

"Aren't the cities using the electricity?" Khayo asked.

"Perhaps it's a different city that takes the power," Suman guessed, pulling his shoulders up slightly.

"There must be something we can do. We need to try speaking to them again. Maybe-" Tauko stopped.

Khayo was shaking his head to the side. Everyone was

looking down at the floor.

"Am I going crazy?"

No one at the table could come up with a promising idea to hinder the dam's construction, and the next week, a similar conversation became pointless even faster. Several of them tried to gain entry into the construction site, but every time were turned back downhill.

So as the winter carried on, the dam was discussed less, their fate seemingly accepted with a silent withdrawal from the topic, and soon the neighbors were more concerned about the coming spring planting. The dam steadily rose, and Ukali was seen less and less. He would occasionally ride his motorcycle up the main road, but the village appeared deaf to the sounds of the engine. He would sometimes try to join a group of farmers as they were playing cards, but he was usually too drunk to participate. If Tauko happened to be dealt into the hand, he would instantly leave his seat before Ukali could sit down.

If the card games moved inside, they stopped seeing Ukali completely. If he had knocked on the door, they would have let him in, they were neighbors after all, but he seemed to disappear on his own. They heard from others that he often sat in his house, drinking whiskey and watching television all through the night. He never worked anymore and seemed out of breath just walking up the hill into the village. He preferred to drive his motorcycle to buy more alcohol, but eventually, that became too tiresome. Then Jeeps began stopping outside his house, and someone would unload crates of whiskey and beer to his doorstep. Ukali paid them with wads of cash and dragged the crates inside, where the door remained shut the rest of the day. The higher the wall of the dam rose, the more disconnected Ukali became.

☼☼☼

On the first warm day after the new year, the sun shone brightly through Suman's window, who woke to hear only the sounds of birds singing. No bouncing wheels or chugging motor sounds entered the room. He dressed and put on his sandals. Reaching over to a shelf, he picked up a stone that Maya had given him as a present. It was shaped like a heart, and he was determined to chisel a new mantra into it. Stepping out into the sunlight, he felt a pulse of energy creep up his toes. Each step up the road felt easier and more fluid than the last. When he sat down at his hilltop retreat, he removed the stone. He didn't let his gaze drift behind him but kept it down the valley instead. He felt the presence of the dam, but couldn't allow it to disturb him on such a beautiful morning.

In the stone, very carefully, he chiseled an elaborate "Om," followed by Maya's name. Above the characters, he chiseled a flower, and below he wrote in the best handwriting he could: "Flowers are always magic." He kissed the cold rock and placed it on his lap. Then, slowly, he stacked rocks into a small, stone monument, and placed Maya's rock on top of it. A few years later, he would bring her up the hill, show her the rock, and repeat the words his father once told him.

"I'm sure you will find many beautiful things in your life, but I hope that someday you'll remember how much I love this place."

Chetan's words floated down the valley, and when Suman watched the wind that carried the words downstream, his eyes fell on the river. It was still small from the winter freeze, but it seemed smaller than usual. He squinted and saw two tiny dots making their way up the road quickly. The road down the valley had been significantly widened by the construction company, in order to accommodate their larger vehicles, and Jeeps could drive up the road much faster now. After watching the Jeeps for a while, he rose to his feet and brushed the dirt from his pants in one, practiced motion.

Before leaving his hill, he snuck a glance upriver at the dam and suddenly wished he hadn't. Staring back at him was an enormous, concrete wall. Still quite far from where Suman stood, it was difficult to figure out how high the wall rose, but it was the largest man-made structure Suman had ever seen. Men, the size of ants, walked near the top, where several towers stretched slightly higher than the wall of the dam. Huge clusters or rust-colored bars stuck out along the top. A small stream was released at the base of the dam, and a large pipe appeared to be leaving the other side of the dam, and continuing upriver.

He had always been surrounded by mountains, many of them impassable, but this wall was different. Such a monotone, blank face looking down at his village. The chaos of cranes, trucks, and cuts into the hillside transformed the scene completely. It felt as if he could no longer journey up the valley if he wished. For him, the wall marked a new edge of his world and his valley began to feel significantly smaller.

Back on the main road of the village, Suman found himself staring at the two Jeeps he had been watching climb up the valley. On the side of the door were characters from a foreign language and a logo consisting of a water drop with a lightning bolt cutting across it. The Jeep was empty, so Suman continued on walking. He stopped outside a restaurant, where he saw Ukali inside with two men in suits. On the front steps of the restaurant were four more men, all wearing black sunglasses, facing out towards the road. Suman looked in and saw Ukali smile and take a large package with two hands, his greedy eyes giving himself away. Ukali glanced outside to see Suman watching, but turned back smoothly, as if without any hint of recognition.

Suman waited under a tree nearby until the men left the restaurant and drove onwards to the dam. Ukali rose from his seat soon after and walked briskly, almost bouncing in his steps, to his motorcycle parked outside. Suman approached.

"Hello, Ukali, final gifts from your benefactors?"

"Uh, hi Suman. Well, that's it for me. No more winters in this forsaken valley. I'm going back to the city at the start of spring, and I suspect you won't be seeing me anymore. But hey, maybe one last card game before I leave? Heh-heh…"

Taken aback by the way Ukali spoke about his beloved valley, Suman took a moment to respond. When Ukali straddled the motorcycle, he finally said back, "Sure Ukali, see you at the game."

IX

"Jiang?" "Hey, Jiang…"

"…he must still be dreaming…"

The group of high school students watched their friend's empty eyes, as they gazed over the glass-like surface of the lake. The color of the sky drifted through a beige, filter at street level into the blue above them, typical during the dry season in Qinan City, when the smog from nearby factories, car exhaust, and the farmer's burn piles create a three-month-long haze over their city.

Somewhere in the distance, a series of motorbike honks created a vehicular sympathy, while a street vendor's proclamation of fruit prices filled in the melody. Two fishermen, wearing heavy coats, worn-out military caps, and sandals, cast their lines into the water.

"Wait, wait, look at his hand…" Bo said, pointing at Jiang's hand, which held a burning cigarette.

The burning end slowly crept towards his middle and index fingers. Within seconds, the red embers were between his digits.

"Yee-ow, shit!" Jiang shook his hand, before blowing on his fingers. His friends laughed, and Bo pointed at their ill-stricken pupil.

"Where did you go, Jiang?" A student named Hong asked, a trace of sympathy in her eyes.

He began to answer her, but paused, taking the moment to notice how the light from the faded sun shone through her hair. She was 18 years old, the same as Jiang, and he figured she had the type of face that would never lose its beauty. Her black, leather jacket was pulled tight over her fleece sweater, the sleeves almost covering her hands.

The winter hadn't quite finished, but the crowds of locals sipping coffee and tea around the lake suggested that spring had already arrived.

"I was...er..." Jiang lost his words after Hong hatched a small smile before looking down at her cup of steaming green tea.

"Are you worried about your exams, brainiac?" Bo asked, in a mocking tone. "Because if there's anyone who should be worried, it's me. I'm not even sure if I've been going to the right class."

Every student began to laugh, and Jiang's embarrassment dissipated.

"Well, I hope so, or else the answers you've been

stealing from me aren't worth a damn." Jiang's joke made him laugh before he could finish the sentence.

Jiang and his classmates had started meeting along Jaminghu Lake most Saturdays since they began high school. The lake was only a few minutes' walk from Bo's apartment building and surrounded by popular restaurants and cafes. Through the thin leaves of a row of willow trees, a six-storied temple floated above a distant canopy, the tiles of the roof barely visible in the haze.

Li Jie would also normally join his old primary school friends, even though his family moved to another neighborhood before they entered high school. However, he hadn't shown up that morning. Jiang checked his phone, not seeing any missed calls from his friend. Their final primary school years seemed to fly by. Years of being accepted into the world of their new friends - after-school meet ups at Bo's apartment, weekends playing soccer on real grass fields, taking the bus to the cinema for every release of major action movies, homework study groups, field trips to museums and famous monuments around the city - a blur of the wonders of growing up in a modern metropolis.

Jiang had felt that he lived up to his teacher's recommendation all those years ago: he had learned to live in his new environment, and his tolerance for it transformed into a genuine pleasure. Technology advanced quickly in the city. He went to the dentist for the first time and was fitted with metal bars that straightened his teeth, producing what his mother called 'a handsome smile.' People began carrying phones everywhere they went, which gave them access to an endless network of knowledge. Even the lights changed. It became brighter at night, and sidewalks and shops lit up all through the evening. His mother said she felt better outside at night after their own street received streetlamps.

But his father hadn't adapted in the same way. After his release from prison, his father kept his promise and found work immediately. It wasn't glamorous, but six days a week at an appliance factory put food on the family's table. His father was enthusiastic at first, boasting that his foreman had promised him a management position and that they would soon move out of their small apartment.

Years passed and Jiang's father stopped mentioning the promotion. He spent less time talking at the dinner table, and sometimes skipped meals, passing the evening hours with a beer in front of the television. Jiang could hear him cursing his company most mornings and he began comparing everyday troubles with "life on the farm." The family had enough money for food and new clothes as Jiang began rapidly outgrowing all his old ones, but their existence seemed to have reached a plateau. Jiang preferred hanging out at the apartments of his friends rather than heading home after school, content to enjoy the better toys and tastier snacks elsewhere.

"You guys want to go catch that new robot movie?" Bo's words broke Jiang from his daydreams.

"I'm going to catch the bus home. I'm supposed to help my mom out today." Jiang heard himself lying to his friends. He didn't have anything particular to do, but a cloud of melancholia had engulfed him and he felt the sudden desire to be alone with his reflective mood.

"Alright, mama's boy, anyone else?" The other students agreed to the movie and stood up to high-five Jiang as they left their seats. Hong paused, standing over Jiang, and he raised his head up to meet her eyes. Blushing, she appeared to hold back more words than she lets out.

"Um…see you later, Jiang. Good luck with your chores."

"Er…thanks, Hong."

Jiang watched his friends round the corner, then got to his feet, scanning up and down the lakefront. He sighed and walked towards the nearest bus stop. His mind was empty in a way, but also as if it was wandering around a hidden consideration, almost purposefully avoiding something.

He stepped onto bus, number 307, which headed east. At this time of day, and being in the opposite direction of the city center, the bus was filled mostly with old women, full bags of vegetables in their laps. The bus route would pass a major outdoor market soon.

Jiang looked at the old women around and couldn't help thinking about his mother. She wasn't much younger than these women, and he could easily picture her sitting on the same bus, chatting with her friends on the way to the market.

Since the move, she had made several new friends and usually spent her evenings socializing outside their building. She had taken a job cleaning apartments in a more upper-class neighborhood, and when she finished, she usually had little energy to stray too far from their building.

Lately, he had noticed her become increasingly preoccupied with the well-being of his father. During his days off work, his father had stopped leaving the apartment, only getting up from his chair to eat and sleep. Jiang had heard him recently talking about looking for a new line of work, somewhere that valued its employees more.

"Years without an extra cent added to my paycheck. They just dangle new promotions over our heads, like we're the biggest idiots in the world…"

The sudden braking of the bus snapped Jiang out of his thoughts. An old woman, perhaps more than 80 years old, most likely hunched over from a lifetime of farming, was slowly crossing the crosswalk, and had picked the least opportune moment to cross.

The driver, unamused by this show of ancient frailty, honked his horn. The woman, either hard of hearing or indifferent to the angry honking, did not look up from her concentrated, painful-looking steps.

As soon as there was enough room, the driver accelerated the bus and continued down the road, mumbling something indistinguishable under his breath.

The market stop arrived suddenly, with another jolting of the break lines, and the bus filled with chatter. The women, bags in hand, raced to exit, causing a significant jam at each of the three doors. There were no insults or bad manners in the crowd at the doors. It was as if the only way to exit was in the same manner toothpaste leaves its packaging. The women somehow managed to squeeze out, two or three at a time. By now, Jiang was accustomed to crowds exiting public transport at the same time, nobody ever giving way easily, fighting for some imagined prize for first off the bus.

He looked towards the front of the bus for the first time since stepping aboard. He noticed a backward baseball cap. Something about it seemed strangely familiar. Or perhaps it was the mess of hair, sticking out the sides of the cap. The bus took off and instantly swerved around several motorcycles, making everyone standing lose their balance briefly, just enough to make them step forward to regain their position.

The person with the cap looked sideways, following the group of motorcycles, which passed along the right-side windows. Jiang immediately recognized the person under the cap.

Li Jie caught his friend's eyes in the back of the bus, smiled, and carefully made his way through the other passengers to get closer.

"Jiang, you giant egg, what the hell are you doing

here?"

"I could say the same for you, where were you this morning?"

"Ah, I've been traveling!"

The bus lurched to a stop, and both of them recognized it as Jiang's stop. They quickly pushed their way off, onto a narrow strip of pavement, slightly dusted with sand.

They began walking down the sidewalk, skirting around several vendors, who were busy dipping dough into bubbling woks of oil. Another man was sitting cross-legged atop his motorcycle and turned his head towards them. He was wearing the vest of a moto taxi driver, but decided they weren't worth the effort of offering his services. Instead, he reached into the front pocket of his vest, and as the two friends passed him, he pulled out a well-worn, silver lighter. Behind them, they heard him cough loudly, deeply, and spit onto the sidewalk.

Ahead of them, a cluster of apartment buildings loomed above the busy streets below. Jiang felt a sense of belonging walking next to his old friend. The tightness that was forming at the lake began to soften, and the muscles on his face began to relax.

"When we were young, I could always count on you to lift my spirits. You had a way…I guess…of turning bad situations into better ones," Jiang looked at Li Jie, wondering if he had opened up too much.

"I thought the same about you, man. Maybe it was the pair of us. But I understand what you mean… But you didn't ask where I've just been traveling to."

"Right, sorry, where did you go? Probably back to the zoo where you belong," Jiang bumped into Li Jie's shoulder purposely, trying to lighten the nostalgic atmosphere he figured his last words had created.

"I went back to our village man!"

Jiang stopped walking, then noticing it, caught back up to his friend quickly. He remembered when Li Jie planned to visit for the first time, years ago. The opening of his parents' new store had stopped him from making the journey.

"Well, how was it? Does it look like here? What do our farms look like? Is it crowded there too?"

Li Jie stopped walking, reaching over to grab Jiang's shirt, signaling him to stop as well. He breathed in softly, without taking his eyes off Jiang's.

"It is the strangest place I have ever seen. It is totally empty. Well, I guess I saw a handful of taxis, but that's pretty much it. Man, there's less people than when we lived there."

Jiang, thinking his friend was teasing him, said, "OK man, but really, what's it like?"

"I'm absolutely serious. Look at my face, I wouldn't lie about our home."

Li Jie told Jiang about the buses he had to take. How, even when he was only an hour away, nobody on the bus, except the driver, knew where he was going.

"I thought that I was going the wrong direction, that somehow I'd gotten on a bus coming from our village, rather than to it. But the driver assured me I was going the correct way. That bus dropped me off at a brand new bus stop. The glass still had that protective film on it, and it had a detailed map of the new city within one of the glass sides. The funny thing was that I didn't see how the map related to what I saw in front of me. There was pretty long grass growing through the sidewalk, and up along the glass sign too, half covering it. There was a taxi waiting down the street a bit, so I walked over to ask him directions. I could see huge buildings in the distance, but man, I couldn't recognize a single landmark."

"How about the little grove of trees next to the market," Jiang asked.

"Couldn't see one tree from that bus stop. But it gets much stranger, my friend. The taxi driver, who just about jumped off his seat when I stuck my head in his window, pointed straight towards the cluster of buildings and said I was already in the city. When I asked about the giant shopping complex that should be there, he shrugged and said there might be one or two shops open. It didn't make any sense. It's been how many years? Six, right? There should be thousands of people around. But I swear to you, I didn't see one person or car apart from the taxi driver on the way to the first apartment building...must have been a twenty-minute walk. The first apartments looked

153

completely deserted. Then, as I passed the first few, the rest of the city came into view. I mean, I keep saying city, but what's a city without people? Is there a word for that? Some sort of pile of metal boxes?"

Jiang shrugged. "You didn't see anyone, except that taxi?"

"Maybe a dozen or so more…signs of life. I saw some laundry outside one apartment window. A handful of taxis were parked outside the shopping mall, which looked half-finished. It still had enormous yellow cranes sticking out of the backside of it. It had one shop open, on the ground floor. Pretty much a convenience store. That was the only person I really talked to. It was an older man. He said he'd always lived in the area, but I didn't recognize him. He said that three years ago…yes, I think three years ago, people began moving into the city. But it was far less than the numbers we heard. A few hundred he said. Then, once construction workers started leaving, it meant that finally all the buildings were finished. I think he said there were about fifty apartment buildings. Well at least, they considered the city must be ready to receive the rest of the residents. But no one else came. Some people were working for the city, so they were busy sweeping, cleaning up trash, watering trees, and all that. But most of the rest had moved to the city early to open shops. Toy stores, appliance shops, restaurants, and so on. But not enough people came. Shop owners couldn't exactly buy from their neighbor's shop when they had no income themselves. Now and then a couple or a small family would move into a building, last a few months, then move away.

He said no one liked to live in a ghost town, and I don't blame them. It was pretty damn creepy, Jiang. Huge buildings, signs everywhere about this and that, which didn't seem to exist: a water park, a zoo, a futuristic shopping mall with a roller coaster, five star restaurants. I didn't see any of those. I walked around all day but really didn't want to be stuck there at night. The only things on the road were the taxis and one motorcycle. I tried to imagine where our houses were, but it was all just concrete, and too difficult to get my bearings. I noticed the canal, with some bridges over it, but only small tree saplings. There's no telling where our swimming hole might have been. Man, it was the weirdest place I've ever been."

Jiang felt as if he should say something, but his brain was still processing what he'd just heard. His mind was repeating Li Jie's story, both he and his mind unsure how to react. He was angry and pretty confused. But neither feeling called him to speak up. Li Jie watched Jiang closely, then attempted to answer what Jiang may have been thinking about.

"I would say there's no need to go back there again. That's not where we are from. I've been thinking about this all day now, trying to figure out why our home would be destroyed for some farce of a metropolis. But there's nothing back there for either of us."

When they arrived at Jiang's apartment building, they shook hands and looked directly in the eyes of the other. Both realized in that moment how much value the other truly had in their own life, and that brief acknowledgement was confirmed in each of them without the need for additional words.

"Jiang, before you go, I want you to meet some friends of mine. When are you going to be free?"

Jiang hadn't heard much about Li Jie's friends from the other school. He had always assumed that since Li Jie still joined them every Saturday, he hadn't made many new friends.

"I'm not doing anything now actually," Jiang admitted. "I just was on auto-pilot mode, going home for no reason."

"You nut!" Li Jie laughed, slapping Jiang on the shoulder. "Cool then, let's go. I told them I'd come tell them about our village when I came back. It sounds strange, but they already knew what it would be like. They know things, Jiang. I didn't believe them, but now...well, you'll just have to come hear it from them."

On the next bus, Jiang sat by the left window, as Li Jie, sitting next to him, hummed an old pop song. Jiang watched the traffic coming in the opposite direction. He tried to count the intervals between each vehicle. He realized that not a second went by without something whizzing by the window. *Amazing*, he thought. *How could one city be so full and another be empty like that?*

After they got off the bus, Li Jie led Jiang down a narrow alley between a motorcycle repair shop and a convenience store. The alley twisted to the right, then to the left. A small whiteboard with illegible handwriting dangled off a rusty wire on a corner. The concrete on the corner was cracked open, revealing several clay bricks. Someone must have broken a small hole into one, then fed the wire in and around the exposed brick. Then it looked like they accidentally used a permanent marker on the sign and tried to scratch out the ink.

As they moved deeper into it, the alley became more narrow and darker, with old apartment buildings blocking out the sky above them. A few thin palm trees reached over the walls and green water stains seeped from several cracks. Through a closed gate, Jiang could hear several chickens. Hens were calling their young to a pile of feed on the ground.

After they turned again to the right, they came to a wooden gate. Li Jie lifted a metal rod that secured the gate into the concrete, and pushed the gate forward, waited for Jiang to enter, then shut the gate behind them. They stood in a courtyard covered in potted trees. Jiang spotted a couple of dwarfed banana trees with tiny green fruit, three unbalanced-looking papayas, a five-foot-tall persimmon, several flowers, at least a dozen types of bonsai trees scattered underneath the fruit, and a wall of bougainvillea.

In front of them was an old house, with a tiled rooftop, overgrown with moss and two car tires weighing down the corners of the roof. The house had a small porch leading to the garden, with several rusted chairs pushed up against wood railings. Jiang looked around the courtyard, then up to the buildings surrounding them. The house felt completely out of place. It was some sort of ancient green oasis lost underneath the modern, looming metropolis.

Li Jie noticed the surprised look Jiang was wearing and

nodded back. "Amazing right? It's been here before the city. Steven told me his grandfather refused to leave the house when they built the neighborhood, so they just built around him, while he watched out the window."

"Steven?" Jiang was thrown off by the foreign-sounding name.

"Ah yeah, he likes to be called by his English name. Says it's easier to talk to foreigners that way."

"Does he go to your school?"

"Officially, yeah, but he doesn't show up much." Li Jie knocked on the front door. Jiang heard movement from inside. The door opened a crack, a chain lock tightened, dangling under a pair of eyes that peered out. The eyes studied Jiang, then grew much wider as Li Jie stepped forward, waving. The door shut quickly, the lock slid and released, and the door swung completely open.

"Li man! You're back! Who's your friend?"

A young man, not more than a few years older than either of them, inspected Jiang from head to toe through a pair of thick, wire-rimmed glasses. His hair was shaved at the sides, and hung long and loose in the back, almost touching the collar of a black, buttoned-up shirt. His jean pants stopped just above his ankles, and his bare feet looked like they hadn't been washed in days.

"Steven, this is Jiang, from my same village."

"Jiang…Ji…ang…" Steven tested out the name, then turned again to Li Jie. "Can we trust him?"

"Of course, man."

Steven stuck out a hand towards Jiang. "Alright, you cool, right, Jiang?" Jiang looked over at Li Jie, unsure how to respond. He took the outstretched hand first, shaking it firmly once.

"I'm cool."

Steven grinned widely. "Cool. Come on in guys, I have some friends over too. They'll be excited to hear about Li's trip too."

Li Jie and Jiang followed Steven through the house, towards the back rooms. The front room was dark and filled mostly with boxes and shelves of books. A stack of papers covered a yellow sofa, and a cat slept on top of the sofa's backrest. Faded portraits of an old man and a couple hung on both walls of the room. All the curtains were drawn in the front room, but as they neared the back of the house, the space opened and filled with light. They passed a kitchen, its counters and sink full of dirtied dishes and used cooking pots. Jiang couldn't see a sliver of space where the counters were empty.

After the living room, the house suddenly filled up with plants. There were vines running up window frames, fern-like plants shooting their long leaves from pots alongside the walls, hanging pots overflowing with foliage, which reached silently toward the floor. The white ceiling was replaced by what appeared to be an old plastic roof, slightly yellowed from years of exposure to the outside elements, but transparent enough that the light from the sky illuminated the room. A dining table, also filled with papers, and two large filing cabinets sat on the edge of a third room. Closed, wooden doors flanked each side of the room.

Steven led them out a sliding door, then down a two-step decline into the rear garden, which was surrounded by a low brick planting box, out of which vegetable greens pushed over the rim of the bricks. In the far-left corner, a makeshift chicken coop of wood pallets protected several hens from a curious orange cat. Under a second, transparent roof, was a large, round table, with two high school-aged boys, two girls, and an older woman sitting on wooden stools.

"Hey Mom, everyone, this is Jiang. Li's buddy." Steven picked up a small bench near the brick garden and handed it to Li Jie and Jiang.

"Welcome Jiang. Li Jie, my dear, would you two like tea or juice?"

"Green tea's great!"

"Same, Madam…er…please." Jiang said, setting the bench down.

"You can call me Auntie." Steven's mom poured the boys each tea in brown clay cups and passed them across the table.

"Li, how was the trip? Any surprises?" One guy sitting next to Steven asked, smirking slightly. He was wearing a black t-shirt, with large bold letters across the top, a circular eagle logo, and surrounded by several names. It was in English, but Jiang didn't recognize the words.

Li Jie laughed a little, throwing his hands in the air, then pretended to bow towards the other boy.

"You were right! Oh, I'm not worthy! I'm not worthy!"

The rest of the table laughed along with Li Jie, including Jiang, although he didn't quite understand the joke.

"Now you see, Li-man," Steven interrupted. "Progress is production. It doesn't have to be functional, it just has to look good on paper."

Steven's mother nodded her head in approval. "It's all about the economy, you know. They figure that if we increase the size of the property market, and bring jobs and new industry to an area, our economy will boom. But there are problems with this…they build before they really consider the potential job market. They offer huge incentives to someone to move to a new city, and promise low-cost apartments, plenty of work, but when someone arrives, all they see are empty shops around them and empty promises of new factories about to open. Even if someone moves in, they are probably scared off in a few months and go back to where they came from."

"If there are even people to go, right mom?" Steven

waited for his mother to answer, raising his eyebrows towards Jiang.

"Of course. They expect millions more people to move to cities and try to predict the future. But they are looking too far ahead. When there's finally enough people to fill the apartments, the buildings will be degraded to the point that nobody would want to live inside them. But that doesn't really matter. Construction looks good for investors. If we report new developments throughout the country, it looks like progress." Steven's mother leaned back on her stool, taking a sip of her tea.

Jiang looked around the table, trying to decide if the question turning over in his mind would sound stupid or not. He looked at Li Jie, who was shaking his head slowly. Li Jie looked over at Jiang and then seemed to read his mind.

"Tell him why they don't report this in the news." Li Jie told Steven.

"Money, Jiang. Millions and millions of dollars in building contracts. If everyone knew that the projects were worthless, they would see through the reports. Officials get rich for allowing developers to build, developers get rich off investors. Sometimes investors get screwed, but overall, the money going into the projects look so nice on paper, that any bad news is swept under the table."

"What about us?" Jiang asked. The group watched him, waiting for more. "I mean, what about villages like ours? My father says he could make more money on a farm than in any factory here."

"He's right, Jiang," Steven's mother began. "But who are you? Just a poor boy, from a poor family-"

"Spare him his life from this monstrosity!" Steven belted out in song, thrusting his arms in front of himself. The table chuckled a little, and Auntie smiled back at Jiang, seeing his confusion.

"You know, Jiang, over the last three years, we've used more cement than the United States in the last 100 years. That costs a lot of money. That's an achievement…an incredible amount of urban growth. Something that will stick in the minds of the world far more than how much corn you grew in the last three years. We are playing a long game of economics with the world, and this was one move. They have told us that it was for the people, for all of us." She looked around at the table and sighed. "I'm afraid this was done purely for business, for numbers in the bank."

Jiang lowered his head, looking down at his cup of tea, and swirled a few loose tea leaves that sat at the bottom of it. Li Jie was watching his friend closely, thinking about how to take the spotlight off Jiang.

"So, what can we do, Auntie?" He asked finally.

Steven's mother let out a slow, deep breath and turned her head upward, searching for something through the yellowing, once-transparent rooftop. A light shadow of a bird sailed over the plastic.

"We can accept it and get a job at the nearest steel factory," a girl wearing khaki pants and a purple sweater responded, laughing. The others laughed along with her. Jiang looked back up from his tea. The girl looked about his age, but she didn't remind him of any girl he knew. The way she dressed and the mascara on her eyes made her seem far more mature.

"Or," she said finally, "we can fight…"

X

*Time to learn to tout...*Ukali rolled this new word between his ears as he walked along the street. He couldn't figure it out. When he turned the corner, just past the university building, he saw the gang waiting outside the bar. He was suddenly self-conscious that he was still wearing the same clothes from the night before, and he could smell alcohol seeping from his pores.

"Hey, man!" Rollie greeted him with a high five, cigarette smoke still steaming through his teeth.

"Looks like my first night after whiskey," Jet observed Ukali's rough-looking appearance.

"Whoa, I can still smell it. No matter about your clothes...dirty clothes always help the gig. But we got to do something about that smell," Rollie said, reaching into a pocket.

He produced a small paper pouch that smelled of aniseed.

"Here, chew on a few of these while we walk."

Ukali shoved a handful of green candies in his mouth. The taste was strange at first, but the more he chewed, the more he enjoyed the flavor.

The gang started walking towards the tourist center, and Chimp, assuming his tour guide voice, began to explain.

"I assume, my esteemed and freshly minted colleague, that you probably don't remember much after the temple last night, but here's the deal. We're what they call touts. I don't know where that name comes from, so don't ask. More importantly, what we do, is spot the greenest looking tourists we can and approach them."

"Ahem, for reference my friend, green is like a newbie…they just got to the city," added Jet. They walked quickly while they talked. A rush of morning motorists blurred around Ukali, adding to the speed of everything in front of him. Noises from shops opening for the day accented with bolts of honking.

"Right. Usually, the bus station is a good spot, but really anywhere in the tourist district, or when they're leaving the burning ghats. Basically, anyone who looks like they haven't been here very long. Because the secret my friend, which you must never speak to them about, is that they don't really need our help. We are sort of middlemen, between them and a hotel, between them and a restaurant, or someone to help them find a walking guide to the mountains."

"They pay to walk?" Ukali figured he would rather pay not to walk anywhere.

"They pay a lot. Those guides, who take them deep in the mountains, they make a decent living from it. But it's tough, you have to deal with a bunch of people who can hardly tie their boots, let alone climb a mountain. But that gig's not for us, a certain group from the mountains runs the whole show. And trust me, you'd rather be in the city. Our jobs are quick, either rewarding or not, but either way, you know if you're going to make a buck or not as soon as they look at you…at least after you've been at it awhile."

"What's a…buck?" Ukali tried the new word, which felt rough in his mouth.

"Right, right, that's an English word, for money. We'll be teaching you English along the way. They never speak a word of our language, maybe 'namaste' or something, but they use it at weird times. Anyway, when you follow us today, listen to the words we use, and we'll write them down for you later."

"So, these tourists pay you to bring them to a hotel?"

"Not exactly, sometimes they give you a tip, but that's pretty rare, so rare you almost want to hug them. But the hotels, the restaurants, the guide outfits, they break us off a cut once the tourists are happy and comfortable forking out their bucks to them. We go around when we're finished and collect. Now it's a competitive city, so you have to be careful. Some hotel managers say the tourists got a lower price than they actually paid, and give you less. You're welcome to make a fuss, but sometimes they don't stand by their word. We can retaliate and never bring business there again, but nobody wants that, so it usually works itself out. So, today, our young apprentice, you just hang back, smile and nod if they ask you anything, or look at us. We'll do all the talking."

The group was walking on pavement again, which meant they were back in the tourist district. Ukali's mouth was dry but began to normalize as the dust settled on the improved infrastructure.

"The bus stop isn't too far now, but we might do some stops along the way. Here, hold these, and give them to me if I ask. Stay with me, and Rollie and Jet will do their thing."

He handed Ukali a small stack of brochures for hotels and restaurants, full of colorful pictures, but obviously well-worn. Ukali folded them along the pre-folded lines across the middle and shoved them in his back pocket.

"It's not dishonest...what we're doing?" Ukali wondered aloud, almost wishing he hadn't. He didn't want to seem weak in front of the gang.

"Not at all. How else are three, no, four, young bachelors going to make it in this town? These tourists fly thousands of miles here on big airplanes, heavy with cash, and they can afford to part with a few extra bucks. And the hotels and restaurants appreciate the work, even if they grumble when handing over money....That's right, you didn't take the equivalency exam, did you? I'll tell you, half of those textbooks were in a different language for me. I can read, write, work, but I never learned anything like that back in my village. This is the way, man. At least, until Rollie makes good with the dream."

"What's the dream?" Ukali turned towards Rollie.

"No, sir, you're nowhere near ready for the dream yet. Take me out to dinner first, baby!"

The other boys cracked up at Rollie's reply. Ukali smiled. The gang moved fast, talked fast, and he felt immediately accepted in this exotic new group of friends. It had been a long time since he felt this good with his peers.

"Boom, show time…" Rollie trailed off in a whisper, tugging at Jet's arm. Ukali started to follow, but Chimp held his arm. The other two boys approached two, white-haired tourists in tan pants and abnormally large hats. They were holding an outstretched map in front of themselves and arguing about something.

"Good morning sir, can I help you?"

Jet's voice faded behind them, as Chimp and Ukali kept walking, with Chimp keeping his eyes forward, a smile on his lips and determination in his eyes.

They stopped at a newspaper kiosk. Chimp glanced over his shoulder.

"Still talking, there we go. See, Ukali, there's an art to this thing. If you run up to a tourist and say, 'Let me take you to a hotel,' they recoil in fear. What, some strange local boy is talking to me? And he wants to take me somewhere? No, I have a plan, I know what I want. I don't need a boy's help!"

Ukali laughed at Chimp's impression of a tourist in shock.

"But, like what they're doing now is fishing for leads. They see what type of thing they can help them with. It's all honest, really. I do want to help them. I want them to enjoy this place, and keep coming back. But I also want my cut. Those guys are helping them find something on their map. Maybe it's a restaurant, maybe a hotel…could be anything. Ah, alright, here we go."

Rollie and Jet gave Chimp a wave and started walking away with the tourists. Jet hung back from the group and curled his arms inward, like a bad imitation of a monkey.

"Nice," Chimp said. "They're going on a tour. That could be a good gig, but it's a toss-up. They'll lead those two old folks up to the temple, maybe tell them a bit about the temple, kind of like a temporary tour guide. If they are making themselves useful enough, the tourists won't mind if they stay with them. Sometimes, they'll leave you at the gate and wave you away. You can stand there with a palm out for doing them a favor, walking out of your way, but sometimes you're stiffed. It's a rough place to be, but best not to make a scene. Always be polite, maybe you can look sad, then half of the time, one of them will come running back down with your tip."

Ukali was enthralled with this fast-paced, multi-directional business. He wanted to be in it, up close.

"Let's keep moving," he said to Chimp.

Chimp winked at him and they continued towards the main bus stop. Tourists lined the streets now, on both sides of the road. A couple stopped to admire hanging clothes outside a door until a vendor spooked them by approaching too eagerly. Others tapped singing bowls with wooden mallets, putting the bowls up to their ears. The trekkers were easy to spot. They were wearing the most clothing, carrying the largest packs, and walked as if they already knew where they were going. Others, donning cameras around their necks, stopped to photograph men selling fruit or monkeys walking across wires.

"OK, now we're getting close to the bus stop, look for big bags on backs or rolling suitcases. Those are easy to hear." Chimp chuckled to himself, but loud enough to let Ukali in on the joke.

"There." Ukali pointed to two girls, struggling away from them, with huge bags riding low on their backs.

"Hey! Don't point man…that's OK, they didn't see you. But don't point at a tourist. You wouldn't call out a monkey before you made a move, would you?"

"I'm…not sure."

"You wouldn't. Believe me. Whatever, let's do it. Just smile and pass me brochures when I tell you. And just say 'hello' when you see them."

"Hell-oooo, hello," Ukali practiced the new word quietly as they caught up to the girls.

"Hello friends!" Chimp said, now walking beside the two girls.

"Hello." Ukali's greeting felt odd and redundant.

"Can I help you with something? I know the city. Local guy. Hotel or something?"

"No, thanks, we're fine," the girl farthest from Chimp replied. Ukali figured it was finished and started to slow down.

"No worry, no hurry. I'm not asking for something from you. Just help the hotels and help you. I know all the hotels. What kind you like?"

The words didn't flow as well from Chimp's mouth as the native speakers, but Ukali understood he must be doing well since they were still talking. He was eager to start learning this new language, but for now, he had to hang back and listen.

"I said, no…"

"Jen, it's fine, we've been walking long enough, let's just get somewhere for tonight and put these damn packs down."

As soon as the second girl stopped speaking, they both stopped walking. Ukali almost bumped into Chimp when the group came to a halt.

"Which kinds of places do you have?" The first girl spoke, looking at Ukali. He didn't understand it was his cue, and he looked at both of the girls, his mouth already wide with a smile. Their hairlines were wet with sweat, and he saw red lines on their shoulders, giving away the true, painful weight of their bags. He stopped himself, looking at the ground. He didn't want to stare. Then he remembered his instructions. He nodded at the first girl, then again to the second, smiling wide. Maybe too wide, he figured, adjusting the corners of his mouth.

"Excuse my friend. No English." Chimp spoke again and motioned at Ukali. "Let's see those brochures, buddy."

Ukali remembered the stack of papers in his back pocket, he reached behind him and pulled them out, handing them over to Chimp.

Chimp shuffled through the stacks, while the second girl said, "Something cheap, and not far away."

"No problem," Chimp said, lifting up a brochure. On the top, in large, red letters, it proclaimed, 'MOUNTAIN VIEW ROOFTOP' and 'BEST PRICE,' with colorful photos of rooms with beds and a picture of a mountain Ukali knew to be actually quite far away.

"Sold!" The first girl spoke again, clearly affirming their collected decision for the group, and followed with, "Lead away, local guy!"

Chimp led the group, with the two girls behind him. Ukali followed in the rear, but not too close. He pretended to be interested in the contents of a nearby shop if one of the girls turned to look in his direction. They turned one corner on the left, passing a restaurant that overflowed into the street, with a scattering of tables, each full of tourists sipping tea and smoking rolled cigarettes.

Not long after, Chimp ducked under a red awning and the rest of the group followed him in.

"Hey, Sanjay. These two girls would like a room. Give them something with a view away from buildings, they liked your brochure." Then switching to English as the girls neared, he continued, "Your best price for them. They are very tired."

He waited off to the side, as the girls talked to Sanjay. He told them something, then they handed over two small blue books, which he copied information from, then took several notes of cash in exchange for a set of keys. He then gave a nod to Chimp, who turned to face the girls.

"OK friends, goodbye. See you later."

"Oh…thank you. See you…" The first girl spoke as her friend busied herself stuffing her blue book back into her bag.

Ukali thought the parting was abrupt but Chimp nudged him and lowered his head out the door. Unsure how to say his own farewell, Ukali gave a quick bow, which was returned with a smile from the first girl. They walked back down the street, rounding the corner again before speaking.

"That's it, man. Can be easy as that. We were lucky we only had to go around the corner."

"They didn't seem to care about your help very much."

"I don't care, Ukali. Look, they could have found that place eventually, so whatever. They, for some reason, decide to pack their whole houses in those bags and walk up and down the roads like yak herders in a blizzard. They probably got hassled by some tout, who was too aggressive in the last city, so they are tired. Whatever, the sooner I can drop them off, the better. But pretty cute, right? I saw one smile at you." He bumped Ukali on the shoulder, almost knocking him off balance.

Ukali blushed and tried to change the subject.

"So, how much did you make?"

"Hey man, I'll give you a piece, even if you did nothing but nod your head off." He mocked Ukali, bouncing his head up and down. "But yeah, Ukali, we'll see what the girls end up paying, usually five or ten percent. Should be enough for you to buy me a beer."

Ukali laughed. Ten minutes was all it took to make a beer? His head began racing to multiply how much they could make in an hour, in a day, a week, a year! Of course, they wouldn't always be successful, Chimp had mentioned that, and they had to eat and walk between meeting tourists. Even at a few hours a day, it was more money than he imagined he could spend. He immediately felt hooked to the prospect of more quick money.

But the rest of the day was slower than it had started. He learned what losing a tourist felt like, after minutes of talk with some backpackers led to nothing, while a bus full of the tourists disappeared. People shook their heads at everything Chimp said, stepping around him, as if he was blocking their paths, and sometimes they furiously negotiated a price without coming to an agreement. Buses came and went. Once more, they walked a tourist to a hotel, but it was just one man. On the way back, luckily, they talked two young couples into following them to the 'best restaurant in town.'

They weren't the only ones working either. At the bus stop, there were almost a dozen touts, fanned out around the arriving buses. Chimp told him that if they stayed a little further from the bus door, tourists had time to breathe. They could look around, realize they had no idea where they were, then maybe they would want help. Some touts would run right up to the doors of the bus, blocking them from leaving the bus, bombarding them with 'Hello madam,' 'Sir, taxi to a hotel for you,' 'Hello, what are you looking for?' Many of those times, tourists just pushed by these touts, their faces growing more red as they collected suitcases under the bus and repeated, 'No, no, no.'

Ukali saw that each tout had luck eventually, but as the day wore on, more buses left them empty-handed than otherwise. He looked around at other touts across the street and once saw a tout throw down a brochure in disappointment.

He met all kinds of tourists at the bus stop. He met happy tourists, who were covered in smiles when they could be pointed to a hotel. Some were quite insistent on finding something called "A.C." He met upset, angry tourists, who waved them away with their hands, refusing to meet Chimp's eyes. He met tourists who weren't new in the city, the ones who smiled and shook their hands and declined their offers immediately but calmly. There were locals who got off the buses, but they were almost as well-dressed as the tourists. They would immediately head for a waiting taxi and saved their bartering for inside the cool vehicle.

Ukali and Chimp worked the bus stop until the sun was high above the city, and then Chimp led them down a street, away from the tourist center. They wove through a few street vendors and a group of students waiting for a bus. Soon they came to a rough-looking restaurant, a real hole-in-the-wall sort of place, with black and tan grease streaked across old white tile walls.

"This is the best, and cheapest food in the city, Ukali, another secret from the pros."

A man, wearing a sufficiently stained apron, tossed fist-sized balls of dough from hand to hand, stretching them easily, rapidly. He then slapped the dough against the inside of an oil drum, which a roaring fire flickered its hot flames just under the rim. The inside of the drum was coated in hard clay and the dough stuck to the sides, until the man, barehanded, pulled them out in a quick, expert motion. He periodically submerged his hand in a bucket of water to cool off the heat that still clung to his palms.

A boy, a few years younger than Ukali, put two metal bowls of steaming lentils on their table, two bubbling brown drinks and a small pile of naan bread. Chimp ate hungrily, spilling hot lentils over his fingers without noticing. He sipped the bubbling drink and then looked at Ukali, noticing his confusion.

"Ah, man, it's cola. Not alcohol, don't worry" He laughed kindly.

Ukali tasted the drink. It was cold, sweet, and the bubbles reminded him of beer, but cooled him even more. He started in on his own meal, breaking off a piece of naan to scoop the hot lentils onto.

Before he put the food to his mouth, he was slapped hard on the back.

"What's up!"

It was Jet. Rollie followed close behind, pausing to stamp out a cigarette.

"Ah, boys, how was it?" Chimp asked, a wide smile pulling up his cheeks.

"A bust man. Left us at the gate of the temple, but picked up another pair on the way down to the ghats, and got five bucks after Rollie told them a long ass story. Damn, it was long, man."

"Worked, right?" Rollie replied, motioning for the waiter. Looking inside, he nodded at a tourist sitting in the restaurant. The tourist, wearing a faded blue hat, a well-worn t-shirt and pants, and green-strapped sandals, was pouring white sauce over a pile of potatoes. His friends anxiously waited for him to hand over the bottle, so they could also pour the sauce on their meals.

"Must be good shit!" Jet said, and sent a two-fingered peace sign in the direction of the tourist, who returned it, smiling with cheeks full of potatoes. Jet turned back to the group. "How'd it go with you two."

"Not too bad, he'll get it quickly. The girls like him, so that will help, after walking around with your ugly faces all year," Chimp said. The other two laughed.

"Casanova!" Jet said, looking around for support.

"Casanova, casa…nova. Yeah, it'll do," agreed Rollie.

Ukali was wiping oil from his lips with the back of his hand, looked up and asked, "What's that?"

"Ah, my dear, green Ukali, it's some guy from Europe, he is real lucky with the ladies. We have your nickname, sir." Chimp agreed as well.

XI

During the spring planting ceremony, Suman's village was alive with energy. The collective endurance through the coldest winter in recent memory bestowed upon the villagers a potent sense of camaraderie. What would have simply been an appreciation of the passage into a warmer season was transformed into a vivid awareness of the power seasons could have in each of their lives. The celebratory mood encompassing the valley was as much derived from relief as it was in anticipation of warmth to come. Evidence of such feelings was obvious from the ceaseless chatter in the crowd. Excited voices, the clinking of glasses together, and howls of laughter filled the atmosphere of the afternoon. Children played enthusiastically on the swing, screeching with joy with every sway of the giant structure. Some of the villagers had organized a dance and performed it with intricate costumes they had been making over the previous few weeks. Some played instruments, while others danced in circles, lifting the ends of the outfits high in the air.

After some hours, the festive jubilance relaxed into a pleasant buzzing of general happiness. Dancers found their way into broad circles on the ground and food was passed around. Suman squeezed in, shoulder to shoulder with his neighbors, for a friendly game of cards. During one hand, he held several good cards and the pile of dal beans was piling up in the pot. He started to figure he had a chance to win. He hadn't won a hand in quite a while and began to tap his leg nervously. He turned over his last card to reveal an ace, the best card in the game. But before the other players could turn their cards over, a bottle of whiskey slammed on the table and the cards scattered onto the ground. The table looked up to see a grinning Ukali swaying above them.

"Evenin' gent-men. How about a las' toas' to yer pal, Ukali?" Ukali said. "You know, yer 'ceiving electricity soon, and I see ya enjoyin' yer cell phones. Nooo need ta thank meh. I been thanked by these gent-men," he continued, gesturing to the two men standing next to him. They were leaning on each other, evidently responsible for the disappearance of half a whiskey bottle.

Tauko placed his hands on his knees and was about to stand up to leave when one of the men in suits started speaking.

"I'm going to try that swing, it looks like more fun than I've had in this whole damn place," he said, punctuating with a belch.

He walked unsteadily toward the swing. The farmers stood up to watch the drunk man lightly push a child aside and step onto the swing. Ukali laughed and the group watched with unsure expressions. The man started rocking the swing back and forth and climbed higher in the air. He let out a roar, and Suman could swear he smelled the whiskey-tainted breath from where he stood. The swing bent with a moan as the man propelled himself higher.

"Crazy bastard," the other foreigner declared, before taking a long drink from the bottle. A loud snap echoed through the celebration like a glacier breaking apart. The rope snapped near the knots and luckily for the drunk man, he was at the bottom of the swing's rotation. He fell stomach-first onto the ground, as the middle beam of the swing broke at the same time. The bamboo and man collapsed into a cloud of dust, both grunting painfully. The children screamed and ran for their parents, as Ukali jogged towards the drunk man. Before he reached him, the man jumped to his feet and thrust his arms in the air.

"I'm Okay!" he yelled back at his colleagues, and Ukali stopped mid-stride and laughed uncontrollably. He patted some dirt off the man when he got to his side, and they wobbled back to the card game.

"So, how 'bout two toasts; one to mah 'parture and one to the crazies' man in the valley," Ukali suggested. Suman looked for Tauko's reaction, but his friend was gone. The farmers reluctantly raised their cups and glasses and wished Ukali a pleasant journey.

"When are you leaving?" A man wearing a thick coat of yak hair asked of Ukali.

"Soon 'nough my friend, I jus' need to sell mah house," he replied, swaying slightly.

Suman left the group and found Sanjana, who was busy consoling a frightened Maya.

"Are you alright?" He asked Maya.

"I don't like that man," she said, and her mother looked up at Suman.

"That's alright, do you want to know something?" Maya nodded through her tear-streamed face. "I don't much like that man either," Suman said. Maya wiped her face and giggled quietly.

☼☼☼

On the last day of planting freshly thawed-out soil, Suman sat down, exhausted, on a rock in his plot of land. He took a handkerchief and wiped sweat from his forehead. He eyed it afterward and raised an eyebrow at the amount of dirt now caked on the cloth. He brushed off dirt from the top of his thighs and watched the dry soil drift into the air by a light southern wind. He removed his shirt and shook it out, letting the wind carry more soil away. As he let out a deep sigh, he looked over his plot; little moist beds with each loved seed safely tucked in for the season. The rains had been lighter than normal, but luckily the piping from the river and springs was still bursting with water.

He was content to know that the bountiful harvest would still bring ample food for his family, and hopefully plenty left to trade for yak milk and cheese.

At that thought, he remembered that he had brought a small piece of cheese to work that day. He removed it from his pocket, and slowly untied the cloth around it. He nibbled a small corner of the cheese, and let the piece melt in his mouth.

He couldn't imagine life without cheese and in particular yak cheese. He never enjoyed buffalo cheese as much. It usually clogged his sinuses. His wife didn't eat as much yak cheese as he did. She claimed that sixteen years living primarily on yak products with her nomadic family was enough for several lifetimes. But for a farmer, without any yaks of his own, he savored every bite.

He took his time eating the cheese, pausing occasionally to watch a small bird attack a larger bird. They swooped near the earth, darted downhill, coming together and spinning free of each other with such quickness and agility that he was convinced it was a dance rather than a fight. The battle of a small creature against a larger one reminded him of a familiar struggle. He grimaced when he considered the dam upriver.

Although, he wasn't yet sure about the repercussions awaiting those downstream from the wall, the most aggravating part of the dam for him was just its existence. The blank face of the wall unnerved him, and occasionally he felt that each time he saw it, the wall had shifted, and was actually creeping closer to his village.

But what first was a disturbance to the rest of the villagers was now a more accepted and tolerated fact of life. If the dam was mentioned in conversation, Suman had noticed, from the onset of spring, generally villagers had become indifferent to the activity upriver. Recently, electricity had been installed, giving light and power to homes throughout most of the day and evenings. The newly established restaurants, which had been continuously patronized by the construction crews, frequently needed electricity for lights and refrigeration. Through his wooden window shutters, Suman could usually hear the clinking of beer bottles and the rattle of pots and pans coming from the restaurants. With electricity giving more ability to new commerce, as well as entertainment through televisions, the activity at the dam was eventually squeezed out of the village consciousness.

Suman noticed that while the spring usually meant a great contrast to the winter atmosphere of the village, a different phenomenon was underway. His neighbors began to stay indoors almost as frequently as they did during the colder months. Instead of hearing the chatter of his neighbors on their front porches, he instead began to hear the buzzing of televisions behind closed doors. Once, he even heard a loud, "Hello," when walking home, turning to answer the voice, he realized his neighbor was talking on a phone, completely unaware of Suman's presence.

On his walks home from his plot, Suman also noticed a change in the routine so delicate and acute, that only its abrupt disappearance had brought his awareness to it. There was an older woman, the grandmother of one of his daughter's many friends, who always spent her evenings on an old, wooden chair outside her front door. The chair seemed to have aged exactly in tune with her brown, rough skin. The yak fur of the chair had most likely never been replaced and had about as much hair as the woman's chin, which happened to be just enough that it was noticeable.

Throughout Suman's life, he couldn't recall if he ever heard this woman speak, but he certainly could picture her smiling, her cheeks pulling her lips towards her ears, uncovering a handful of betel nut-stained teeth.

His path never passed her front door close enough to warrant a conversation, but he would always notice her, almost subconsciously, from the last right-hand turn descending the hill. He could see the colorful stripes of her dress and could just make out which direction she was looking. It had been so many years of the same presence by a distance, that he couldn't remember the last time his attention had been purposefully focused in her direction. It was always peripheral.

On one particular day, Suman paused on the last corner of the path and found himself gazing at an empty chair. As she was an older woman, his thoughts immediately turned towards an issue of health. She was perhaps the oldest person living in the village, and Suman knew that a day like this would be inevitable. Suman never felt sadness if he learned of an old neighbor's body lying down for that ultimate rest, for he knew that they would finally know something that any living person could not know.

The greatest mystery of humankind would be finally within their grasp. Leaving the earthly plane for something higher, something more vast, and what Suman was convinced would be more beautiful than anything they could possibly imagine. Suman decided that he might as well go check on her, at least for her family's sake.

He approached the woman's home, and as he neared the front door, he saw that there weren't any yak hairs left on the tired old chair, just a square of sunbaked leather. Then as he reached the door, he heard the sound of voices from inside. They seemed farther away than possible, inside such a small structure, and suddenly laughter erupted through the walls. He put his ear to the door. The voices were clearly foreign. Then, another set of laughs, this time sounding identical to the last.

He walked his hands to a small window, a few feet over from the door. Through a narrow opening in some fabric curtains, he saw a television, alive with sound and color. The house was dark inside, except for the television, which thrust rays of light out of its front opening, illuminating a sofa, a table, and the old woman in a pixelated glow.

The woman seemed to be alive after all. Suman breathed a small air of relief outside the window, partially fogging up the glass. But as he watched the scene, an uneasy sensation crept through his chest. He couldn't take his eyes off the woman's face. Her mouth hung slightly ajar, neither giving away a smile nor a frown. Her eyes appeared unblinking, fixed to the center of the television. Her cheeks were left motionless, almost heavy. She looked much older than Suman remembered. He waited for a confirmation of life, watching her chest until he could see it rising with breath.

Suman stepped back, away from the glass. He heard the sound of laughter once more. He felt a bit guilty for the invasion of privacy, but the strange feelings subsisted. He tried to make sense of the scene he had just been watching. He knew that the woman did not speak a word of another language. Yet, her attention was completely focused on a box of foreign chatter, as if she was also plugged into an electric outlet. She was a part of the television, and the television looked as if it was the only real living creature in that room.

He confessed to himself that he didn't know the woman well enough to make broad judgments, but wondered if she had the same, fixated gaze when she sat in her chair. Had he stopped by to greet her in the years prior, he may have known the answer better. As Suman continued walking home, pulling his body away from the house, his mind remained stuck there, still watching a living ghost in a room filled with voices neither of them could understand.

While he walked, he couldn't help but worry about changes prevalent in the village, especially the infrequency of interactions between his neighbors. Especially after his work, he should have heard laughs coming from groups of people, talking, eating, playing cards, or drinking apple brandy during the sunset. It made the town feel alive, glowing with energy from its inhabitants. But the energy that year appeared shut indoors, and only those without television sets were still venturing outdoors in the evenings.

As his own house came into focus, his contemplation of the issue faded without any solution, and he noticed his fingers had become stuck together. A chunk of unfinished cheese had melted in hand.

He put the last piece in his mouth and then looked up to see Tauko coming uphill. Suman waved, but Tauko didn't return the gesture; he appeared quite unsettled.

"Hello my friend, are you finished planting?" He asked of Tauko.

"Nothing will take in my soil, dear Suman."

"What? I assumed you began planting already. You should have told me, Tauko."

"I know, but I never imagined it would take this long. My soil is as dry and hard as the road we walk on."

"Is there water for your irrigation?"

"There is some, but the earth remains dry. The sun dies it out too quickly." Tauko was right. Suman had been noticing that the weather was hot enough to be mid-summer, but planting had only just finished.

"I'm sorry my friend, you can take water from my land, and if needed, you will share my crop of course."

"You're too kind, Suman, but I'm not giving up. My father's plot always comes late, maybe harvest will just be late this year."

"Do you want me to help you?"

"Thanks, but no my friend. I have always finished the job myself."

"You are too proud Tauko. I am your friend, and I am here to help." Tauko nodded and sat down on a rock near Suman, and reached into his pocket for a cigarette.

"Those don't help, you should stop doing that to yourself."

Tauko grunted and lit his cigarette. "I need something to drink, Tauko," Suman said. "I'm going back down to have some water. Will you join me?"

"I think I'll stay awhile."

"Okay, well don't worry my friend, things will come around for your crop, and don't forget my offer." Tauko forced a smile and gave a nod.

As Suman walked down the hill, he looked back to see Tauko looking in the direction of the dam. He couldn't tell if it was the sun on his face, but Tauko was red as a chili.

Suman hardly saw Tauko over the next few weeks. When they passed each other on the street, Tauko only talked briefly but seemed distracted. He mostly grumbled about his plot of land and the work to be done. Suman hoped that things would turn around, and his friend's usual happy smile would return. He had space enough in his own plot to plant extra vegetables for his friend and spent extra hours tending to a late addition of seeds, trying to boost the new crop with buffalo fertilizer.

Eventually, sprouts began to show above the surface of the additional crops, and between that and his own yield, he figured it should sustain both of their families. He might have to do without yak cheese or Tauko without his cigarettes. He shook his head at the idea. In the end, he would rather never eat cheese again, if it meant Tauko could have what he needed to be happy. Although he despised his friend's new habit, if they truly gave him peace of mind, wasn't he better off?

XII

So it was, Casanova, Rollie, Chimp, and Jet worked the streets the whole tourist season together. In the mornings Casanova studied English. First the basics, then phrases, and eventually he was doing some talking while they touted.

It wasn't long before he could walk up to any group or solo traveler, unleash a few words of that new language, and if they said anything or stared at him, he learned he could continue. Usually, the silent treatment was a locked door that not even the smooth-talking Chimp could pick.

"Hello, do you want a hotel? Very nice hotel. Cheap for you."

Eventually, he added more words to his sentences, and every time, he felt his rhythm being ironed out. He noticed the more fluid his speech, the longer a tourist might listen to him. He even picked up some Mandarin words, one of the languages of the Chinese tourists. Every now and then, a group of four or more tourists from Beijing would step off a bus, or emerge from a restaurant. Casanova also learned that after a meal, some tourists were full, possibly drunk, and maybe more inclined to walk it off down the street, to see a temple, ghat, or browse one of Chimp's many clothing shop connections. Mandarin was a little easier to handle in Casanova's mouth than English. Words didn't feel as lopsided on his tongue, but English was where the best tips were found.

He studied hard when he wasn't working. He saw how quickly Chimp and the others could get tourists on the hook, and he wanted to know what that confidence felt like.

Then by the end of the season, he led the approaches, with his mentor, Chimp, standing back and offering help when it was appropriate.

"Hello miss, can I help you? Don't worry, no money. I can show you a restaurant, cafe, or perhaps you are climbing mountains?"

He added the mountain climbing bit each time he approached young groups or old couples, obviously in town for temples and picture taking. He figured why not flatter them by pretending they were there to stand on a mountain peak.

The climbers were well-adorned with shiny equipment and could easily be spotted from far away. They looked either fresh and excited, or completely exhausted. Some were miserable and sat in restaurants on street level and drank cold beer. Others touched their glasses of beer together in celebration, on an outdoor patio two or three floors above street level. Always there was a local guide, lingering somewhere around the groups, probably thinking about the next walk he was about to make.

Casanova and the gang usually worked the edges of the tourist district, unless they happened to catch a few lost-looking faces nearer the center of town or by the ghats.

They all lived in a small room together, started each day with tea, and ended almost every night with beer, and occasionally with a whiskey bottle in their room. Sometimes, they woke up late, tired from a late night with beer and hazy walks around the city. Those days, they might not work, and would instead lightly argue over who would go outside to bring back food.

Casanova, it turned out, was a natural at touting, or at least Jet declared him as such. He could approach tired tourists and talk them into a long walk, or convince a couple that his restaurant was the most romantic in the city. More than once, Chimp was just about defeated, watching his words bounce off closed ears, as if the tourists had heard every word a thousand times, until Casanova stepped in. He shifted the direction of the conversation, moving the focus away from the discernible desperation in the tout's voice and to the tourists themselves.

"Where are you from? Do you like my city?" The questions immediately brought answers, since who couldn't help but answer a question about oneself? Ukali hardly understood what the replies were, but he noticed the more the tourists began talking about themselves, the longer they were inclined to speak. A shift in methodology commenced, although a few months overdue into the season, but still soon enough for the rewards of the latest approach to show.

They split their earnings evenly, unless someone made a considerable score alone. But even then, the victor usually bought the beers that night. The rest of the gang tried the recently-tested angle of tout attack that Casanova introduced. Instead of jumping quickly to the point, which could save time if the touted party was uninterested, Casanova led with questions about the tourists. He figured this technique masked his true intentions and the targets thought that he was just a curious kid, still getting used to the tall, light-skinned strangers roaming his town. It seemed to pay off at a higher rate than the other methods, but Chimp, who was still the aged master, had to point out a myriad of factors that could influence the outcomes too. Perhaps the economy of the tourist's home country was rising and they were loaded down with even more cash than last season, or perhaps Casanova was just good-looking enough to keep folks talking. But, whatever the reason, the foreign money was coming in steadily.

Casanova felt at home with the gang, and it didn't take long before he pushed the idea of attending a university or taking tests far from his mind and welcomed every frosty glass of beer as a deserved bounty for the day's work. Why should he slam his skull against a textbook every night rather than enjoy himself? With hard currency in his hand every day, he couldn't imagine that more classes would make him feel any better. Time moved quickly, and the season felt stretched into one long day, and he thoroughly enjoyed it all.

When the season finally cooled down, he noticed less and less tourists roaming the streets. There were far fewer people to offer tout services to, and even those remaining seemed as cold as the weather.

Casanova and the gang started going to a new dance club that recently opened up. The atmosphere inside was always full of energy. A DJ in the back corner, playing records under a large green and yellow tapestry, played new mashed-up versions of pop songs into the room. Foreigners and locals mixed on the dance floor or sat on floor cushions in the back, sipping beers and fermented millet drinks. The price of the drinks was far more than the gang was used to, but for the excitement of the place, they always agreed it was well worth it.

One night, Casanova was dancing alongside Jet and Rollie to a classic pop song, when he noticed a blonde foreign girl dancing alone. He shuffled his feet closer to her and tried to make eye contact. When he did, she smiled at him. Amazed, he looked behind him, to make sure she wasn't smiling towards someone else. When he saw no one else looking at her, he turned to face her again. He moved closer, and pointing to his chest, asked silently if she wanted to dance together. She nodded and waved him closer.

As the next track transitioned through the last one, the tempo of the music increased, making the girl throw her head back and laugh.

"I love this song!" She shouted to him over the sound. Casanova had never heard the song before, but smiled wide and began to shake his body faster, catching up to the rhythm. They danced through the whole song together; Casanova tried to impress her with an improvised spin move, and the girl pointed to the ceiling and mimed the chorus each time it came around. Casanova felt like he was dreaming. It was the best night yet in his new city.

When the song ended, the girl motioned away from the dance floor, raising her eyebrows in a question. Casanova nodded and followed her towards the bar.

"Nice moves! Can I buy you a drink?" The girl asked, setting an elbow on the counter of the bar.

"Ok, same as you," replied Casanova. She smiled and turned to the bartender.

"Two lemon and mint juices, please," she said. Turning to Casanova, "Sorry, I don't drink alcohol."

"Cool," Casanova said, trying out a new English word.

"So, what's your name," she asked. "I'm Monica."

"Ukali," he said. "Nice to meet you."

"Hey, your English is good, Ukali." She spoke in a thick accent. *Could be England or Australia,* he contemplated.

"Thanks. I practice a lot."

"So, you live in Kathmandu?"

"Yes, but I was born in a small village, in the mountains."

"Cool! The mountains are so beautiful here." Ukali wanted to invite her to his village but decided it might be too soon to suggest it.

They touched their glasses together and took a big sip. For Ukali, it was more refreshing than any beer. He felt beads of sweat run down to his chin. The heat of the room felt more intense the moment they stopped dancing.

"It's hot here," Ukali said, wishing he'd thought of something better to say.

"I know," she said, laughing. "Because we set that dance floor on fire!"

Ukali laughed with her, although he had no idea what she meant.

"So, tell me about your village," She leaned against the bar.

Ukali began to describe his village, the mountains, the river, even the buffaloes. Her eyes seemed to brighten with each description, and he found it hard to focus on his words. She was the most beautiful girl he'd ever spoken with. She wore a long, colorful, loose dress, and several strands of brown, prayer beads hung around her neck. Her blonde hair was braided in several places, and red beads were threaded into the braids. She seemed to inch closer when he spoke. He wondered if he was speaking too softly, but not wanting to make her move backward, he kept the same volume.

"It sounds incredible, and why did you ever leave such a beautiful place?"

Ukali was silent for a moment and decided that he didn't want to speak about his father's death, or about the distance that grew between him and his former classmates. He decided to go for the simplest answer.

"I wanted to start the university," he said.

"Cool, what do you study?"

He hadn't realized what her next question would be. He considered telling her about his gang, and the touting. But based on the last few months, decided that not all the tourists appreciated touts. Instead, he said, "Business."

"How long will you stay here?" He asked, wanting to quickly change the subject.

"I don't know," Monica said. "I have an open ticket." She smiled at him. He could see her pearl-white teeth shining in the lights above the bar. It was a perfect smile, like every part of her. "Say," she began. "Ready to dance again?"

"Yes!" He said, thinking maybe he sounded too eager.

They danced to several more songs, some as fast-paced as their first dance, and some much slower. During the second slow song, Monica reached for his shoulders and noticing his bewilderment, moved his hands to her hips. He had never touched a girl his age before. Her dress was softer than it looked. He could feel her hips moving slightly underneath it, and he felt his body warm up with nervousness. When his shoulders tensed up, she pulled him closer, moving her mouth near his ear.

"Relax," she said, and his shoulders slowly dropped. She tilted her head and kissed him on the cheek. Pulling her head back from his, she watched a huge smile wash over his face. He looked away quickly, feeling his cheeks warm with a crimson brown blush, then looked back at her, finding her eyes staring deeply into his own. He heard a whistle over his shoulder, knowing it was Jet or Rollie's, but tried to ignore it. They danced through a few more songs before she led him over to the bar again.

"You're great, Ukali," she said, bluntly. "What are you doing tomorrow?"

His mind was still on the dance floor. *Doing, doing, what could I be doing?* He had to blink until reality slid back into view.

"Nothing," he finally came up with.

"Perfect, well…since you know this place better than me, how about you show me around?"

"Cool," he said. "Sounds…perfect."

She kissed him on the cheek again. "I don't travel with a phone," she said. "So, let's just meet in front of this place tomorrow morning, maybe eight o'clock?"

"Eight o'clock," he repeated.

She leaned in to hug him. He felt the small of her back as they embraced, it was sturdy and soft all at once and fit neatly in the palms of his hands. He wished they could remain connected like that forever. When they did move apart, he sprung back forward quickly, planting a kiss on her right cheek. She smiled and gently placed her hand on the side of his arm.

"Wonderful to meet you, Ukali," she said, turning away and leaving him alone at the bar. Suddenly three other girls joined her. One nudged her in the arm and whispered something in her ear. They both giggled and looked back towards Ukali, who was still standing in his blissful fog at the bar. "See you, Ukali!" she shouted across the room, and her group walked towards the front door. Ukali watched them all the way, feeling a small pain deep in his chest as she vanished through the entrance.

He couldn't help but smile to himself, almost laughing when he turned to catch his reflection in a mirror behind the bar. *How had it happened? How had such a beautiful creature kissed me, twice!* A completely new sensation seeped through his chest and his mind raced around images of her, twisting and turning around scenes of the dancing, the kisses, the hug. He could almost still feel the warmth of her hand on his arm as he stood shaking his head at his own reflection.

"Casanova!"

Jet's hand came down hard on his shoulder blade, knocking some air out of his lungs. Rollie arrived by his side, grabbing him around the neck with one arm and messing up his hair with the other. Casanova moved out of the hold and lightly bumped Rollie with his shoulder, looking down at the floor while holding back a grin that threatened to give him away.

"How the hell did he do that?" Chimp asked, leaning over Jet's shoulder. Jet slammed a hand on the counter, and shouted towards the bartender, "Four whiskeys, sir!"

The following morning, Casanova strolled up to the front of the club ten minutes before eight. The gang teased him about arriving too early as he was leaving their apartment, but he decided he'd rather wait longer than risk being late. Besides, he wanted to see her round the corner and walk towards him. He wanted to watch her in the light of the morning and have a good reason to stare while she approached. He sipped a chai from a clay cup. The steaming hot tea burned his tongue a little on the first sip. It was always that way in the city. Tea would either scald his mouth or be too cold, and usually lukewarm chai meant it wouldn't be as fresh.

He checked his wristwatch and saw he only had a few minutes before her arrival. He whispered English words to himself, practicing the first words he would greet her with. Should he tell her she looked beautiful? Was it too forward? Should he ask about her night or make a joke? He couldn't think of something clever to say in English and his head hurt a little from the night's whiskey. "Play it cool," Rollie had told him. *Cool,* he thought. *Be cool.*

He began walking several steps up the street, then turned in the opposite direction, facing the streets behind him. He wondered which corner she would appear from. He kept pacing for several minutes then stopped himself. *Don't look impatient.* He leaned his shoulders against the wall next to the club's door, lifting one foot behind him, and planted the sole against the concrete. He whistled a little to himself, still hearing the d.j.'s last song in his head.

A few more moments passed and he checked his watch again: 8:15. He wasn't worried. He knew that tourists were often late, especially in the mornings. He couldn't count how many times during the season he was about to abandon a tour of the burning ghats after waiting 30 minutes for a group of customers. But they always showed up, eventually. He lowered his foot from the wall, made small circles with his ankles, stretched his knee, and then put his other foot against the wall. This time a little plaster came off of a crack. He hummed a few lyrics from the pop song, feeling his foot tap softly against the wall behind him. Tiny bits of chalky plaster bounced off his ankle. He looked from corner to corner down the street, placing a bet with himself that she'd come from the right side.

More time passed, and he began pacing again. He'd finished the chai and it already began to press against his bladder, telling him he would need to relieve himself soon. He considered the predicament and wondered if it'd be better to go into an alleyway at that moment or excuse himself after she arrived. A few minutes later, he figured he still had time to duck behind a wall briefly. In an alleyway off to the left, he wrote his name with his stream under a mess of graffiti.

He couldn't read the writing at all, thinking that the message must have not been that important if the artists hadn't bothered to make the letters clear.

He skipped back around the corner of the alley, expecting to see Monica waiting by the entrance, but she wasn't there. Walking up to his position at the front door, he checked his watch again: 8:45. He was sure they had agreed to eight o'clock, but as the time moved closer to the next hour, he wondered if her own watch was an hour slow. Fifteen more minutes wasn't much longer to wait, especially now that his bladder was empty.

But after another long half hour, he was shaking his head at the time on his watch. How long was he supposed to wait? He was unsure how etiquette worked with a foreigner. With the gang, if anyone was late, they never expected each other to wait long. An absent friend meant they were either not coming or that they would meet up later. He considered Monica, her face, her hair, her dress, those perfectly white teeth. She was worth waiting for, but he couldn't help but think that at some point, he was a fool for staying there. He decided that his limit would be two hours. He knew his gang would be having breakfast after ten o'clock near the bus stop.

The final minutes passed excruciatingly slow; each second dragging on like a tortoise stuck in a pit of mud. With every moment that passed he became simultaneously sad and angry. He became worried about facing his friends again, walking up to the breakfast cafe alone, humiliated after hours of waiting for nothing. He felt angry at her, and at himself, for liking her so much that he wanted to keep waiting. Then again, maybe she had been delayed by something awful. Maybe she was in an accident, or was sick, or was helping one of her tourist friends. He felt ashamed at assuming the worst, especially if it turned out she was injured in any way. As the clock neared the next hour, he grew impatient, wondering if he should start walking somewhere, maybe with the chance of finding her in need of help. He saw his watch count up the last few seconds, and at the exact two-hour mark, he took off in a sprint down the street.

At each intersection, he peered down the streets, straining his eyes, hoping to catch a glimpse of her coming out of a building, or perhaps holding a map, completely lost in the maze of streets. He looked above the street at the second intersection and saw a large advertisement for the club, with a large red arrow pointing behind him. *It couldn't be that hard to find…could it?* With the idea that she was lost feeling less likely, his mind wandered through horrible images about what might have happened to her. He knew that many tourists became very ill in Kathmandu, after drinking the water from a tap or eating food they had never eaten before. He hoped she wasn't violently ill in a dimly lit room somewhere. He would never know where to look. As his mind wandered, his feet moved him towards the bus stop. He wondered if she was indeed sick, if she would go to the club looking for him the next day. Or maybe the day after. He decided that he could just make it the routine for each morning: drinking his chai outside of the club at eight o'clock.

When the breakfast cafe came into sight, he saw his friends pulling apart pieces of potato paratha with their hands. Steam rose from the table after each section of the bread was torn open, and a cloud of steam and smoke hovered over Rollie's head, as he put pieces to his mouth with a cigarette still stuck between his fingers.

Jet looked up first, meeting Casanova's eyes, then nudging Rollie next to him. When Casanova saw them watching his approach, he felt his eyes water a little, the emotions of the morning suddenly taking hold of his head. His face felt hot, his mouth was dry, and he became conscious of how he appeared to the gang. As he got close enough to hear them, Rollie spoke first.

"This doesn't look good. What's up, Casanova, my friend? Where's our lucky lady?"

The whirlwind of emotions merged themselves in Casanova's cheeks and tied up his tongue. Instead of speaking, he just shook his head several times, as if he was trying to shake out every bad thought, sucking in air through his teeth, and holding back tears.

"She didn't show up?" Chimp asked, his mouth stuffed with paratha and red spices.

"Two hours!" Casanova blurted out. "Two hours and nothing. I don't know if I'm supposed to be angry or worried about her."

"Ah, look at that, guys, Casanova's in love!" Chimp bumped Jet's arm, laughing through the food in his mouth. At first, Casanova felt insulted, but as his friends joined in on the laughter, he couldn't help but laugh too, a smile breaking across his blushed cheeks. His emotions slackened, and his tear ducts were clearing up.

"Oh, whatever. I thought that it might just be a big payday. A private, all-day tour around town. She looked like a big tipper!" He lied to the bunch, who kept on laughing.

"Ok, sure man, whatever you say," Rollie said, winking at him. "Don't tell us you weren't already thinking about introducing her to your mom." Jet and Chimp brushed tears from their eyes, unable to control a violent roll of laughter from their stomachs.

"I'll just try again tomorrow," Casanova said, shrugging.

"I knew it. This guy is in deep!" Rollie said, mopping up the oil on his plate with his last piece of paratha. "He's totally obsessed!"

"I can not fiiind youuu, I was looking in my dreeeams," Chimp sang out, borrowing the words from an old romance movie. The rest of the gang, including Casanova gave in, laughing and holding their sides until Jet fell off his chair, pounding his palm into the dirt while yelling at Chimp to stop.

After the jokes subsided and the gang pulled themselves together, they decided that as long as Casanova wasn't busy chasing his girl around the city, they could head to the bus stop and start working. Rollie paid for the group's breakfast, then reaching his arm over Casanova's shoulder, said softly, "Don't worry about it, man. Foreign girls are impossible to get. We're just proud of you for dancing all night with her anyway. Better than we've ever done."

Casanova felt his body and mind relax at the quiet support, but deep in his chest, he still wondered where Monica could have been at that moment. He moved his arm over Rollie's shoulder and together they marched off towards the bus stop, matching each swinging of their legs so that they stepped on the outside at the same time. Jet and Chimp followed close behind, and Casanova could hear Chimp still humming the old love song.

When they approached the bus stop, a dozen or so tourists were pushing their packs into the lower storage compartment of a bus. Brightly colored jackets under waves of messy hair and pale skin moved around quickly, as they shuffled through the door of the bus. When the gang neared that particular bus, Casanova noticed the back of one tourist's head had blonde braids held together with red beads. The blonde girl was hanging off the arm of a tall, male tourist; he had his arm on her waist, holding her tight against his body. Casanova strained his eyes at the pair, while his mind told him there was no way that it was the same set of braided hair. But then the girl moved her head slightly to the side. Casanova stopped in his tracks. The profile was unmistakable. It was the same flawless curve of a nose above perfect lips. The same lips they had touched his cheeks the night before. He watched in horror as those same lips lifted back towards the other man, kissing a different cheek. The two boarded the bus, vanishing from the world outside it.

Casanova's feet dragged forward slightly, unsure whether to chase Monica onto the bus or not. A hand grabbed his shoulder as he moved. He turned to see his gang watching him. Rollie's hand squeezed his shoulder gently and Chimp stepped forward to add his hand to the other shoulder. Jet shook his head and clicked his tongue.

"Man, I'm sorry…" Rollie began, but before he could say more, Casanova turned, pushing past his friends, and ran away from the whole scene.

"Forget her man!" Jet yelled after him, but he let the voice drift past, and turned his attention forward. He felt tears freely run alongside his nose and onto his upper lip. His head hurt, and so did his chest. What had been a warm feeling in his heart so recently was replaced by a sharp, stinging pain. Each breath hurt more than the last. His pace quickened. He shoved past a tour group, which was walking in mass towards the bus stop. He heard murmurs within the group as he bumped shoulders with one man. He wanted to lash out at them, grab the straps of their packs and pull them to the floor. Anger built up inside him uncontrollably as he struggled to find a sense of what he'd seen.

Blurs of people, cars and shops flew past him as he walked directionless through the city. He didn't know where he was going and he didn't care. Somewhere inside him, almost instinctively, he remembered the frustration that surrounded him during his first day in the city. He remembered the first bar he visited with his gang, and the cold beer that lifted his spirits. He wanted a beer. He wanted whiskey. He craved a different state of mind, void of any pain or feeling at all.

He ducked under the awning of the first building that advertised beer. An unlit neon sign boasted "Everest Beer" on tap. The lighting inside of the bar was dim, and a few, sad-looking men sat at the bar, nursing large glasses of draft beer. He pulled up a seat next to them and signaled for a beer. When it arrived, he took a large gulp, feeling the cold and bubbles move quickly to his empty stomach. Immediately he felt the hint of numbness spread throughout his body. He took another large drink from the glass, holding the glass to his mouth until he had to pull it away to breathe again. Then he repeated the action until the beer was empty. After asking for another beer, the bartender looked at him with a concerned face but pushed another glass in front of him anyway. The effect of the beer washed through his body as he took a smaller drink of the second glass.

Several beers later, he found himself feeling dizzy on the edge of his seat. He stumbled towards the toilet, swinging open a thin, metal door that led to what wasn't much more than a hole in the floor. There was a cracked mirror above the sink, and seeing his reflection, he turned away quickly. His face was red and his eyes were horribly bloodshot. After relieving himself, he found his way to a table in the corner of the bar. His head swayed slightly as if it was balancing on the deck of a boat. He could hardly hear the voices coming from the bar and the lights above the bartender were blurred and painful to look at.

A voice came from his side. It was the bartender asking for payment. He hadn't even noticed the man walk towards his table. He fumbled with the bills in his pocket. He had brought enough money for an entire day with Monica, hoping to treat her to lunch and plenty of chai. He handed two paper bills to the bartender and asked for another beer.

The bartender said he could only continue drinking if he also ordered food and a bottle of water first. A restaurant across the street regularly brought in dishes for the customers. Casanova fished out another bill and asked for two plates of paratha and deep-fried vegetables. When the food arrived, Casanova picked at the plate until the bartender was satisfied enough to fill another glass of beer.

Hours passed in the dim lights of the bar, and soon his table was full of plates and empty glasses of beer. Every time he imagined Monica, he lifted the next beer to his mouth, waiting for the alcohol to push his thoughts far away. Eventually, the bartender approached to tell him the bar was closing. Casanova used the side of the table to balance as he stood to his feet. The room began to spin around him and he shoved a number of bills at the bartender, who followed him to the door. When he emerged from the bar, the sky was dark and a few lights shone on the street. When he inhaled the air outside the bar, a force of nausea sent shivers from his stomach simultaneously to his knees and head. He rushed around a corner and emptied his stomach into a small bush. His legs shook uncontrollably as he hunched over, his hands resting on his bony knees. After heaving twice more, he stood up straight, looking at his surroundings. He had no clue where he was.

He drifted down the street, looking for a recognizable landmark. His wandering must have lasted an hour until he found himself again in the tourist district. From there, he stumbled towards his apartment building.

He opened the door of this apartment and instantly heard the snoring of his friends from their mattresses on the floor. He kicked off his sandals and fell onto his bed, immediately sinking into a deep sleep.

In the morning he opened his eyes to an empty room. He found a note explaining his gang had gone to the bus stop again to work. He briefly considered leaving the apartment to meet them, but he couldn't stand the idea of returning to the scene of what he felt was the worst betrayal he had ever experienced. Instead, he stayed on his bed for hours, turning over all the reasons why Monica may have been hanging off the other man's arm. The previous morning, he had wandering thoughts of a future with her: taking her to his village to be married, then renting a room in the same apartment building as his friends, taking her to all his favorite places around the city, and endless fantasies of a long life together. But that morning, he only felt angry and hurt. He wanted to leave the city. He felt ashamed for expecting so much from one kiss and was nervous to face his gang again.

When night came again, he left the apartment finally, in search of the nearest shop to buy beer. He bought several large bottles and a plastic bag filled with salty snacks. When he returned to their room, his gang was sitting in a circle on the floor. They had gloomy faces and he immediately knew there hadn't been any luck touting that day.

"Hey, there he is, what's up Casanova?"

He felt tears welling up in his eyes and he wanted to tell them about his previous day in the bar, but something stopped him. Maybe it was his shame at falling for a girl he hardly knew, or not wanting to add to what appeared to be a terrible day for them all. He shook it off and feigned a smile.

"Nothing," he said instead. "Who wants a drink?"

"That's our man!" Jet said, standing up to high-five and take the bag of beers from his hands. Casanova felt his mind push Monica further away.

"Forget her, Casanova. You can do better," Chimp began.

"Leave it, man," said Rollie from the other side of the room.

"No, seriously, he has to know this. Look, Casanova, it isn't about you at all. Those girls, they just want one thing."

"Money…" Chimp popped a beer cap off a bottle with a lighter.

"That's right. Money, my green friend. And you may have a little. But you need a whole lot more to hang onto a beauty like that. See the tourist she was with. I guarantee you he has more money in his pocket than you've made all year. He can swoop in and whisk away any lonely girl for a month-long honeymoon, and what can you offer her? This apartment? With three more roommates?"

"Alright, alright, he gets it, now can we talk about something else?"

"Fine," Casanova said, sitting down on the floor. "I'll make enough money that she'll be sorry if she ever sees me again. I'll buy that whole damn club someday. But for now, I feel like having a beer."

"Sounds good to me." Chimp reached over to touch his beer's neck to Casanova's. Rollie and Jet shuffled over to join in.

☼☼☼

The next day, he woke up with heavy eyelids, and his whole body felt glued to the mattress. The only thing that kept him from sinking back into his dreams was a growing stomach ache and a heated argument coming from behind him. It was Rollie and Chimp.

"I don't care if you go, man. But I'm just saying it's too soon. Wait for the dream to be realized, at least."

"Screw your dream, Rollie. You've been saying that for almost three years now. We save just enough to live and drink every night. And you spend more than your share rolling those damn things."

Rollie had just started rolling a cigarette and suddenly threw it at the wall. "I buy these with my own money, Chimp, you crazy bastard. You...you just have no patience."

The tension in the room was thick, and Casanova wanted to step in the middle of the argument, but instead, he tried to mediate from the doorway: "What's the dream?"

"This dreamer..." Chimp began, but Rollie cut him off.

"I have a vision, an idea perhaps. The businesses that do the best here, aren't the hotels or restaurants, and as Chimp knows, definitely not the touts either."

Chimp moved to sit on his bed, and stretched out, forcing out an exaggerated moan.

"It's the mountain climbing," guessed Casanova.

"Of course, but that's out of our league, man. I'm not as big of a dreamer as some people think. I have realized it's the cafes. All they do is serve drinks and cakes, and charge ten times the cost of making them. Those guys make a killing. Always financing new signs, new tables, new sound systems, and upgrading to better locations. That's the future for us...we just need to...save a little."

"How much do we need?" Casanova wondered.

"More than we have, even if we quit drinking and smoking," Chimp said, lying on his back.

"Quite a bit to get started, but we'd get the money back easily in a season, then from there, it's all profits, better clothes, girls even…" Rollie trailed off, lost in thought.

Chimp rolled his eyes from his bed, stretched his back, and appeared to be waiting for a reaction from Casanova. To Casanova, opening a cafe immediately made sense. He'd read the menus in some of them, especially the more popular spots, when he wondered why a place was so crowded. He was shocked to see that people could easily spend his entire day's wages on a juice. One juice.

They didn't drink that night, and Casanova turned over constantly in his bed while the others snored from their own. He thought about his friends, the cafes, the season, which despite the recent heartbreak, had been lots of fun. He also thought about how to maintain the peace within his new gang of friends. Ultimately, he decided that it was up to him to wrangle a solution out of his mind.

His thoughts swirled from the city into the thin air above it, and off towards his high mountain village. His mother came into focus. He never thought about money much growing up. They could have sold their buffaloes and been rich, but then what? They would have just used the paper to light fires. There wasn't much to buy when he was young. He saw images of his father. His father and the buffaloes.

He sat up. His mind furiously raced around an idea. Could it work? How could he do it? What would it take? What should he do? Yes. Yes, it could work. He had to tell someone. A loud grunt bellowed from Rollie's mouth as he rolled over. Casanova slid out of his blanket and crawled over to his bed. He shook his friend gently, then more roughly. Rollie stirred in his sleep. Then opened his eyes, focusing hard on the abrupt transition from the dream he had left to Casanova's face almost touching his own.

"Rollie, I have an idea."

XIII

On the third Saturday of February, Lie Jie knocked on Jiang's door. Jiang could hardly see his friend in the darkness of his cavern-like hallway. Before he could speak, Li Jie held a finger up to his mouth. He moved closer to Jiang.

"The Revolution begins tomorrow," he whispered, and Jiang felt the hair on his arms rise. They stared at each other for a long moment. Somewhere behind Jiang, a fluorescent bulb flickered, mixing the shadows on Li Jie's face. Jiang thought he looked years older than he was. Turning, Li Jie left quietly down the hallway, wearing a serious look but his eyes giving away excitement.

That night, Jiang couldn't sleep. He couldn't stop his mind from playing over the events that led him to this point. He rolled from side to side, twisting up his blanket between his legs. His head pounded and his mouth was dry, but he didn't want to drink anything. He didn't want to move from the bed; he just wanted sleep to come. But every time he shut his eyes, he saw some scene from the past.

First, it was his eviction from the farm, his father being beaten, that violence on his village road, the man on fire, the far-away look of his mother. Images that hadn't bothered him in a long time suddenly were as real as the day they occurred. His existence the last few years revolved around his new friends and the city he had grown fond of.

Then the meeting at Steven's house. The group of activists, all oozing a degree of cool and mystique that Jiang had never seen before. Steven's mother, sipping tea and spinning thoughts around the table like some sort of philosopher. Li Jie's tales of their village turned into a city of ghosts. Imagined scenes of businessmen shaking hands behind closed doors, pictures of Jiang's village behind them, envelopes of money passed between hands. Then Jiang saw blood. Flashes of red pooled over his memories.

The group had shown him horrible images; video footage allegedly hidden by the government for decades. Police shooting at students, civilians, a lone figure standing in front of a tank in the middle of the capital, and military troops patrolling the streets. Steven had said just watching those videos would forever put his life in danger. The faces around the table at Steven's place were serious. The energy was tense and defiant. But Jiang insisted. He wanted to see proof of what they had been speaking of. The footage was graphic, he had never seen such violence outside of the films he watched. It was worse than any video game because it was real. Jiang's mind had struggled to believe what his eyes had seen. But they all assured him it was true, and he did ultimately trust them, especially Li Jie, whose hands were visibly shaking throughout the videos.

Jiang's mind raced through the last several years. His acceptance into his new environment. His high school years full of new friends and an endless progression of entertainment. He had spent countless hours in computer cafes playing online first-person shooters with his friends. He had ordered a hamburger from a touch-screen machine at a new restaurant just the other week. He had learned to eat from the air-conditioned markets. Rows and rows of food he had never known existed, all with brightly-colored packaging. Strange fruit from different parts of the world. His first smart phone. Games, maps, applications that translated his words into any language of the world. None of this exciting world of technology had existed where he was originally from. The new world had provided so many new experiences for him. He considered the words of Li Jie's new group of friends. Would their action destroy this new world? Was it all as bad as they said?

Jiang couldn't decide what to do with the information. Should he trust Li Jie's new friends? He had always been taught that his government was looking out for his best interests. He knew that if he wanted to visit a doctor, he could. If his house was on fire, hopefully a government-paid fireman would come to put it out. But he did notice some imbalance in the city. In some areas of the city, people seemed more comfortable than others. In one neighborhood, people spent their evenings in restaurants and cafes, while in other areas, the people were still working, late into the night. He knew that some folks went home to sleep in their own room, while others shared that room with their entire family. He had always reasoned that his friend Bo's life was extraordinary. Bo's life looked comfortable and money was never as elusive as it was in his own world.

In school, Jiang had learned quite a lot about the rest of the world, historically and topically speaking. He knew about government corruption that was rampant in other places around the world, but how could his own world be the same? Steven and the others had told him that the truth was being hidden from him. He wondered how much about the world he really knew?

He felt his heartbeat in his ears as his mind drew up new images of the old capital protests he had seen on the videos. Would the next day be the same? Steven said it would be a smaller gathering, but there were similar protests planned in at least a dozen cities around the country. Steven had shown him protests that had erupted in several countries in the Middle East the year before. Normal people had taken to the streets, demanding a new, better, and fair government. The amazing part was that it seemed to be working. Steven had said those other protests occasionally transformed into revolution, sparking rebellion from entire cities. Their governments had no choice but to act after that. Sensing Jiang's nervousness, Steven reassured him; he said that their protests would be non-violent, and their goal was just to let their communities stand up and shout demands of the government. They could stand up and demand more transparency from their leaders for example. Jiang liked this part. He believed Li Jie and his new friends about his old village's transformation, but he wanted to hear it from the state, or at least some local official. People deserved to know the truth.

Steven and the group had given an important task to Jiang, which only fueled his nerves. For some reason, Li Jie had told Steven and the others about Jiang's recent hobby of photography. Jiang had only been using a camera for less than a year, and he only really bought it to take pictures with Hong, ever since she had become obsessed with some photography app on her phone.

Steven said that Jiang's task was simple, but to Jiang, it felt like the most dangerous job for any of them. Surely, if the police wanted to cover up a story about a protest, then they would be looking for photographers. He remembered a story about the photographer who took the picture of the man in front of the tank, how he hid the film in a hotel room toilet. It all seemed so intense. How would Jiang, more than any of the more seasoned activists, be able to hide a memory card after the protests? He pulled himself to the side of his mattress and swung his legs over the side, moaning as he stood up. He had unplugged his clock, in order to stop looking at it, but now he wondered how long he had been rolling around without sleep. He walked up to the heavy curtains in front of his bedroom's one, tiny window. He saw a hint of light behind it and pulling it back, he revealed the neighbor's concrete wall, with the first light of the day slowing creeping into the space.

☼☼☼

Later that morning, Steven thrust a Fujifilm f300 into Jiang's hands as they hurried down a quiet street. Lie Jie and six other boys were ahead of them.

"My camera's bigger than this…" Jiang began.

"We want small, man. Easier to hide." Of course, Jiang felt that was obvious. "Don't worry, Jiang, it's going to be easy. Just shoot as much as you can, then if the police move in, switch the memory cards, like I showed you, ditch the camera, and walk away." Steven moved his mouth sideways, speaking in a loud whisper and keeping his eyes forward. "Just don't run."

They turned a corner, making a wide bend around a woman setting up metal tables and an older man connecting propane to a stove on wheels. The man looked at Jiang. His eyes narrowed as if he knew what the boys were up to. Jiang swallowed hard. He felt a knot form in his stomach.

They were getting closer. A surge of men, women, and younger students pushed out from several alleyways in front of them. The street led to a popular, large square, flanked by government offices and international chain restaurants. The February air was still brisk enough for winter coats, but some protesters wore their best suits. Some held signs with slogans that said "Long live democracy," and some held national flags. The crowd thickened as Jiang's group funneled into the square. There were several foreigners and locals with large cameras slung around their necks. Jiang watched one photographer look through his lens, click the shutter, and then look quickly to the sides and behind him. The photographers looked excited and nervous at the same time.

The crowd grew. Bodies bumped into bodies, and heads swiveled to the sides, looking, waiting. A flag whipped in the wind behind Jiang, a corner of it snapped against his ear. He stepped forward, deeper into the mass of protesters. Jiang was just tall enough to see over the heads around him. Checking behind him, he spotted several men hanging off street lamps. He turned on the small camera and held it above his head, snapping the shutter several times while rotating the lens in different directions. The beauty of digital film. He knew he could filter through the photos later, easily cutting out the blurry ones.

A bullhorn floated above the heads around him, finding its way up a set of stairs outside a restaurant. Jiang could see through the glass of the restaurant. Mouths paused mid-bite, watching the growing mass outside. A waiter stood by the door; a skinny boy nervously standing guard, hoping the protesters wouldn't break into a riot and spill through his door. The man with the bullhorn reached the top of the last step and swung around, facing the crowd. He looked to be in his mid-30s. A scarf hung loosely over an open blazer jacket.

"Brothers! Sisters!" The crowd grew quiet, turning to face the man. "We're here together for one reason! To say that enough is enough!"

The man paused, gazing around the crowd that now watched him closely. "Our demand is simple. We are tired of authoritarian rule. We are exhausted by long hours, pathetic pay, unsafe and unfair working conditions. We can't stand that our country stands on our backs, and makes our future for us. We want a say. We want a voice!"

The crowd cheered together after each sentence. The faces around Jiang were hungry for more words. "We want democracy!" The man belted out the last words so fiercely, the horn screeched with the sound. The crowd exploded in applause and cries of approval. The man's final words evolved into a chant, springing from mouth to mouth through the masses.

Jiang's finger bounced off the camera's button, his hand raised high above the heads in front of him. He pointed it at the man, who leaped off the stairs and disappeared. He swung the lens behind him, the shutter snapping wildly as the chants filled his ears. He felt the crowd surge forward, away from the restaurant.

"Jiang!" Li Jie's voice barely crossed the few feet between them. "Let's get up to the front, man!"

Jiang followed Li Jie through the bodies, twisting their arms around as they sidestepped around a stranger's feet. Jiang spotted Steven and two of the other boys ahead of them. A white sign with hand-drawn words drifted past them. Jiang tried to take a picture of the woman and the sign, but more people funneled through a gap before he could. Ahead of him, the back of Jiang's head disappeared amid a dozen others. The chants deafened any thoughts inside his own head and as he joined in, he couldn't even hear his own voice. He felt his heart racing. The energy around him was incredible. Over a hundred voices yelling in unison, almost shaking the earth below them.

Somewhere in front of the crowd, a new wave of excitement rolled backward. People were moving faster now. Jiang heard screams over the chants. His heart threatened to leap out of his chest. He wanted to scream too. He needed to scream or he thought his screams might explode out of his ears.

Suddenly the screams became sharper. There were yelps that were quicker than before. Something like a dog if you tugged on its ear. Jiang leaned on his toes, trying to get an eye above the crowd. He saw people moving backward, back into the people that were still on the forward surge.

He trained his sight forward, squinting his eyes, trying to make out a row of black shirts at the head of the mass. In front of the wall of black, a few heads fell, lost to the sea of bodies. The chants in front of him stopped. A snapping sound flew backward, almost like a gust of wind. Then more sharp sounds. Snaps and thuds of blunt objects on skin. Jiang's stomach lurched to the side. He felt the panic in the crowd before it began. His position among the protesters was closer to the front now, and he saw the black shirts were uniforms. A row of helmets blocked the momentum of the marching crowd. Police.

Jiang fought his legs' instinct to run. The job Steven had entrusted to him immediately became clear. He pushed ahead. Some protesters pushed with him, but most were moving back, shoving quickly past, trying to gain distance from the violence. The front of the line was only several people away from him. He spotted a cop in full riot gear swinging a wooden stick at the bodies in front. The stick slammed against the thigh of student, buckling the student's knees. Another cop grabbed the straps of a backpack and dragged the student behind the line of police. The panic in the crowd roared and the protesters began to turn in retreat. Jiang kept his camera in front of him, taking as many pictures as he could. He heard a scream next to him. A woman lay on the ground, a rush of feet stumbled over her, as she held her arms over her head. A man bent to help her when he was struck by a stick in the back, tumbling his body over the woman's. The crowd shoved past Jiang, pushing him away from the scene. He moved to the side, trying to get a shot of the front line.

He recognized Steven, shoving his way towards the police. Jiang tried to follow, moving slowly against the stream of people running backward. He held out the camera just as a stick collided with the side of Steven's head. Steven's body collapsed on the ground and was dragged forward by four hands. Jiang looked up from the camera, locking eyes with a cop. The cop moved towards him. He knew he had to get out of there. If they took his camera then his mission was lost. Luckily a group of protesters moved between him and the cop, and Jiang hid behind the motion. He turned quickly, joining the rush of people that ran back. Cracking sounds and screams deafened all other sounds.

He ran back and the crowd became thinner. The protesters were splitting up, finding escape routes out of the square. Jiang wasn't sure which direction to run, but let the shoulders around him guide. An old man crossed in front of him. The man's body was limp, carried by his armpits and legs by two other men. A bloody wound cut across the man's forehead. Jiang tried to take a picture but was bumped from behind. The camera shot out from his hand, bouncing on the ground below. He ducked down, looking for it. More people bumped into him as he tried to push between legs, darting his eyes across the ground. He heard the camera slide across the pavement and saw a pair of feet barely miss the thing. He leaped forward, grabbing the small strap of the camera with one hand and pushed off the ground with the other hand.

When he looked up, he was around the corner from the restaurant where the man with the bullhorn had started the chanting. The metal grate of the restaurant was closed and he couldn't see anyone inside. The crowd's momentum picked up and he let it move him towards an alleyway. He spotted a raised planting box on the corner, and moved towards it. Jumping on the box, he surveyed the scene behind him. People were running in all directions. The police were spread out in the crowd, grabbing at shirts and shouting orders. A photographer was being led away, a cop holding the back of his neck with his hand. The photographer's head was bent downwards, a broken camera hanging pathetically off a strap around his neck.

Jiang searched the faces of the crowd for his own group. There seemed to be as many police as protesters. The bulk of the crowd had already run away. Torn banners and signs littered the ground over a fury of feet. Then Jiang recognized his friend. Two police were escorting Li Jie away from the steps of the restaurant. Li Jie's shirt was ripped and the collar was stretched out so that Jiang could see his bare chest. Li Jie's face looked unhurt but it was streamed by fresh tears. Jiang wanted to yell after him but noticed several cops moving towards him, their eyes fixated on Jiang's hand holding the camera.

Leaping off the box, he joined the crowd through the alleyway. As he ran, he fumbled with the camera's memory card slot. He switched out the card with the second one in his pocket, bending mid-stride to slip the first card inside his left sock. Looking up he saw the crowd split down two streets. He rounded the corner and froze.

A cop was standing with his legs wide, and a wooden baton held in front of him. Through the riot helmet mask, Jiang saw a man's eyes watching him. Jiang looked around him. The rest of the crowd had flung itself away from the corner, moving across a two-lane road. People jumped over the road's center divider. Jiang looked again at the cop who suddenly felt closer to him. Slowly Jiang raised the camera, showing it clearly in front of him. The cop took a step forward. Jiang dropped the camera. It fell to the concrete, breaking on impact and sending the battery skidding between them. A long moment held in the short distance between them. The cop met Jiang's eyes again and nodded towards the road. Jiang spun around and bolted to the road, catching up to a group that was crossing the road. He kept running until he was across. When he looked back, the cop picked up the camera, tucking it in a pocket on his leg. Jiang looked away and started to run again. When he got to the next cross street, he kept running.

When he couldn't hear the sirens anymore, he finally stopped. With his hands on his thighs, he coughed between breaths. He felt his pulse through the skin on his neck. The thumping pulse was going faster than any time he could remember. When he brought his hand down, he noticed it was shaking. *This is insane.* His vision blurred for a moment, his head felt light, and he reached for a nearby street lamp to brace himself. The adrenaline of the morning began to fade, and it was replaced by an unfamiliar motion of nausea. *Where's Li Jie right now?* Jiang shook away images of Steven's body being dragged away. But it was only replaced by an earlier scene of his father being taken away from his old village's road.

He reached towards the top of his sock and tapped the memory card, making sure it was still safe. He knew he needed to send it off as soon as possible, at least before he went home.

At the post office near his apartment, he scribbled the address Steven had recited to him, *Time Magazine, Rockefeller Center, New York, USA,* and slipped the memory card and a small note into the envelope.

Paranoia gripped Jiang's mind as he walked the next two blocks home. Several times, he ducked down an alley and waited, watching for someone to come following him. But no one came. He had succeeded. Steven was gone. Jiang didn't expect to see him, or the rest of the group anytime soon. Li Jie was somewhere, hopefully having escaped the police roundup. But as far as Jiang's role was concerned, he was done for the day.

As he struggled with his key in the door of his apartment, he felt exhaustion coming for him. He wanted to lie down. He wanted to process the morning and put his head on a pillow.

But when he opened the door, his father was standing in front of him.

"Jiang." His father's eyes were locked on the floor. His large, farmer's hands hung at his side. "Your mother's sick, she's in the hospital."

XIV

Casanova stood on the edge of a concrete curb next to a bus stop a few blocks from his apartment. He balanced his front toes over the edge and lowered his heels to compensate for the forward motion. The curb was chipped away on either side of his feet, but a few splatters of yellow paint remained where he balanced.

"Here it comes," Jet said. "Going to miss you, Casanova."

"Ah, it's Ukali again, isn't it? Don't want to be Casanova around a bunch of water buffaloes, right?" Rollie thumped Ukali on the shoulder softly with his fist.

Chimp had left for his home village the previous morning but promised to stay in contact with his gang through letters. The high tourist season was finished anyway, and Chimp said he needed to get away from the city for a while, breathe some fresh air, and take a break from the monkeys. He said that if the monkeys had a slow winter, they wouldn't expect him when he came back, full force and even crazier.

Rollie stuck a small wad of cash in Ukali's coat, along

with a quart of whiskey.

"For the cold…and boredom," he said. "But don't drink it all at once, you thirsty bastard."

"I'll see you all in a few months." Ukali picked up his small backpack and walked towards the bus. After about eight hours, he would find another ride further north. Rollie told him that there were plenty of seasonal traders that would leave from the next town, anxious to share the cost of travel back to their own villages in the mountains. Ukali passed the driver and found his seat near the back of the bus.

Ukali turned to wave from his seat, but his friends were already walking down the street. He watched Jet slug Rollie in the arm, just before they rounded the corner, past a stall selling hot tea, packets of aniseed, tobacco, and newspapers.

His plan felt simple enough. He would convince his mother that in order to pay for university studies, he needed money, fast. They would sell off all the water buffaloes and he would leave her with enough cash to hold her over until he could send more money to her. He reasoned that if he mentioned the cafe idea, she would think he was crazy. Selling tea would sound like a waste of time to anyone in the village since they always drank theirs for free.

The trip back to his village took him two days. The trio of motorcyclists he got a ride with were reluctant to take him at first, but his whiskey sealed the deal. They made room for him, on top of a pile of new blankets from the city. The two motorcycles that trailed his driver carried crates of beer.

His village looked tiny after living in such a large, busy city. From the back of the motorcycle, Ukali breathed in deeply. The air was fresh for sure, Chimp was right, but the quietness of the valley unnerved him a little. He immediately missed the buzz of the city. It's constant noise. The honking of horns, the calls from vendors, and the barking of hundreds of street dogs.

The motorcycle dropped him off at the bottom of the path that led to his home. As promised, he turned over some of his cash to the driver. The whiskey had long been finished by the other traders.

There were no lights on in his house. The sun was already going down, and he expected his mother would have lit her lamps already. He climbed the old, stone steps up to the front door. Long grass grew in between the stones, and the chairs in front of the house looked cold and lonely. He knocked on the door. He couldn't hear anyone stirring inside the house.

She must be at a neighbor's house, he thought. He pushed the door open. There was no use for locks on doors there. The house was quiet and cold. The breeze behind him blew dried grass and dust past him, onto the floor. He dropped his backpack off at the door and walked to the single table that occupied most of the room. He put his finger on the wood and brushed away a thin layer of dust.

Where was she? Could she have been so lonely without me that she was staying somewhere else? He knew his mother had always been social, and he hardly saw her without friends nearby, chatting about anything, passing the time.

He walked down their path and went to the nearest house, where a woman about his mother's age lived. That woman's husband had died long before his father, and the two were always visiting each other, sharing old memories, good and bad, of living with the men in the valley. There was a light on in that house, and when he approached, he could hear a pot filling with water. He knocked on the door and heard the water stop.

The woman opened the door, her tired eyes opening wide when she saw him.

"Ukali. It's you. Come in, come in," she pulled him inside gently. She seated him at the table. "Are you hungry? I was just starting to cook."

"Thanks, maybe. I was just coming over to ask if you've seen my mother."

She was resting her hands on the back of the chair across from him. She pulled out the chair and sat down. She leaned forward and her face seemed to morph unpleasantly. It was a look he had never seen her wear.

She began to speak and with every word, Ukali's heart became heavier. His elbows started to shake where he had them bent on her table. Then his hands. His eyes were wet and his throat began to close. He looked away, at the wall next to them. The woman explained more but only heard pieces of her speech.

"…her heart…a month ago…so sorry…"

Ukali didn't remember leaving the house, but he soon found himself standing down by the river. It was a cold night, and he shivered in a thin coat, which was far less than what the mountain climate called for. His eyes had dried, but the inside of his head and chest wouldn't stop pounding, like a fist on a door. He sat on the corner of a rounded rock, looking at the river. He wasn't watching the river; he wasn't watching anything. He just stared ahead of him.

He considered joining the water. He considered jumping into the glacier melt, and letting it numb his whole body. He was alone. Suddenly, he was just an orphan standing in the crisp air.

At some point he climbed the path back to his childhood home. The house felt empty and small. He laid down on his parent's bed. Somewhere between a spell of dizziness, he fell asleep.

The next day, he almost couldn't move. He laid on the bed, which only a month or so ago, had comforted his mother to sleep. Or did she sleep? Was she thinking about him when she left his world? Was she thinking of her only son, who left her, only a few years after his father left? Did his actions chip away at her beating heart, making it tired and unwilling to continue pumping blood throughout her body?

He stayed in the bed most of the day until there was a knock on the door. He rolled over and tried to ignore it, willing the person to disappear with his silence. But the person knocked again. He eventually shifted off the bed and listened. Silence. The person had left. He could have gone back to bed, but curiosity stirred him. He walked to the door and pulled on the old, heavy, wood. The easy light of an early evening met him, but he still had to squint. The house had been completely dark, and the wood shutters stayed closed all day. When his eyes adjusted, he saw a boy, no, a young man, walking down the path, not far from the door.

"Suman?" Ukali's voice was raspy and foreign sounding to his own ears.

Suman stopped walking and turned around. He walked back towards Ukali. Suman was the same age as Ukali, and they had always been in school together. Sometime after his father died, Suman was the last of his friends to drift apart from Ukali.

"Hey, old friend," Suman said, reaching to embrace Ukali. Ukali wanted to recoil, to remain in his cloud of sadness and suffering, but when it happened, the hug felt warm and welcome. "I just wanted to see you. I heard you were back and I wanted to say that if there's anything you need, at all, my house is open to you. My wife agrees. You can sleep in our extra bed anytime you'd like."

Ukali's throat tightened, he didn't want to speak about his mother to his old classmate. But he managed to let out several words from the empty space inside him.

"You have a wife?"

Suman smiled. "Yes, sometime after you left. We

haven't spoken for a while. She's from a yak herding family, but is tired of watching animals eat, like you were."

When Ukali laughed quietly, he noticed his eyes were wet. He turned his head away and wiped a few tears with the back of his hand.

"That's great, Suman. I'm happy for you. Thank you. For now, I want to stay here."

"I understand. So, you know then, my house is your house."

A few days passed until Ukali gathered the courage to visit Suman's house and meet his wife. He learned that they had tried for a child but nothing happened yet. Suman's mother was anxious to have a granddaughter, as she was starting to feel older. Suman's father had also died when they were both young. So, it was just the three of them living in the house.

Suman's family was growing, and Ukali's had shrunk down to just himself. While he tried to feel happy for Suman, he couldn't shake a lonely feeling inside. With every word Suman's mother spoke, he thought of his own mother. When they talked of children, he thought that his father would never meet any children he might create, if he ever met a woman. Furthermore, he felt a vast void between him and his old classmate. Suman wanted a simple life. But Ukali had seen another world, and liked it. He felt too big for his small village. Everywhere he looked, he saw places he had been with his parents. When he heard buffaloes calling out to each other, he felt sick with pain.

He soon remembered his plan, his mission, his gang back in the city. That was his future, he decided. He didn't want a wife and daughter in a tiny valley. He wanted cash, enough to impress any girl that he met. He wanted to vacation somewhere tropical. He wanted chaotic, dusty streets, late nights drunk with his friends, and enough money to party in a club anytime he wanted. As the following days passed, he stopped visiting Suman's home, politely declining any invitations, and set about his plan.

His father's buffalo had been temporarily taken into a neighbor's herd, but the neighbor said he would hand them back whenever Ukali wished. He was only keeping them until Ukali came to claim them.

He tried to sell them to that neighbor first, but that man had no money to part with. It turned out, most people in the village didn't have a lot of money or a reason to buy them either.

The snows approached, and Ukali kept the buffaloes in their indoor stables, safe from the cold. He let them out to feed, but his mind was so preoccupied with selling them, that he often forgot to let them out until one started making a fuss.

No traders visited the village all winter, and Ukali spent his days shut inside his house, going over his plan, drawing designs for the cafe with old pencils and scraps of newspaper. But he grew bored of these constant daydreams and needed to occupy his time in other ways. He scribbled a letter to the gang on the back of an article about the rise in tourism. He cited the article, telling his friends that business would explode once they set up their dream cafe. In his final sentences, he wrote:

'Dream Cafe, that could be the name. Better than Chimp's Crazy Cafe anyway. Signed, Casanova.'

Ukali counted the money he had left, pulled out a few notes of paper money, and walked into the village. One neighbor had begun selling beer out of their house. He bought two crates of beer, which felt much colder than anything in the city. He carried them, one at a time, back to his house. He opened the first bottle at the table and took a big sip from it. It was brutally cold, hardly necessary for the weather outside. But his chest warmed nonetheless. Once again, he felt his mind clear of the negativity that consumed him, and his daydreams about the cafe and future became more abstract. He laughed to himself, thinking about what he would do with all the cash they made. He kept drinking. Then he laughed at himself, as he stumbled around, beginning to feel tipsy and a little crazy with the visions of the future.

The winter passed faster with every crate of beer he dragged through the snow to his house. He began to eat less, finding his stomach full enough with the nearly frozen beverage. His mother still had food stored it turned out, and the supply of potatoes, onions, and dal was plenty to fill his stomach between sessions of beer drinking.

By the time the snow started melting, he had almost spent all his money on beer. He waited impatiently for the first traders to arrive. He sat outside the house, on the old chairs, and watched the road down the valley. It took weeks for the first motorbike to cough its way up the narrow road. By then, Ukali was long out of beer. He felt bored and agitated without the liquid escape.

He waved to the first motorbike from the end of his path, making the driver pull over. The driver struggled to balance his load of goods as he came to a sudden stop. The driver shook his head. What did he want with a buffalo? Buffalo meat maybe, but he didn't have the time to butcher one. He would leave the next day, hopefully, loaded with lightweight cash for the ride back down.

Of course, Ukali never considered that buffaloes would be more easily transported back to the city in the form of meat. He had seen his father butcher a calf plenty of times and he knew he could manage. He left the driver to continue his drive into the village and went looking for his father's knives.

He found a dust-covered box of butchering knives in a crate in the corner of the main room. He removed the longest, sharpest one. More of a sword than a knife, he thought, and walked out to the stable. There were four smaller buffaloes in the herd, and he led one outside, behind their house. The snow was melting, but still thinly blanketed the cold ground. He tied the neck with a rope, and pulled it tight towards a tree. He put a handful of grass in front of it, and as it started to eat, he reached for the big blade. He lifted the heavy metal above his head, breathed out deeply, then brought the blade quickly down on the animal's neck. The sword had stopped at the bone, and the buffalo began thrashing around. Blood squirted all over both of them. He remembered his father making the cut in two short blows, but it took Ukali another five to finish it off. The animal fell, its legs still kicking in the snow, thick, dark blood pooling down its neck and soaking into the white ground.

The butchering took him most of the day. He set aside the least delicious pieces for himself in a rock basin next to the house. He washed each cut in a bucket of icy cold water. The cold weather would preserve the meat until the next day. He wrapped the better pieces of still-warm meat in newspaper and stacked them neatly on top of each other. The innards, he dragged uphill, leaving them for birds and other scavengers to pick through. He tried to label the newspaper bundles, but the wet meat soaked the paper and any pencil marks faded away.

He kept the meat in a cold, stone-lined hole, underground, just next to the house. He removed a few pieces of old meat from the hole that he realized his mother had left. They smelled rancid, even after the cold winter, and he tossed them on the pile of innards.

Then he waited. The next day, two motorcycles came up the road, and one stopped at his waving arms. He was lucky, the driver was interested in bringing meat back with him, saying he could almost double his money after selling off his newspapers and beer. Then the next day, Ukali received a crate of beer and a fistful of cash for most of the calf meat.

He counted the cash in the house that night. It was a good start, but nowhere near the amount he needed. The next day he would butcher another buffalo.

But, after the day of work, the following day brought no more traders, and Ukali waited, frustrated at the delay, drinking beer from the fresh crate. He had drunk four beers by sundown.

He stood up from the chair, a little lightheaded at the sudden heightening of his inebriation. *Tomorrow*, he thought.

But he waited in vain the next day, and the day after that. His crate of beer finished, and he worried that the recently butchered calf wouldn't last much longer.

Finally, on the fifth day, a group of traders appeared. They purchased the meat, although at a discounted price. The traders knew what fresh meat looked like.

Nevertheless, he replenished his beer supply and Ukali added more notes to his stack of money. He decided not to butcher another calf until more traders came up the road, figuring he could convince them to wait until he butchered the calf fresh.

But a week passed slowly and there was no sign of traders. Then another week, and when his beer finished, he walked into the village to buy more. At the neighbor's house, he asked when they thought more motorcycles would come. The neighbor told him that they always had a rush when the snow melted, but it could be a month or two before more showed up. Ukali was shocked. How could he hold out for so long? The season of touting would start soon in the city, and he was ready to get back and begin the dream with his gang.

He sat at the table in his house and stared at his fresh crate of beer. *OK*, he reasoned with himself, *I have to ration this. Every two days, I can have one beer.* It was simple enough, but he knew the boredom that came with waiting alone in the empty house. What else was there to do?

He visited Suman several times, but their happy family just made him feel lonelier. He walked on the hillside above his house. He threw stones into the growing river.

One day, when walking back home, he heard a buffalo calling out. Of course, he hadn't let them out all day, and they must be more bored than he was.

He removed the wooden poles that shut them in their stable and walked with them down to the river. He watched the familiar mud bath rituals and listened to them eat away at the new grass, vibrant and fresh from the snow melt. He leaned on a twisted tree trunk, seeing his father's silhouette in his own shadow. Ukali, the buffalo herder. He felt as far as ever from the city.

A week passed, then a second. Several traders ventured into town, but none wanted meat. They were all after cash, just like him.

He followed the water buffaloes along the riverfront, watching, waiting. Another week passed as he felt less and less interested in the boring lives of the herd. He knew inside that he was meant for action. Born to hustle in the busy streets, not wasting away, watching slow-moving animals.

One day, a trader appeared just as Ukali was carrying a crate of beer to his house. This time the trader waved first, stopping his engine in order to speak without the rumbling sound.

"Are you Casanova?"

The word sounded strange in that setting and it took a few seconds for Ukali to realize that he was this person the trader named. The man handed a letter to him, then declined his offer of fresh meat.

Ukali tore open the letter as the motorbike chugged along into the village.

'Casanova! We are sorry to hear about your mother. Jet says to remind you that he is on his own too, and things will be easier each day for you. Chimp never returned to town. No word or anything. Probably out chasing monkeys from his parent's garden or something and too busy to write. The season is in full swing. Where are you, man? You sounded certain about the buffalo deal. Hope you're not making your Casanova moves on anyone up there. Send us a word, thirsty man! We are saving a little cash too. I only smoke in the evenings now, and damn that Chimp, he was right, it helps with the saving. Talk soon-Rollie.   P.s. Hurry, Jet is talking some crazy shit about taking a job in the desert somewhere to work construction.'

The letter brought Ukali back. He imagined the streets, the fast-paced life, then to the fading dream, and his ever-shrinking pile of money under his parent's bed. He needed to sell buffaloes quickly.

He left his crate of beer just inside the doorway and started down the path. He visited every house in the village, offering meat, live buffaloes, old tools, anything that might sell. Only one old man bought a few knives from him, but after wanting to first trade pickled chilies, they settled on a small amount of coins.

Ukali counted the money that night. He figured if he sold the next two calves quickly, it would be enough to go back. Not enough for the cafe, but a good start, and he would find more money with half a season left of touting. His friends would be happy, he thought. Happy enough at the reunion that the rest of the money wouldn't matter yet.

But each day bled into a week, and weeks turned into another month watching his herd graze.

Frustrated, he had started drinking more often. He stopped caring about the money as much and put half aside for the cafe, and decided the rest would be for beer, some food, but mostly beer. He knew he was happier drinking, so why torture himself?

One night, drunk from perhaps one too many, he swore he could hear a motorcycle down the valley. He decided that he could use his tout skills to talk a trader into buying the meat, no matter what. So, he went outside, and under the light of a nearly full moon, butchered a calf. While he cut the meat, he polished off several more drinks.

The next morning, he woke up, curled up on the corner of the bed. He was in a cloud of rough morning sobriety. He didn't realize his plan the night before until he noticed the dried blood on his pants. He flung open the front door and went searching for the trader. Through the entire village, he found no motorbike. Had they left already? No, a neighbor informed him, there hadn't been a trader the night before, or that morning.

Distraught, he walked back home and immediately took a beer from the crate. He drank quickly, greedily, until he was lubricated enough to go into to town to buy more beer. He continued to drink for several days, only pausing to sleep and eat occasionally. No motorbike came, day after day, until his pile of cash looked alarmingly thinner than he remembered. He started eating the meat from the stone hole next to the house, and traded most of it for other food and more beer from his neighbors. They were happy to have the meat, but he didn't share their smiles. He felt a giant space between himself, the man with dreams of city life, and simple farmers.

The summer finished and the weather cooled. After butchering another calf, he drank through the first weeks of autumn.

One brisk morning, he decided he had enough of the village. He could gather up his belongings, sell, trade, or give away the herd, and catch the first ride back to the city. *Forget the cafe.* As long as he was touting with Rollie and Jet, he would be happy.

Two days later a motorbike rolled into town, but this time the driver had another letter for him.

'Ukali,

I hope you're still alive somewhere. When we never heard from you, we figured you might have gone back to herding or something and decided against touting or a cafe dream. Jet left. He was hired by a foreign company to build houses in a country somewhere west, in the desert. Haven't heard from him. It sucks to be alone in the city now, and I've also decided to return to my village. It was a good ride, but maybe Chimp knew something we didn't. Life sounds easy in my village. It's a big trip, so I'll probably already be on my way when you read this. Good luck, whatever you're doing. Maybe see you someday.

-Rollie'

Ukali stared at the letter until the dimming light of the sunset made it impossible to read anymore. He wanted to shout down the valley, to write, to do something to tell Rollie to wait. But he knew it was too late. How had he forgotten to write a reply to the first letter? To tell them he was coming? He didn't think that they, the kings of the tout world, would leave that wild city.

He considered going back to the city anyway, to start touting again. But each time he reflected on his memories there, they sounded empty without the gang around the relive them. He drank from his crate of beer. His busy mind led him late into the night. It was impossible to sleep, despite his heavy eyes and no matter how many beers he drank.

He figured that he could still sell meat and start a cafe. When it was successful, his friends would hear about it and come back. Yes. That's all he had to do. Wait, and realize their dream. Make enough money for Jet to leave the desert and send enough beer to Rollie's village, to make him remember the good times in that wonderful, chaotic place.

Sometime the next day we woke up. The sun was already high in a cloudless sky. He didn't remember falling asleep. Maybe it was all a dream. The letter. Rollie's words. But he soon found it, crumpled up under the table. The words were real.

He felt trapped in his house. He had to get out. He walked to the stable. The water buffalo were grazing around it. He hadn't locked them in for the night, but they came back anyway, waiting for their two-legged master to lead them to green patches of grass. He walked back to the house, picked up a beer, stuffed it into his back pocket, and returned to the herd. He shouted at them, announcing his presence. They immediately started towards him. He walked in front of the giant animals. He walked down toward the river, on a trail well-worn from years of his father passing the same direction. A male charged past Ukali, towards a muddy hole by the river, smelling the murky water. Satisfied, the bull crashed into the water, covering himself up to the neck with refreshing liquid. Mud began to dry on the animal's back, under the midday heat of the sun, and one by one, the rest of the buffaloes found a bath of their own.

XV

The public hospital on Jingwu Avenue was enormous, stretching down an entire city block. Jiang felt disoriented as he followed his father down the brightly-lit corridor. They twisted through a maze of hallways and numbered doors until they came to his mother's wing.

She shared a room with three other people, but only her bed had its curtains drawn. When they pulled back the curtains, he saw her eyes widen, almost sparkling under the fluorescent light on the ceiling. Even from several feet away, he could hear her breathing. Heavy, painful-sounding breaths. A tube stretched out from under her nose, and another thinner one rose from a needle in her arm. A machine next to her beeped occasionally, and her pulse bounced across a small black screen, like a tiny green snake. She shifted her weight until she freed one hand from her covers. The skin on her arm was much more pale than Jiang remembered.

"Jiang...my boy. How...are you?" She stuttered out with a small, raspy voice.

"Just fine, mom. But I think I should ask you that."

She smiled and looked around the room. Then rolled her eyes toward the ceiling.

"They say it's a rare one...just bad luck."

"Merkel carcinoma." Jiang's father affirmed from behind him.

"It's funny. They say I spent too much time outside. I never considered that to be dangerous." She laughed a little with a tiny snort as a punctuation.

"I'm sorry...I don't know what to say..." Jiang shifted uneasily in place.

"Don't worry. They have ways to stop it from spreading more. I may be old, but I'm a lot stronger than they think." She smiled at them, then reached a hand to Jiang. He stepped forward and took her hand. It looked impossibly small in his.

"Tell me, Jiang. What did you do today?"

"Oh...nothing much. Just hung out with some new friends."

"Good. That's really great...you adapt well...unlike this grump," She nodded at his father and winked. "Cherish the time with friends...take it from someone...who misses her friends all the time..."

"Jiang, let's go get your mother something to eat." His

father had put a hand on Jiang's shoulder.

"Oh hush…I'm fine…"

"It's no trouble, come on." Jiang's father led him back in the hallway, and after shutting the door, spoke to Jiang softly.

"It's cancer, Jiang. It's a bad one, but the doctors say they have a chance to cut it out with surgery."

"But?" Jiang knew his father well enough to sense where a conversation was heading.

"But…it's expensive. Something this serious is only partially covered by the state. We have some savings, but I need your help. After this, we might not have much left."

"How can…"

"We need to find you a job. Quickly."

In the cafeteria on the ground level of the hospital, Jiang and his father hunched over a newspaper, skimming through job announcements.

"Dishwasher…1600 a month…no, no. Hotel lobby…1750…clerk…reception…stock boy…let's see, Accountant, 4000!"

"Dad, I don't even have a degree."

"Right, right…well, here's something. Security, 2500,

overtime bonus, promotions available. Possible travel. That's not a bad start, Jiang. It's more than a minimum salary."

Jiang looked down at himself. He was one of the taller boys in his class, but he didn't have much weight on him. The chaos of the morning was really the only violence he had been close to. He never considered himself to be a strong person.

His father nudged him.

"Come on, I know you're not scared of anything. Just wear a big jacket. With those long legs, you'll tower over anybody."

Jiang took a sip of a coffee. "Alright, I'll go for an interview anyway."

The next day, Jiang found himself sitting in the lobby of a large, brick office building. The company that was hiring was a private security firm, which provided security for everything from private events to major industries. He tapped his foot on the floor, bouncing his knee a little. He looked at the round clock above the reception desk. The hands on the clock didn't seem to move at all.

His mind wandered away from the lobby. He still hadn't heard from any of his new friends, or Li Jie. He had no idea what was going on with the movement. He wanted to go see Steven's mother and hear some news, but he knew he needed to be where he was. His family needed him, and at that moment, Jiang needed to sit and wait.

A television in a neighboring room played the morning news. He didn't hear anything about the protest. That was expected. Steven had told him that the local media wouldn't cover an event like that, which is why his photographs would be helpful. With foreign media coverage, Steven said other governments could support their movement. Another protest was planned for the following weekend, but Jiang worried he would now miss it. The world felt far away. What point did the movement have when his mother was sick? How could he have time to be chased by the police when he needed to fight for his family?

"Jiang?"

A woman, probably no more than a few years older than Jiang, wearing a tight-fitting white skirt stood by the reception desk. She looked at Jiang and the two other men who sat on either side of him.

"Jiang?"

He stood up and raised his hand, feeling like a lost kid in the world of adults.

"Um, that's me."

"Come with me, please."

He followed her down a hallway, past closed office doors. White walls and metal doors, windows with the blinds pulled down. He could hear muffled voices behind the doors. She moved quickly ahead of him, her high heels tapping rapidly. He almost had to jog to keep up the pace. She didn't look back at him once. The ponytail on her head bounced almost as fast as her feet moved, and he tried hard not to let his eyes drift down to her swaying hips.

Suddenly she stopped at a door. He almost collided with her when she stopped. She knocked three times on the door, and it swung open. A man in a dark blue suit showed them in. She introduced Jiang, then without even a slight glance at him, left the room, shutting the door behind her.

The man motioned to a chair for Jiang to settle into. There was another man behind a large, oak desk. He was looking through several papers. The first man reached for Jiang's resume, then slid it across the desk. The other man grabbed the paper without looking up.

"Hmm, ok, good. Yes, ok. Ok," the hidden face said. Jiang cleared his throat and then wished he hadn't. Both men looked up at him.

"He has a decent build. Looks like a smart kid."

"Yeah, he could do, right?"

"I think so."

"Jiang…"

Jiang looked at the man behind the desk. "Um, yes sir?"

"Sir! That's good. Alright. From what I see, you haven't finished school yet?"

"No, sir. It's just that my mother, she's in the hospital, and-"

"Fine, fine. Alright, Jiang. We have a really important position that needs to be filled immediately. But you'll have to travel a bit."

"Um, well-"

"But you'll receive a big signing bonus. Send some money to your mom, and start you off right, how does that sound?"

"I mean…where-"

"You look like an adventurous kid. I see a spark in your eye. You're not from here originally, right?"

"No, I'm from a village in-"

"I knew it." The man standing leaned toward Jiang. "A country boy. That's perfect. You'll love this then. Think, mountains, a beautiful little village nearby. Easy, safe work. High salary."

"Yep, he's the one." The man behind the desk flipped through the pile of papers.

"Indeed. I like him. Doesn't talk much, which they'll like."

"Yep."

"Well, I could-" Jiang began.

"Yes, well, take a look at this contract, and see what you think." They handed a paper to Jiang. The salary was written at the top in bold. **Minimum 3500 Yuan, signing bonus of 5000!**

Jiang started to read the rest of the paper. 'Role: Temporary Security Detail for Energy Consultancy, Inc. Rural, mountain location. Standard hours of watch and patrol…'

"So, how's it look, Jiang?"

"It seems, um…interesting."

"Interesting! I like this kid. It's an adventure of a lifetime. Say, tell us, have you ever traveled abroad?"

☼☼☼

From a chair next to his mother's hospital bed, Jiang broke the news to his parents. He had found a high-paying job. It had happened incredibly fast, and he wondered why he had even bothered to go to school at all. Now, he could give his parents the signing bonus and send money home each month.

He would be a security guard, but he assured his mother that it was a safe place, although he was pretty sure he couldn't even find the place on a map. The only catch, he told her, was that he would need to travel far away. In fact, he'd be somewhere in the Himalayas.

"Where?" His mother looked over at him. A bouquet of flowers behind her distracted Jiang from her eyes. A slight breeze from the open door made the pink and purple peonies dance on the bedside table. He was content to shift his gaze from his mother to the flowers. Every time they locked eyes, he couldn't help but fixate on the wrinkles next to her eyes and above her cheeks.

"Himalayas, mom. It's a mountain range in the south. I read about them in school. It's where Zhumulangma Feng is, you know, the tallest mountain in the world. Our tallest mountain. The pictures look beautiful."

A rush of cold air drifted past Jiang and over the hospital bed. His mother shifted her legs underneath the blanket and smiled at him. As the peonies shuttered against the draft of air, Jiang felt the hair on his arms stand against the inside of his shirt. *The Himalayas,* he thought. *Why not?*

XVI

The fire underneath the aluminum pot was the only light in Suman's kitchen. The orange and blue flame gave him just enough light to see the wood counter next to the stove. He crushed moringa leaves and mint with his thumb and fingers, letting the pieces fall into his clay cup. Upstairs he could hear Maya snoring softly.

Sleeping was never so much of a task as it was a natural response to the night. With the night, usually came a serene energy that ran through Suman's body, as it did with most people whom he knew. Every farmer knows the sun is a fundamental requirement for plants, but when the sun disappears from the sky, true growth begins. Once tired-looking leaves stretch out wide and stems and trunks thrust upwards in the cooler night air. Standing in his kitchen, eyes fixated on the gently pulsating stove flame, Suman wondered if his recent insomnia was stunting his growth.

After pouring the steaming water into his cup, Suman found his way out to the street. There were still a few hours until the sun would hint at its return and cast its glow on the thatched roofs around him; roofs that lost all individuality in the night's muted tones of dark blue shapes.

The air was cool and still. It was the type of moment when a person could feel that they were the only living creature awake in the world. As his family slept in the rooms behind him, so did most villagers, animals, and insects in his valley.

He began walking through the sleeping village, hearing nothing but a few birds still reminiscing about the day before. Or maybe it was just gossip. He always wondered what birds spoke about at night. He counted seven distinct chirping sounds. Pressing his lips together, he tried to whistle back at them. His mocking whistle cut through the night like a foreign tongue, something alien that didn't belong. The birds stopped their chatter. Suman paused in his stride. Then the birds began again, seemingly ignoring this imposter in the night.

He ventured uphill, making quiet tap-tap sounds as his sandals snapped against his heels. He hummed a quiet tune: an old folk melody that he remembered from some herders. It was soft, romantic, longing. He felt energy in his stride.

Up ahead, he noticed something in the middle of the road. It looked like an animal curled up against the still-warm rocks that freckled the dirt track. It was difficult to determine which type of animal it was. He didn't move and assumed it was asleep. Still, he approached it slowly, fanning towards the outside of the road, giving it space.

As he came closer, he realized it was not an animal at

all, but a person curled up in an oblong ball. On the ground, just out of reach of the person, was a bottle of something. He quickly realized that it was Ukali. He began to hear a soft snore coming from the cluster of limbs and clothes beneath him. Thinking of the other villagers in the morning, he decided to rouse Ukali gently awake. He tapped on his old friend's shoulder. When nothing happened, he smoothly rocked him forward and back, until he heard a grunt.

"What…what…who's that?" Ukali murmured.

"Ukali, it's Suman. You are sleeping in the road. It's dangerous. Let me bring you home."

"Ah…uh…Suman. I am comfortable. Leave me."

Suman tapped his shoulder again. "Come on, my friend, let's go."

Ukali slowly regained a bit of consciousness and began to stir. Suman put an arm under Ukali's and pulled upward.

"Ok, ok, come on, come on," Ukali said.

Suman lifted Ukali to his feet, then swung one of the half-sleeping man's arms over his own shoulder, spreading a leg outward to take the weight.

"This way, Ukali."

They turned and began the descent to Ukali's house. Ukali stumbled occasionally, making each step forward appear to be a great undertaking.

The birds increased their chatter, watching the two men shuffle below the trees. Suman and Ukali passed Suman's home, and Ukali shifted his weight towards it, catching Suman off balance. Suman caught his step in time and brought their momentum downhill again.

"Let's…beer at yer place, c'mon." Ukali's words were broken and mumbled.

"Another time, Ukali. We're almost home."

Walking up the steps to Ukali's house, Ukali suddenly started to sniffle. Suman could barely hear it over the river sounds below them. Then Ukali broke down. He snorted inwards, gasping slightly, through a sudden outpouring of tears and sobs.

"I…Suman…so sorry. We been friends…long ago. What happened…What happened to me. I don't know….I don't know," Ukali said between each sob, coughing throughout.

"Don't worry, Ukali. Don't worry."

"No!"

Ukali twisted out of Suman's arm, stumbling backward. Suman reached out, preparing for Ukali to fall. But Ukali stumbled into a stance. He hunched in a half bow, his knees shaking. His tears and mucus flowed freely down his face. It was twisted and sad in the light of the moon.

"I'm sorry. For everything. I am...lonely. So...lonely. This..." Ukali pointed to his house. "This is my mother's. Not mine. I should be in the cafe."

Suman furrowed his eyebrows and turned his head behind him. *What cafe?*

"I should be in the cafe. Making chai for beautiful women. My friends...gone. Everything's...gone. I'm-"

Ukali bent forward and began to dry heave. Suman stepped back, as Ukali unloaded a night's worth of alcohol on the grass between them. He heaved twice more then looked up.

"Damn it. Damn...I'm sorry, Suman. My friend. I'm sorry."

Ukali stumbled and turned to face his door. Suman reached out his arms to Ukali's back but paused.

Ukali turned the knob of the door and pushed it inwards.

"G'night Suman." The door slammed behind him.

"Goodnight Ukali. Don't worry. It will all be ok."

XVII

Jiang had never been on a train before, although he had learned quite a lot about the country's railways in one of his classes. He understood that the train was traveling on a track that was part of over 150,000 kilometers of railway lines within China. That particular train was part of the largest network of high-speed rails in the world, totaling over 40,000 kilometers. He learned more recently that the railway construction was full of corruption, and ex-officials pocketed a couple billion dollars worth of funds meant to go to the development of the railways. The corruption reminded him of his village turned ghost city, but at least this development appeared to be functioning fine enough.

When he found his bunk in the compartment, he saw it was shared with three older men and someone was using his bunk as luggage storage, the 20-hour journey suddenly felt much longer.

When the man on the bunk below his noticed Jiang, he grunted recognition of this lone, student traveler, and slowly moved his suitcase and bags from the top bunk. Jiang thanked him as the man returned to a laying position, his cell phone sounding the morning news for the whole compartment.

The other two men had their top bunk folded upwards, and they sat on the bottom bunk, an arm's length apart, content to pass the first hours sitting, rather than laying down.

Jiang decided that he could wait to lay down, and after dropping his two suitcases on his bunk, set off to explore the train. When he walked down the corridor between the compartments and windows, the train was much cleaner than he had expected.

The security firm had hired him out to a prominent hydro power company, which had paid for Jiang to have second-class accommodations for the train journey, and he wondered what the third-class looked like. At the end of his train car, he found himself at a glass door without any handles. He pushed at the door, and nothing happened. He stomped his feet a few times, thinking that it might be automatic, like those in a shopping mall or supermarket. But this didn't work either.

Confused, he tried to remember how he got on board. Of course, he realized that the train car door was open when he entered, so no handle needed pulling. Then a young girl, probably five or six years old came skipping up behind him. She stopped and tilted her head to the side. She was contentedly chewing gum and a cell phone, wearing a pink case, dangled from a bright yellow string around her neck.

Jiang pushed on the door to demonstrate that the door

must be broken, and looked at the girl, shrugging.

She stepped to his left, balanced on her toes, and pressed a button, which was illuminated with a red light. As soon as she pressed it, it changed green, and a hissing of compressed air came from inside the door. The two glass panels parted and the door was open.

From between the two cars, Jiang could hear the steady mumbling of metal wheels on tracks and a light wind pushed the little girl's hair over her face. She stepped through the void, unaffected by this strange technology, and waited for the next door to open for her.

And I am the high school student, Jiang thought. He followed the fading whistle of the girl down the next corridor until he found the next door, and repeated what she had shown him. The next button turned green without much pressure from his finger.

After several cars, he came to a glass door with a picture of a coffee cup on it. He had found the food car, and from the brochure, he knew the economy class was through the following doors.

The food car was bustling. Each table was overflowing with men in suits, drinking coffee from plastic cups, which seemed to be slowly melting and changed shapes as they held them by the rim. Groups of families ate noodles from Styrofoam cups, releasing steam that was evidently fogging up the car's windows. At the counter, a lone woman, perhaps fifty years old, worked in a busy but fluid motion, filling noodle cups with boiling water and plastic cups with tea and coffee. Several men stood smoking by the windows, next to a large, red text, demanding that smoking was forbidden on the train.

Jiang thought about ordering a coffee, but decided after several hesitant steps, that there was nothing he needed extra energy for on this journey. He walked through the food car, its noise amplifying the longer he lingered, and found his way to the next door. A large text read, "3rd Class, Economy Comfort." Below, someone had scratched the words, "Lies" on the glass. Below it, written in ink, was "You're a liar."

I think you're both right, Jiang thought, inwardly pleased at his mediation. The doors hissed open and the noise of the cafe dissipated as the new sounds from economy class filtered through the second glass door. Jiang noticed the temperature change as well. He felt sweat begin forming on the back of his neck and under his arms.

The "Economy Comfort" car was busy. The passengers were seated on bus-styled benches, and bags were sat upon, stuffed under seats, above heads, or in the aisle. He watched one man, far on the other side of the car, slowly and clumsily shuffle his way through the aisle, trying his best, probably, not to step on luggage.

Throughout the car, people spoke in full volume on their phones, sometimes trying to speak over the conversations next to them. A lady in a blue dress, yelled into her phone's receiving end, as she stuffed a finger in her opposite ear. Everywhere were children playing games on their phones or mothers trying to force rice cakes in the mouths of their youngest. Somewhere a dog barked, then yelped as it was reprimanded.

It appeared that Jiang's train exploration had reached its terminus, and he started to shift his feet around to exit the car. Suddenly drops of liquid hit the side of his face. He felt the warm moisture on his cheek and a salty smell crawled up his nostrils. To his left, an older woman was fanning herself with a red rag. In between fanning, she used to rag to wipe sweat from her neck, then commenced the wet fanning.

She met his eyes, before rolling hers up and away from him, not interrupting the process of cooling the air around her. He wiped his face with the bottom of his t-shirt, then made a large step towards the door, before more flying sweat could find him.

Jiang found his bunkmate snoring loudly when he returned to the compartment. The other two men seemed unaffected by the noise and busied themselves in a calm, political discussion, something that only people in agreement seemed able to conduct. Jiang swung himself up onto the top bunk and opened the front pocket of his suitcase. He pulled out a phrasebook on the Southern language. He scanned the introduction quickly, already vaguely aware of the differences in customs and history through his secondary school classes.

Without wanting to draw attention to himself, he practiced the new words in his head and closed his eyes to repeat the translations. He glanced at his watch, a knock-off luxury brand his father had given him that morning. 19 hours to go. Plenty of time to study. Although he was only to be a security guard, his placement was going to be amid a large-scale dam-building project. It wasn't something he would have studied through in his next years of school, but it was interesting nonetheless. Among his other belongings, he brought two books on dam construction and hydropower, as well as a book about two local mountain climbers who had summited several of the tallest peaks in the region.

The day passed with Jiang reading his books, sleeping, and sometimes waking to find that he had somehow rolled into an open book. The uncomfortable hard binding of a book brought him quickly back into the waking world.

Occasionally, he would walk up and down the corridors of the train cars, but never going farther than the sleeping cars, and never venturing into the first-class compartments, which had an attendant standing guard.

Sometimes he watched the passing countryside through a corridor window, amazed at the vast emptiness between each town. His country was enormous, he thought, and to think he had never journeyed more than a few hours by bus from where he was born.

Adventure, he thought. Maybe he was the type of person who was destined to see the world, cross vast landscapes, and find meaning within the changing landscapes. The world of schools, the protests, and even his school crush seemed to fade far into the past. He wondered about Li Jie, worried for his mother, but he couldn't help but feel excited for the journey ahead.

His mind wandered to the other passengers. *Who were they? Why were they on such a long journey?*

He couldn't help but feel pity for the youngest ones, so enthralled by the images on their phones, finding more entertainment in them than this modern feat of engineering that careened them across the country at such high velocity. He imagined his father, motionless in front of his television at night, escaping from the cruel reality that thrust him into their new home. Were the other passengers, who were glued to their phones, also escaping from the world around them?

His busy mind soon brought repeated yawning motions to his jawbone. His watch revealed that it was already 9 o'clock. In five hours, he would arrive at his stop. From there someone would meet him and bring him deeper into the mountains to some strange new world. He stole another glance out the window. Sharp mountain peaks were hazy in the distance, south of the train. He found his way back to his bed, and after climbing in, fell into a deep sleep.

XVIII

Somewhere far away, deep in the recesses of his muted consciousness, Jiang was climbing a skyscraper's antenna. The view over the city was fantastic. From the top of the building, he could see everything. A giant mall, stretched over the horizon, a water park, overflowing with water, splashing onto car windshields below, and in the distance, his swimming hole, its junipers blowing gracefully in the afternoon wind. He said to someone next to him, "Isn't it incredible?" When met with no response, he looked to his side. No one was there. Looking to the other side, he realized he was alone on the antenna. The wind picked up around him, and he struggled to hold his grip. Far below him, dust blew through an empty city. Windows were shattered, and only blowing pieces of trash drifted across the empty lanes of a road. He lost his grip against an angry gust of wind and fell. A knocking sound repeated, sending shock waves up, through the air around him. The concrete ground of a deserted metropolis rose towards him, quickly. Then, everything went black.

He opened his eyes. The transition from his dream was fast and confusing. A man in a uniform was knocking on his train compartment's window. The man held up his watch, signaling the time. The train. The dam. *I'm here.*

Jiang scrambled to gather his belongings, stuffing his books into his suitcase. He looked through the opposite window as he opened the door. It was dark outside, and he couldn't see anything but a dimly-lit, concrete platform.

He shuffled to the door, which was resting open, silently. He stepped out onto the platform, and the sounds of his luggage landing echoed down the walkway. No other passengers exited the train.

Is this right? He wondered, looking around him. A hiss from under the train made him jump. The wheels of the train started rolling to life as the door behind him shut with a mechanical gasp.

When the train pulled away from the station, he saw, across the tracks, a few streetlights illuminating a road. Under one, was a jeep, the lights on, and he could hear the soft idling of the engine, the warm fumes of the exhaust billowing in the brisk, early morning air.

As he approached the jeep, the front door opened and a man in a brown uniform stepped out. He waved towards Jiang, yawning and covering his mouth with his other hand.

Jiang got close enough to recognize a symbol on the uniform. It was the same water drop and lightning bolt, the two-toned logo that was on the brochure tucked away in his suitcase's front pocket. The brochure of the power company.

"Jiang, welcome. Tired, eh? These damn trains, always getting here at unforgivable hours. Don't worry, there's coffee in the Jeep." The man reached out his hand and introduced himself as the assistant head of security, Huang.

Huang and Jiang pulled out of the train station down a dimly lit road. Jiang was impressed that Huang knew where he was going. Huang took several, unmarked turns easily, and handed Jiang a warm Thermos. Jiang started to pour coffee into the removable lid but Huang stopped him.

"Don't bother, just drink it straight from the bottle. It's about to be bumpy. We're not far from the border now. You have your passport and work documents we sent, correct?

"Er, uh, yes. Yes, I do. Are we crossing a border?" Jiang finally realized why they had requested he bring his passport. He had figured they'd be close to the border, but not actually cross it.

The jeep neared a grouping of lights in the distance. Two concrete, simple houses on either side of a red and white, retractable gate. When they came to a stop before the gate, a soldier appeared from one house, a machine gun slung over his shoulder. For almost three in the morning showing on a clock behind him, the soldier looked very attentive.

"Morning. Papers, please."

Huang collected Jiang's papers and passport, combining them with his own stack, and handed over the pile to the soldier. The soldier walked, stiffly upright back into the house and closed the door.

"So, first time down here?" Huang broke the silence in the jeep.

"Yes, sir. But I've been studying a lot about the area…"

"Never mind that. But good, you're familiar. The locals are nice, anyway. Serve pretty good food, and the accommodation at the dam isn't half bad. We even installed hot showers last month. Beauty of making your own electricity I suppose. But you'll learn all you need to know soon enough. I think you'll be helping out my team for the duration."

"I don't have much experience, honestly…"

"Ah, alright, you'll do fine. But wait, you mean you haven't built a dam like this before, have you?"

Jiang looked at the man's serious face. Huang didn't wait for him to answer but burst out laughing. "I'm just messing with you. It's easy work, really, just have to make sure only authorized people are walking around. But never mind, you'll enjoy yourself plenty. I got to say, the mountains here have been growing on me lately. First it was just all snow and hills to walk up, but lately there's something about the size of them. Makes you think…"

The soldier returned with their papers before Huang could continue his musing, and handed them through the window, motioning them forward without a word. Huang waved and nodded his balding head to the soldier, who watched the jeep as it passed through the open gate. Jiang looked in his sideview mirror, to see the soldier still standing in the middle of the road, as the gate slowly lowered down before him.

They quickly came to another border post. This time a different flag flew above the gate. It was red and in the shape of two triangles. Each triangle had a symbol of a sun, one that rose out from a crescent moon. The process was repeated with a soldier who had slightly darker skin than the one before, but besides that, had very similar facial features. Afterward, the soldier handed them their paperwork and smiled.

"Welcome to Nepal."

The road became dirt almost immediately after the border post and began to snake up and over a front range of mountains, and soon shadowed giants of peaks blocked their view of the night sky.

There wasn't a single light in the distance. Jiang mistook this as the landscape being completely void of any human life. But deep in the looming embrace of the mountain ridges, families slept, yaks stirred in dreams of thick green grass, and villages breathed in the night air in unison.

They were climbing the dirt track higher. Somewhere, the sun was hiding, ready to emerge over a ridge line to the east. Yet, even as dawn neared, the air was becoming colder. Jiang's head drifted off somewhere in a semi-present, hazy space. He felt that he was awake, the beat of his heart increasing from the coffee, but his brain acted on impulses that hinted at a dream state. He assumed he was awake for the entirety of the drive, but he couldn't be sure. Hours passed without many more words from the man next to him. Sometimes, Jiang jolted into wakefulness, suddenly aware of how far away from his home he was. He began to worry that Huang might have fallen asleep too. But when he turned to look, he saw the man's same, relaxed, wide-eyed focus on the road ahead.

Hours passed, maybe four, probably more. Once, Huang pulled over to refill the jeep with faded red jugs of diesel, which were strapped to the back of the vehicle, next to a spare tire that looked like a desperate substitute for real tires. Huang pulled out another Thermos from the floor behind the driver's seat, along with a large, circular tin of warm rice buns. They ate the breakfast in silence. It seemed that Huang conserved all this energy for the drive, as he rarely spoke a word. Jiang declined the second Thermos, figuring that the contents should be reserved for the person in the most control of the fast-moving vehicle.

Outside, houses began to appear. They had descended a mountain pass for the last hour or so, and the vegetation became lush and vibrant, almost tropical. Thick, healthy plants burst out of the earth along the road, and large trees extended their thick arms over the undergrowth. Then a sharp turn around a corner and thatched roofs came into view. They dotted the steep slopes of the jungle-like hills along the road. A river joined the road just before a new ascent on the road.

The houses clustered near the river banks, and fresh soil, with vein-like rows, emerged in organized rectangular shapes next to each home. Thatched roofs on the hills above them became more frequent and their partially obscured, mud-colored walls contrasted the green landscape. Impossibly steep terraces of gardens fanned away from the houses, towards rocky outcropping. A cluster of homes formed a village and the road passed through the center. Over the next ridge, the sun finally found them.

When passing through the first village, Huang decreased the momentum of the Jeep slightly, and Jiang could see people standing in doorways watching them pass. A few children chased the vehicle. They wore sweaters, some new, some old and tattered, and each with a distinguishable different tone of dyed color. Dogs barked from chains next to houses, frantic in their exclusion from the chase the children led.

The village disappeared as quickly as it appeared, and the Jeep climbed higher, then after crossing a newly constructed bridge, it began traversing the edge of a new valley on the right bank of the fast-moving river. A small, unsafe-looking pedestrian bridge, dwarfed by its modern successor, swung slightly above the current.

They climbed higher. The four-wheeled traction of the vehicle was at home on the rocky, steep incline. Only on sharp turns, could Jiang feel an inner wheel slip and then regain traction on the difficult terrain. The flora around them changed as well. The lush green turned lighter and the plants along the road shrank. Each turn, showed Jiang that there was no end to the heights these mountains could reach. Each time he imagined that he must be in the highest valley on Earth, his naivety taunted him. Until, finally, the ascent relaxed, and the road balanced into a relaxed, winding, slightly upward motion. Stretches of pasture increased the distance from the river to the road. A herd of buffalo grazed near the water, some soaking in muddy holes in the pasture. They seemed bigger than the water buffalo he grew up with. One of these would have been impossible to skirt around on his rice-berm bicycle tracks. He saw a herder, snoozing under the shade of a large rock, just a stone's throw away from the group of buffalo.

A new village came into view. It was smaller than the one before, at least in the sense that there were fewer houses. The houses were farther apart, some at the end of long dirt and stone paths leading up the hills surrounding it. In the distance children played on a single bamboo swing, several waiting for their turn behind the current swinger. A man with crossed arms watched the jeep roll by his house. His presence felt serious to Jiang, but there seemed to be a resting smile on his face, but Jiang couldn't be sure it was directed at him.

Once through the village, Jiang saw the dam, towering over the river below. A line of lighter-colored rocks, laying on top of each other dotted each side of the water. He spotted the high water mark where the grass met the rocks. The concrete face seemed out of place after the beautiful, yet arduous drive from the border. It, and the bridge below, were the only signs of industrial construction since the train station.

"Yeah, pretty impressive, isn't it? That's it, we're home."

Huang let out a small chuckle, his fatigue showing slightly with a fading sigh that tailed the end of the laughter.

They pulled up to a chain link gate and Huang honked the horn twice. A man, also dressed in a brown uniform, stepped out of a tin guard house, waved at the Jeep, and pushed the gate open. The wheels of the gate bounced along a strip of metal on the ground, kicking a few pebbles to the side.

Huang rolled down the window as they passed the guard.

"Back so soon, Huang? I thought you would've fled home by now."

"What?" Huang said. "And leave you here on your own? You wouldn't notice an intruder if you were sitting on him."

Huang left Jiang in front of several trailers, which were painted white and topped with tin roof panels.

Jiang walked up a wooden ramp to a door that read 'office,' his suitcase loudly announcing his arrival as it rolled behind him.

He opened the door of the office to a row of four desks, each with a man or woman sitting behind it. One man was talking on a landline, and another had his feet on his desk, talking to the women. They all stopped talking when he walked in. Jiang stood in the silence for a long few seconds. The phone clicking shut was louder than it should have been.

"Who are you?" The man with the phone asked.

"Jiang, sir, from the security firm. Uh, Huang dropped me off."

"Yes, yes, of course, I forgot that's today. Well, hello, Jiang." The other three people continued their conversation, something about voltage. The man walked out from behind the desk and Jiang gave him a bow. He reached for Jiang's hand, who shook it with the strongest grip he could muster.

"I trust the drive was alright?" Jiang nodded. "I'm the head of operations here and as you can see, we're quite busy." This got a small chuckle from the group behind him. "So, Jiang, I'll show you to your room and give you a quick tour. Then you can rest until your shift tonight."

"What will I be doing, sir? I actually read up on dam construction on the train, and learned quite a bit."

The man laughed a little through his nose. "We give the rookies the night watch shifts here. Standard procedure, and since the dam's completion, we lost some staff to other projects. So, we need help at night. It's all very simple, but I promise, there will be plenty to learn later. First thing, tour, sleep if you can, then ten hours on watch. Alerting the staff to any disruptions in the turbines, intrusions, and so on."

"Intrusions, sir? From people?"

"Yes, the villagers you passed have been welcoming enough, but we know from past projects that there could be someone disagreeing with these types of projects."

"Yet, they still love their televisions and new electrical sockets," one of the women commented.

"But they're simple farmers and don't really grasp the idea of how many people this electricity reaches. Tens of millions of homes powered by one river. They've never even seen one hundred homes," the man next to her added.

"If that," the woman replied.

The Head of Operations led Jiang outside, onto a graveled cut-out on the hillside. Jiang had to strain his neck upwards to see the tops of the mountains above him. Sheets of rough-looking ice, white and blue clung to rocky edges, threatening to fall onto everyone below. Brown rocks dotted snowy saddles in between jagged peaks, partially obscured by clouds. To Jiang, the clouds looked like wisps of white hair on an enormous head.

Jiang and the man continued to another set of trailers. One marked, 'female' and the other 'male,' each one had an adjoining trailer for showers and toilets. He showed Jiang his bed, and Jiang slid his suitcases underneath. Back outside, they walked over to a door embedded in a concrete pillar. Inside was an elevator to the pump house, which contained the generator. The pump house wasn't visible from the trailer up above, but Jiang noticed the thick cables rising from over the edge of the dam to a separate power station near the trailers.

After a slow descent, they arrived inside the powerhouse. His new boss led Jiang along an indoor catwalk above the generator, and inside Jiang could hear the deafening hum of the turbines, spinning, working water current through its huge blades, converting the rotations into electricity. They could barely hear anything over the noise of the generators, so they pushed open another door and stepped onto the deck of the pump house. A series of catwalks created a maze of metal around the pump house, where Jiang saw several people in yellow helmets moving around, holding clipboards in their hands. Over the edge of the catwalks, the concrete base of the pump house towered high above the river and a stream of out-flowing water splashed into it.

"There you go, Jiang. A basic tour. We can save a longer tour for when you're better rested, but let's take the elevator back up and let you sleep off your travels. We'll need you alert for your shift tonight. And you probably know by now, Huang can make a strong cup of coffee if you need one."

"Thank you," Jiang replied. "What's your name, sir?"

"My name? Well, everyone around here calls me Captain. Sort of an assumed role on our stationary, concrete vessel here. So, let's keep it at that for now."

"Alright, Captain. Thank you for the tour." Jiang followed Captain back to the elevator and found his bunk in the Menes dormitory.

The first night on watch was colder than Jiang anticipated. He sat on a swivel chair, high above the pump house, in a concrete tower with large windows. To his left, he had an intercom system, a red warning button, and several switches to turn on flood and searchlights. In front of him, needles on an instrument panel sat happily at the center of their meters. To his right was a small television set, VCR, and a stack of old movies he had never heard of. He spun his chair around slowly, using his feet to push against the plastic legs of the chair for momentum. Behind him, the slow bubbling and dripping of a coffee machine gave off puffs of steam and an aroma of coffee drifted into the air.

He immediately felt bored. He wished that he had brought his books into the tower with him, but he had decided that he didn't want to look unprofessional on the first night. He noticed a stack of books in the corner of the room and realized it wasn't uncommon to read on duty. The books were romance novels, undoubtedly corny and full of emotions that he didn't want to think about in his little room deep in the mountains.

He paced around the room, and then feeling a bit stir-crazy, climbed down a ladder to take in some fresh air. The night was piercing cold and his new, brown uniform hardly protected his skinny figure. He walked circles around the tower to stay warm but eventually gave up and returned to his chair.

Minutes passed slower than he ever considered possible, and he passed the time humming a few songs. His eyes grew heavy and he began to yawn. He checked his watch. It was only 11 pm. He still had nine hours to go until he was relieved.

He decided to put a movie in the VCR. It was a story about a soldier lost from his company. The soldier stumbled on a village in a lush mountain setting, falling in love with a local woman, of course. When the company came to arrest the mayor of the village, the hero of the story was conflicted. Jiang found himself able to predict every scene before it happened. The movie wasn't in color, it was made too long ago, and the dialogue bored Jiang more than his humming. He stretched during the closing credits and filled a cup to the brim with hot coffee. Each sip brought a little more alertness back to his head, and he tried to see out of the windows. The lights from the room made it difficult to see, but when he put his face to the glass, he could make out a few stars, almost straight up, looking much closer to the peaks of the mountains than anywhere else.

Jiang's shift finished finally, not long after sunrise, and he was relieved by a sleepy man carrying a notebook and several books.

Jiang slept through most of that day and woke just in time to eat dinner with some of the staff. He didn't talk much, but they asked him the usual questions about his home, his studies, and his family. One man was surprised to learn Jiang was originally from a small village. So was that man, who urged Jiang to visit the village downriver when he had a chance. The man whispered that the food there was much better.

A week passed with Jiang sitting guard all night in his

lone watch tower, above the rumbling turbine below him. Nights were a little easier once he brought his books with him. After he finished them, he began to write. First a journal, then some sort of autobiography. He wrote about his childhood, the move to the city, and analyzed his life experiences.

The time in the tower gave him a lot of time to reflect, to wonder, to draw a few conclusions from his short time in the world.

The dam made him think deeply about humankind's engineering feats and what he had seen growing up. The life in his childhood home clashed roughly with existence in a city of millions. Steven's group had mostly talked about politics, but environmental issues had also come up. They spoke about the misuse of resources fueling an urban world while farming villages like his own disappeared. He wondered what that group would think of his new work. Of course, it was money he was after, it wasn't some personal ambition that led him there. He wondered if the dam was actual progress for the world, or would it also destroy villages like his own? What was real progress anyway?

Could the world really be progressing into something better if it was simultaneously destroying the old world? He reasoned that his family was certainly happier in their former home. His father was content on his land, even if he was poor by modern definitions. Being thrust into a crowded city seemed to be negatively affecting his mind and perhaps it even damaged his mother's health. Personally, he had adapted to the new life. He was young and malleable. His new schools had taught him quite a bit about the modernization of the world, and it was always shown in a very positive light. He knew that a hydroelectric dam would give off less pollution than an old coal power plant for example. It was the better option to provide power to modern civilization. But he wondered, would the better option be less power consumption to begin with? Furthermore, what was the end result of the progress his teachers spoke about? What were they all striving for the world to transform into?

He felt tired and lonely with his thoughts. He drank more coffee and tried to change the narrative in his mind. He was working, saving money, and after his mother recovered, perhaps someday he'd use the money to live somewhere deeper in the countryside. This was the current path he was on. He didn't choose it necessarily, but somehow it came to him. Why swim against the flow of life?

Jiang laughed at himself in the tower. He ruminated that maybe he should study philosophy. He then wondered if someone heard him laugh, alone in the room, they would probably think he was going insane. He moved to put another movie in the VCR. He let another old movie, with a simple, predictable story push his thoughts away. He sipped his coffee and turned off his busy mind.

XIX

Suman's plants were growing tall, and it looked like it would be a decent harvest. Nothing compared to the previous year, but enough.

Late one night, Suman heard footsteps outside. He walked to the window and saw Tauko with a glowing cigarette in his hand. He was pacing in front of Suman's house. Once outside, Suman approached his neighbor.

"I'm sorry Suman, I didn't want to wake you," Tauko began. "I just don't know where else to go."

"What's wrong Tauko?"

"I haven't had any luck with my field and my wife agrees with me. We think the dam has dried up our soil. My son wants a television and he doesn't listen when I tell him that the dam only brings us problems and television won't fill our stomachs." Tauko's voice rose from a whisper to an exasperated high pitch by the end of his sentence. The underlying anger was obvious.

"Be calm my friend, I'll help you. I'm not sure the dam

is to blame. But we will combine our efforts and your family will eat well this year. I've already started..."

"You're kind Suman, but I just came to tell you that I'm going to the dam to stop all of this." Tauko's voice was shaky.

"Relax Tauko, I'll go with you tomorrow. The middle of the night is no time to walk there. Please, wait for the morning, and we'll go together." Tauko took a long drag from his cigarette and chewed over his friend's words. After a long silence, he spoke again.

"Alright, I will wait. I'll see you tomorrow." Before Suman could say anything else, Tauko turned and headed away into the darkness of the night and disappeared down the road.

Suman stood outside his house for several minutes, replaying Tauko's speech in his head. He felt sorry for his neighbor. *Tauko was always a proud man, but eventually, he'll have to accept my help.* He turned to walk inside but stopped when he heard a loud crashing sound from down in the village. Thinking of Tauko, he ran in the direction of the noise. The smallest sliver of a moon made the road barely visible. When he came into town, he could see that several lights in houses were still on. *It could be anything.* He thought, hoping that the noise was unrelated to Tauko. Passing two houses, he saw that most of the lights were from television sets. An eerie hum could be heard from the electric cables outside the houses. He noticed that Ukali's house still had its lights on as well. Then he heard a door slam in the house. He ventured cautiously up to the house, a bit worried that Ukali might be in a drunk fit.

When he reached the front of the house, he found the front window smashed, and small pieces of glass littered the ground. He paused for a minute then decided to knock on the door. It was immediately flung open and slammed against the inner wall. Ukali was standing in the doorway with a large stick in his hands. His face slackened when his eyes met Suman's.

"That crazy Tauko broke my window with a rock," he began. "He said he was going to destroy the dam, then come back to finish me off if I was still here." Suman started to open his mouth, but Ukali stopped him. "I'm not going anywhere until I sell this house, Suman, I won't be intimidated."

"I understand, Ukali, stay here. I'm going to find Tauko. You'll be safe." Ukali shut the door, and Suman heard a bottle open inside. He pivoted around and wondered if Tauko already started for the dam. He jogged up the road and aimed first for Tauko's home. He discovered that the lights were still on, and approached to knock. To his surprise, Tauko opened the door almost instantly.

"Suman, how are you?" Tauko smiled, stepping outside, bringing the door softly shut behind him.

"Are you crazy?" Suman asked, as Tauko lit a cigarette.

"What do you mean?"

"You can't threaten Ukali like that. You'll only make things worse."

"Listen, Suman," Tauko put his hand on Suman's shoulder. Suman could smell whiskey on his friend's breath. "I only told Ukali that he should leave the town. If I take down the dam, then probably his business friends would be very angry with him. I suggested he leave town for a while.

"Tauko," Suman looked him in the eyes. "I heard the window break. He said you threw a rock at him and threatened to hurt him."

"That drunk fool!" Tauko shouted abruptly. Both of their eyes widened. Tauko appeared to notice how loudly he had reacted, and brought his head lower and whispered, "That drunkard threw a bottle at me when I left. He broke his own window. He said not to threaten him, but I was calm, Suman. Really, don't worry."

Suman looked over his shoulder to the street, before returning to face Tauko. He sighed. There was no point in believing either story, he decided. No matter who was lying, it didn't matter. The anger from both of them was poison in their minds. He didn't want Tauko to become more upset than he was already. He put his own hand on Tauko's arm.

"Take it easy, Tauko. I believe you. This anger at the dam. At Ukali. It isn't good for you. You are only hurting yourself. We will help you with food this year, don't worry about that, but please take it easy on yourself."

"Thank you for your concern, Suman. You're a good friend." Tauko breathed in the smoke from his cigarette deeply and blew it above their heads. "I'm ok, I've calmed down since we spoke. I'm going to wait on the dam situation. I need to think more about what I can do anyway."

Tauko kept his eyes focused forward, willing his friend to believe him. He spoke again, "I'll wait for Ukali to leave at least."

"What if he doesn't?"

"That will be his choice. But I think he needs to return to the city anyway. It's all he speaks about."

Suman bowed his head and sighed once more. Looking up at Tauko, he feigned a smile. "Everything will be fine, Tauko. I'm going home, I've had enough excitement for tonight."

"I'll see you, Suman," Tauko replied. "Thanks for checking on me."

XX

Jiang was just over a month into his new field of study: how to survive in a tiny watch tower alone. The shifts had started to pass more easily as each night faded into the next. The secret was to never, under any circumstances, look at a clock until the sun began to rise. He wrote in his journals, reread his books, started on the sappy romance novels, and watched almost every movie on the small television set. He paced himself with the coffee, finding it best to wait the longest he could for the first dose of caffeine. He slept less between shifts, and somehow that increased his alertness. He spent a couple hours each day, before dinner, walking around the pump house, asking questions to whoever was around. At first, they were too busy to talk, but eventually, they warmed up to the young, curious mind. He learned a great deal about this particular river's flow rates, season by season, since the first project scouts canvassed the area.

He watched the reservoir behind the bulk of the dam fill, the level slightly higher each day. He took note of trees at the surface of the water and watched as limb by limb, they were covered by the rising lake. He learned how the staff were measuring the depths of the reservoir as well, and how they released just enough water downriver to slow the growth of the reservoir and move the turbines. Eventually, they told him, they would have a steady rate of inflow that would adjust with timed mechanisms, once the water level reached its capacity.

One day a week, he had a day off. At first, Jiang only wanted to sleep. He laid in bed most of the day, emerging for meals only. Each week he would compose a letter to his parents. He would tell them about the mountains, the river, the trees submerging in the reservoir, the village downriver, although he still only had the one drive-by experience. He always left the watch tower out of the letters. He didn't want his mother to know her only son was slowly going insane in a little box every night. He instead put himself in the role of the people with clipboards, monitoring the turbines and water flow. He invented many tasks for this fictional self, how we would check for cracks in the dam by being lowered down the wall in a harness, which he never saw anyone do, how he inspected the blades of the turbine occasionally, and how the staff were fantastic mentors all enthusiastic with their work.

One day off, he decided that he was rested enough for a change of pace. He finished his letter to his parents during breakfast and asked if he could accompany some of the staff on their walk into the village for lunch. They shrugged. Why not?

At midday, he and four others walked through the front gates and headed down the dirt road towards the village. The scree pile below their terraced workplace gave way to patches of grass, and they started passing small farm plots, minimally bordered with small stone walls. They passed the first village house, mud walls seeming to be baking and hardening in the sun, the thatched roof showing loose strands above the doorway. A single, leather-coated chair, rested by the front door. Two apple trees were budding in the front garden, and a mess of old, shriveled apples littered the grass underneath them.

They passed a few more houses until signs of life appeared. A boy with an old school bag skipped up the road and smiled as he passed the group of workers. An elderly lady brushed a rammed earth landing step in front of her door. Jiang couldn't see any leaves or anything on the step, but the lady kept brushing anyway. A man, possibly her son, smoked a cigarette while smashing dried chilies in a rock mortar, sitting on a hand-carved wooden chair. Two dogs chased a group of kids from its yard, the latter group screamed past Jiang and jumped into the man's front garden, causing him to spill the smashed chilies. He shook the pestle after the children and they continued around his house, laughing.

Two men working on a rusted motorbike looked up from their work and smiled at Jiang. They both wore old, dirty jeans, and he could see the outlines of cell phones in their front pockets. Just over a rise in the road he could see the top of a bamboo swing and could hear faint laughs coming from its direction. A group of women stood outside a house, while one hung clothes on twine, securing each garment with two sticks bound with rubber bands. They returned Jiang's wave, but didn't break their conversation. One lady had a long, flowing dress that reached her ankles, and the others looked to be commenting on it.

"Here we are," one of Jiang's co-workers said, and the group turned at an intersection in the road. A tin-roofed awning, haphazardly connected to a house's mud walls with metal stakes and rope, stretched out over several sets of plastic tables. The tin was secured from the wind with large stones, one for every fourth or so rivet in the tin. The group occupied two tables, and Jiang pulled up a chair from a third table. On the top of the red, plastic table, was a logo for a local beer, and Jiang spotted crates of empty bottles in a leaning stack against the house. He watched the stack, thinking they might fall down any second, but somehow the infusion of bottlenecks and concaved plastic held.

Each table had a bowl of pickled chilies and a smaller bowl of salt in a corner. Without saying a word, one worker held up five, outstretched fingers, and a woman lingering in a doorway, under the awning, got the order. She disappeared into the house and Jiang heard propane turning on, an ignition of flame, and then a battering of metal on a wok. One of the staff looked at Jiang and said something. He only caught the movement out of his peripheral vision.

"Sorry?" Jiang asked him to repeat.

"I said, do you want a beer?" The man was now standing. Jiang had never had a beer before, but he didn't want to appear too young to this group of adults.

"Of course," he replied. "A cold one."

The others laughed. "That's a seasonal order, here, Jiang," explained one. "You might have to wait until winter for that."

"But don't they have electricity now?"

"No refrigerators. I've seen people drop baskets in the river to chill beer before."

Jiang joined in the fading laughter. He didn't mention it to the group, but his father used to do the same thing.

Suddenly the restaurant's proprietor, if she could be called that, emerged with two plates, steam escaping the metal dishes furiously, wafting into the air. She set two down, then returned with the remaining three, the third expertly balanced between the other two. She didn't flinch, but Jiang knew the metal must be scalding hot.

"That was fast," Jiang said. He had never even seen a soft-boiled egg delivered at this woman's speed.

"It's a mystery, kid. Only one stove burner in there also. I've checked," informed one staff member.

The man who went for beer came back with an arm-load, setting them all down on the table, then reached behind him to pass two to the other table. They all touched the bottles in a toast and took a sip. It wasn't as good as he imagined, but Jiang figured he could stomach it. He had nothing to compare it too but he wondered if it tasted like the ones his father drank in front of the television.

Everyone dug into the food with their hands, mixing soupy lentils with the rice and occasionally adding a potato or piece of onion to the combination. They cupped their four fingers into large human spoons to scoop up a serving, then used their thumbs to pass the food into their mouths. Jiang watched and tried to imitate the new method of eating. He spilled hot lentils on his chin on the first try. His stomach growled with impatience. Then, more slowly and carefully, he landed a decent-sized portion into his mouth. It was hot but delicious. He repeated the action. The food became better with every connection with his tongue's taste buds. He couldn't believe the combination of spice and flavor that floated through his mouth, it almost seemed like a shame to swallow such a masterpiece. He ate quickly until the man next to him put a hand on his elbow and chuckled.

"Easy, kid, we're not in a hurry, enjoy it."

"I am. It's incredible."

"What did we say?" A woman at the other table leaned towards Jiang's table. "Best part about working here."

Jiang decided to try the pickled chilies. He had plenty of spicy food at home, and figured his mom's cooking could prepare him for anything. But these, sunbaked chilies, softened and aged for months, gave his mother's fierce competition. First, his tongue was scorched, then his gums and teeth, and when he swallowed the heat spread down his throat, and he felt like a dragon accidentally swallowing its own flame. He fanned his mouth desperately, trying to breathe through the pulsing heat. Someone pushed his beer in front of him and he gulped it, trying to extinguish the fire he had swallowed. This made the group laugh so hard that one man snorted rice through his nose, which only got more laughs. Through his tears, Jiang saw the owner smiling and shaking her head.

When the pain subsided, Jiang offered his chilies to someone else, but quickly noticed they hadn't touched theirs, in fact, most of them moved the chilies carefully out of contact with the rest of their food.

"We've asked for no chilies many times, but she keeps putting them on the plate."

"Probably waiting for another fool to try his luck."

They ate, sipped their beers, and watched the village scenes around them for at least an hour. When Jiang finished his plate, he wondered if she'd make more. He was told that the rice and lentils were endless but anything else would cost extra. He finished off another big helping of rice and lentils until he felt his stomach could burst with joy.

"So, Jiang, I've heard you're from a village like this too, at least originally," the woman from the other table said, setting an empty beer bottle down.

"Well, a village yes, but quite different than this one."

"Tell us about it," she pressed politely.

Jiang told her, and the others, about his family farm, the rice fields, his bicycle, his father working the fields, the smaller water buffalo that roamed loose sometimes, his wooden house, the smells of the fruit trees in the autumn, his swimming hole. Then he began telling them about the men in suits, the packing of bags, the strange new city, and the abandoned city Li Jie had found in place of their village. He didn't realize that he had started to make two of his company tear up a little.

"I've heard about villages like those," the woman said.

"A load of foreign propaganda!" The man next to her bellowed.

"Really," she retorted. "And the boy in front of us is who?"

He shrugged, belched invisible beer gas, and said, "A paid actor." Those at Jiang's table shook their heads slowly, smiling.

"Well, I believe you, Jiang," the woman encouraged.

"Anyone want to head back up," the disagreeing man asked, standing up. Another man joined him, and they walked towards the restaurant's door to settle their bills.

"I remember a teacher I had," Jiang continued. "He didn't want to talk about my family's village much either. Like his world was more true than mine."

"Some people want to ignore the negative things happening in the world, Jiang," the woman replied. "But if everyone turned their backs on trouble, we would all be screwed. People have a strange definition of improvement sometimes, and when the world doesn't naturally spin ahead into the future fast enough, they want to help speed it up."

The man to Jiang added, "But, like our project here, some change is necessary. Some villagers may not like what we're doing, sure, but it's a hell of a lot better than the coal fields and environmental disasters that come with it,"

"True," the woman confirmed.

Jiang asked, "But couldn't this hurt the environment also? When I was on watch last night, I couldn't stop thinking about how much water is stuck behind the dam...and we slowly dish it out to the villagers." He looked at the other staff and tried to gauge their reactions.

"Sure, I see what you're saying. But it really comes down to the greater benefit we can give to people. More people will benefit from this electricity than not. Think about the hospitals that need power. The people that need light to work by, late at night."

"But there must be a middle way," Jiang said. "A solution where no one suffers at all."

"Ah, little Buddha, but isn't suffering just a reaction of people's attachments?"

Jiang chewed the idea in his head. He knew the woman was probably just teasing him, but there was a grain of truth there. But if it was a truth, Jiang didn't know if he wanted to accept it.

☼☼☼

When Jiang reported for his shift that night, he walked slowly towards the elevator. His feet felt heavy in his shoes, lead appendages his skinny legs had to lift with each step. They knew, perhaps better than his mind, the semi-motionless night that awaited him. He was also carrying the lunch discussion with him, unable to shake it or solve the questions it provoked. When he considered that if everyone lived simply, on a farm, everything would be in harmony. But then he talked himself out of the solution, thinking about the long evolution of humankind. The inventions and advancements that helped life become easier, and then how less work outside gave rise to philosophy and science.

Maybe life's questions weren't meant to be solved. But, was this a lazy answer? Were his body and mind too exhausted and just wanted to focus on his shift, the reality of which grew as the elevator lowered him down the concrete shaft? He pushed his brain forward, deeper into the answer, almost feeling his prefrontal cortex confirming and packaging the thoughts into a nicely formed ball of contentment against his forehead. Yes, maybe there wasn't exactly an answer after all. Science was an obvious source to pull from - each time science discovered a new secret of the universe, new questions arose. When those questions were answered, there was even more to ask about. It was a never-ending tornado of inspection fused with understanding. There would be no end to science, now that humankind had let it out into its world. It was impossible to shut down the wonder. It appeared to be innate in people, either a gift or a curse of consciousness.

When Jiang stepped out of the elevator, he suddenly envied the mountains above him. They didn't seem to wonder about much; they knew exactly what their mission was. All they needed to do was continue growing. They grew and watched the crazy human species below them, who were still busy pounding their heads together to figure out what the hell they were meant to do.

XXI

"Dad! Come quickly!" Maya yelled from behind Suman's house. Suman raced downstairs and outside, finding his daughter staring at a rock.

"What? What is it?" Suman asked, panic in his voice.

"Look at it," she replied, pointing to a caterpillar on the rock. Suman sat down next to her, his heart still racing. "It's a caterpillar, my dear Maya."

"It likes our yard. I tried to put in on a tree, but it came back." Suman smiled at his daughter and relaxed.

"Maybe it wants to build its cocoon here." Suman guessed. Seeing her confusion, he explained further. "It's going to change into a butterfly someday soon, then it will be even more beautiful and fly anywhere it wants."

"Will it fly over the mountains?" Maya asked.

"It might."

"Will it come back to our house? Will it remember us?"

Suman answered her quickly before the flood of curiosity poured out completely.

"I'm sure it will...since it likes it here so much."

"I hope so," she said, "Everyone who is nice can come to our house." Then she leaped up, giggling and bounding towards the house, without saying anything more. Suman could hear her call Sanjana inside.

Suman rose and walked into the village. He listened for the raging of the river. A normal sound for a summer day, but he heard nothing. Then he heard a different sound. A quiet roar grew louder. He looked up the road to see Ukali driving his motorbike full speed towards him. Suman stepped to the side of the road as Ukali flew past him. Ukali didn't wave. His red face seemed to show no emotion and he drove straight out of the village, several large bags tied to the back of the motorcycle.

Suman was going to meet Khayo for tea at a restaurant in the village. He wondered if that was the last he'd see of Ukali. He understood that the need to return to the city had been growing inside him for some time. He knew that the fight with Tauko didn't help but it surely wasn't the sole cause of that swift departure. He paused in the middle of the road and wished Ukali, truly, better luck in his next stage of life.

He continued up the road to the restaurant, finding Khayo already seated. Gently bowing to his friend first, he took a seat on a plastic chair. Two hot teas appeared before them. They turned to see the woman who owned the restaurant smiling widely.

"My dear neighbors. The workers from the dam bought all my food from me yesterday. It was a good day. These are free for my friends."

The two men bowed to her, with palms pressed together.

"Thank you, Madam," Khayo said. "We are happy for your success."

She strolled back inside, humming a lively tune to herself.

"Have you seen Tauko this morning?" Khayo had turned to once again face Suman.

"Not since last night."

"I had invited him here today. He didn't look well. He said he had plans to visit his land today and couldn't spare a moment. He also said for you not to worry, he is keeping your advice at heart."

Suman stroked his chin, hanging on the words.

"Suman, which advice?"

"Tauko is distressed about the yields of his land this year. He blames the dam and seems to be on a vendetta against the thing."

Khayo shook his head solemnly. "His land always struggles. In my opinion, they broke ground on the wrong side of the valley."

"I do agree that the dam, namely its bringing of electricity, is not healthy for our village."

"But the lights at night are useful."

"Of course. It helps. But what did we do when there weren't lights?"

"I guess, if we weren't sitting by candlelight, we sat outside, under the stars."

"That's what I remember. And without the television, I think we all talked more to each other."

"That's true as well." Khayo leaned back in his chair, taking a sip from the tea. "But the electricity doesn't affect Khayo's crops. There is less water in the river, true. But it should still be enough."

"Could it be that..." Suman paused. Behind Khayo, he noticed a young foreigner approaching the restaurant. He looked a bit younger than the other workers at the dam, and his uniform hung loosely on his thin body. He looked timid but friendly. His presence felt quite a contrast to the usual large and greasy men who work at the dam.

"Um, hello," Jiang said to the two villagers staring at him. He was immediately conscious of how strange his accent must sound. The villagers smiled and nodded at him. "Is the restaurant open?"

As if on cue, the owner reappeared. She smiled but shook her head at the young man. "Sorry, no food.

Come back tomorrow."

Jiang shifted his weight between his shoes. "Oh, I see. My co-workers told me that might be the case. Thank you." He turned to begin the walk back towards the dam.

"Wait!"

Jiang turned around again to see one of the villagers standing next to the plastic table. Suman opened his arms wide, hoping that his gesture could be understood as a friendly one. Jiang shuffled his feet slightly back to the restaurant.

"If you're hungry, please, come to my house." Suman moved one arm slowly down the road, signaling where that was. Khayo leaned over to Suman.

"Suman, are you sure that's a good idea?" He whispered.

"Everyone who is nice is welcome in my house."

Jiang walked towards the two men. He reached out a small, bony hand to the first villager who spoke. "My name is Jiang."

"Call me Suman. This is Khayo." Jiang bowed softly as he took Khayo's hand.

Suman led them all down the stone-cobbled road towards his home. Jiang walked silently, taking in his surroundings with curious eyes. In a green pasture to his left, slightly higher than the roofs of the village, two older women, maybe around his mother's age, were burning a large pile of brush. The white smoke rose directly upward as there wasn't a hint of wind in the air, yet Jiang could smell the smoke all the same. There was a tinge of sweetness to the smoke and it smelled different than the smoke that once burned in his father's fields. Nearer to his eye, another woman was shaking out a dusty carpet inside a small fenced garden. As their eyes met, she cocked her head slightly and smiled with her teeth exposed. Behind her, a man was trying to pull the trunk of an old tree from the ground. Jiang saw a few digging tools lying next to the partially excavated tree, each caked in dense soil.

They soon arrived at Suman's house, where a woman was sitting outside, drinking from a colorful clay cup. She set it down in front of her, and Jiang noticed as the cup passed her face, her lips turned into a warm, welcoming smile. Jiang realized that she may have been the most beautiful woman he'd ever seen. Her hair was tied in a long plait that rested softly over one shoulder. Her cheeks were long, and elegant, appearing both strong and soft at the same time. Her orange dress, its patterns radiating outward like an erupting volcano, should have distracted anyone from seeing the person behind the cloth, but instead, it seemed to only accentuate her seemingly flawless skin.

"Do we have any food left for this young man?"

Suman's voice broke Jiang's eyes from the spell cast over him. He finally noticed that the woman was indeed looking directly at him. He blushed quickly and searched to see what his feet were doing.

"Of course, anything for you Khayo?" The woman spoke. A sound that drifted through the air more like a melody than a language.

"Thanks, Sanjana. I've eaten."

Sanjana. Jiang practiced her name in his mind. Then he repeated the names of the two men next to him. He sometimes had difficulty remembering the names of those he just met.

The three of them sat around a large wooden table. Suman had insisted Jiang sit with his back against the house's wall, so he could see the view behind them. *What a view he has!* Suman's house, although it appeared older, and most likely had a few more creaks within the floorboards than his childhood home, had an incredible scene in front of it. It was set to the side of the village, and as it sat slightly higher, Jiang could see over the nearest roofs easily. Beyond the roofs, he could see the next hill of the village, a line of thatched-roofed houses, then the dense forest, broken occasionally by an outcropping of gray rocks. The forest spread upwards until it couldn't anymore, then only rock, and eventually rock and snow that pulled Jiang's eyes higher until he felt the back of his neck stretch. Suman and Sanjana's view had everything in it. From the neighborhood they shared, to the highest reaches of the mountains around them.

"How do you get anything done?" He asked, looking back down towards Suman's smiling face.

"What do you mean?" Suman's brow bunched together a little.

309

"If I had this view at home, I would just sit here all day and look at it."

Suman and Khayo laughed, nodding their heads.

"Luckily, the mountains don't go anywhere when we take our eyes off them."

Jiang shook his head once and accepted a cup of tea Khayo was holding towards him. "Still, it's very nice."

"Is it hard work building the dam?" Khayo asked. "Maybe there isn't enough time to look around?"

"I don't build anything. Actually, my job is just to look around." Jiang replied, sipping his tea.

Khayo and Suman exchanged looks. Khayo turned again to face the young man, his head slightly tilted to the side. "What kind of job is that?"

"I don't know. Honestly. They just pay me to see if everything outside looks normal. It wasn't a job that I imagined I would do."

"What job did you think you would do?" Suman chimed in.

"I'm not sure about that. I haven't finished school. I only came here because my mother is ill and we needed the money."

The expressions on both of the villager's faces turned somber. To Jiang, their eyes suddenly expressed pain, true pain, after hearing what he'd said.

"We hope your mother will recover quickly, Jiang," Khayo said. "We are sad to hear of this."

"Thank you," Jiang replies, holding his hand up slightly. "She is starting to do better lately. My work is paying for treatment in a hospital. But I worry for my father as well."

"Why is that?" Suman leaned in.

"Well, since we moved to our city, he spends more time in front of his television than anywhere else. Even in the hospital. He sits in front of it all day, while my mother sleeps."

Suman raised his eyebrows, turning to see if Khayo had the same consideration. There was something to this young man that they were both starting to understand. He seemed to be at ease in their village. It was as if he saw it as they did.

"Where did you move from, when you moved to your city?" Suman asked.

"I am from a village in the countryside. My father was a farmer back then. When I first passed your village, it felt nice to be back in the countryside. But up at the dam, all I hear is mechanical noise, look at cement walls and try not to go crazy. I used to run around without any worry at all, like the kids I've seen here. Except they are running around on the edge of enormous mountains; where we were was pretty flat, but there was a nice little river to swim in…" Jiang suddenly became aware of how fast he was speaking. Alone in his tiny watchtower every night had sure given him the need to speak. He glanced around the table, hoping that his hosts were able to understand his ramblings.

Suman smiled and was about to speak when Sanjana returned with a metal plate of food. It looked similar to the one Jiang had in the restaurant the day before, except the color of the vegetables sitting next to the rice was yellow rather than red, and the pickled chilies were in a separate small bowl. Jiang thanked her as she set the plate down. She rounded the table and sat on the same bench as Jiang, smiling and waiting for him to try the food. He spooned some lentils and rice into his mouth, breathing steam outward at the same time. It was even more delicious than the restaurant.

"Wow, this is incredible. Thank you so much," Jiang said, grinning, and started to mix some vegetables into the rice.

"Try the pickles," Suman said, eyeing the small bowl.

"Thank you, but I tried them yesterday. I think it's too spicy for me."

"Not Suman's," Sanjana began. "His pickles are famous here. They are balanced." Jiang saw Suman's cheeks blush.

Khayo nodded. "The best pickles in town," he affirmed.

Jiang cautiously picked up a small chili and what may have been a radish, gently biting a corner. He waited for the burning sensation, but it barely arrived. It was a delicate spice, and the flavor of the chili shone through the heat. He then popped the whole piece in his mouth and chewed silently.

"It's really good," Jiang said, starting to finger-spoon more rice.

"Allow me to talk while you eat, Jiang," Suman started. "You are not what I imagined when I saw you coming down the road. I have met some of the workers of the dam before. They seemed to be more proud of what they are doing and sure about what the dam provides for us, and for those it gives electricity to. From what I can gather, you probably didn't leave your countryside village by choice, am I right?"

Jiang nodded, chewing happily.

"We were speaking of the dam before we met. Me and Khayo" Sanjana put a hand on her cheek, listening. "Some in our village have grown weary of the effects of the dam on our village. We are not used to electricity. We are not used to a giant mountain of concrete in the middle of our river. Some think it may even have a negative effect on their crops. I was coming to the conclusion that it is doing more damage to the minds of those troubled by it, than to anything else."

"I know what you were going to say," Khayo interrupted. "As Jiang here came to the restaurant. It could be that the disillusionment Tauko is having towards the dam is making his work on his farm worse.

He isn't giving his land the attention it needs because he is preoccupied with his worrying."

"That's correct, my friend," Suman continued. "Change here used to happen very slowly. We don't sit and watch a tree grow, because it takes years to bear fruit. When a wall interrupts our river's flow, it almost feels instant, and we don't know how to handle it. Tauko can't take his mind off the thing. He sees its ugly face in everything. In his son's love of television and in his failing crops."

Jiang swallowed his last mouthful of food. "I know what you mean." The eyes at the table all studied him. "When we left the village, my parents didn't know what to do with themselves. They had their routine in our village. Now they are lost in a huge metropolis. My father turned to drinking beer and watching television, and my mother just worried all the time. I think it didn't help with her illness. I had a difficult time finding my place as well. At first, I hated the city. Then I became enchanted with all the new technology around me. More recently, some friends opened my eyes to the horrible things our government was doing, and I started to worry all the time as well."

"What is your government doing?" Sanjana asked.

"Many things. But what concerned me the most was that our village was destroyed to create a giant city, where nobody lives."

This seemed to interest everyone, so Jiang, between bites, told the table about his friend Li Jie, and what happened when he returned to their village. Then he told them about the protests, Li Jie's arrest, and then about the initial protests and arrest of his father.

"Your father is a brave man," Khayo said when Jiang finished speaking. Suman nodded.

"He is," Sanjana agreed. Turning toward Jiang, she continued. "But not everyone must be that way. I sense that you didn't like being in your protest."

Jiang nodded in confirmation. "I was pretty scared, to be honest," he replied, taking a sip from his tea.

"Here, we may not be facing down your government as your friend and father were. But the dam is a force that is also more powerful than anything we've ever seen people capable of. Our friend, Tauko, has turned himself against the wall. Whether it is the dam or his distracted mind that stops his food from growing, it doesn't matter. He seems to want to fight because it is what some people need to do. My husband, Suman, is different. I married him because I could see that he was different. When things outside of our control go wrong, he adapts and tries to bring us all together, peacefully. Believe me, he is troubled by it as well. But instead of becoming angry or vengeful, he does what must be done for our family. For myself and our little girl. I have the feeling that you are more like Suman than your friend, Li Jie. You adapted. You felt angry at what was done to your village but when your mother needed help, you responded, and here you are. Sending money to help her. Taking a long journey and doing work that you don't enjoy because the health of your family is more important than fighting."

"But sometimes I think I am just not brave enough to fight. I ran away when my father was arrested. I ran away in the protests."

"If you were arrested, how could you help your mother, Jiang? You had to run because you were needed somewhere else. What we haven't spoken about is the force that governs more powerfully than the dam, your government, or anything that people have created."

"The mountains," Khayo said, looking behind him.

"That which created the mountains," Sanjana corrected. "I don't know what you call it where you come from, Jiang, but here we say *Devas,* they are forces in our world and every world among the stars that govern all things. It is the eternal flow of all energy, that transcends life or death, that exists adapt to the swift changes of our world and respect the directions of the Devas, we can remain at peace. When we forget, and fight with worldly forces, we lose this peace."

The four of them remained sitting in their own thoughts that Sanjana's words left for them. After a minute or so, Jiang spoke.

"Do you mean that it is useless to fight?"

"No," Sanjana started, "Somethings are certainly worth fighting for. We all can find ourselves fighting for something. But we should choose the battles wisely, and fighting can mean different things."

"If you choose to fight against something, you can,

Jiang." Suman was speaking, and Jiang turned to face him. "But worry, on the other hand, doesn't always help. I agree with Sanjana. I worry a lot about the dam. But I don't worry about whether or not I can stop the progress of the dam. I worry how I can help my neighbors, what I can do to help my family with these new changes. Deep down, you see, I know that this constant worry isn't helping anyone. It's my actions that can help, and if the worrying won't lead me to action, then I have to let it go, otherwise, it won't be healthy for my mind. If there are forces that are outside my control, then I'll leave it to the Devas, and get on with my work."

After his meal, Jiang shook everyone's hand, bowing deeply to Sanjana for the delicious food and her advice. It was beginning to be late in the day, and he needed to prepare for his shift. Yet, he felt that he didn't want to leave the company of those villagers. Their conversation was more profound than what he was used to with his friends. It felt more like they were versions of himself that had escaped his mind to help him deal with his introspection over the last days, and it felt much healthier having the discussion with actual people than with himself in the lonely watchtower. Still, he said his goodbyes and walked slowly up the hill, once stepping aside to let two barefoot children run by. Smoke began to rise from the chimneys of the last houses he passed. When the dam was in sight, he turned back downhill to face the village once again. He breathed in deeply and held his breath in, waiting several seconds before slowly releasing it. He looked at the mountains above the tiny houses below them. He imagined their Devas could be seen much clearer here than where he came from.

☼☼☼

Back at Suman's house, Sanjana sat outside watching clouds drift over the peak of a mountain. Near the peak, she could see how fierce the wind must be, as wisps of white streaked to the side, as if the clouds were holding onto the rocks for dear life. Closer to her, the other clouds, with their smooth underbellies and brush-stroked sides, glided peacefully down the ridge, pleading ignorance to the violence going on behind them.

Inside, Suman was washing Jiang's dishes and their cups from lunch. Khayo had left them to be able to greet his son on his arrival from school. Sanjana mused about her past and revisited the memories of a young girl from a nomadic family. Change was with them every day back then. They could stay camped in one valley for days or weeks, but there always came a time to pack and continue on to the next temporary home. Their life depended on constant change. If they stayed too long, eventually nothing would be left for the yaks to eat. In return, the land would spoil and take years to return to its richness. Because they had no particular destination planned too far in advance, their lives were a seemingly seamless journey from one destination to the next, and the location where they arrived was less important than the voyage it took to get there. On the road, they encountered constant obstacles: yaks would get injured, flooded rivers became impassable causing them to change course, landslides blocked once trekkable trails, elders would get sick and delay the progress. When they eventually settled in a new valley, it was as if the band of nomads were on a holiday.

When she first moved in with Suman, the lack of change distressed her. She compensated for the lack of movement by constantly exploring different reaches of the single valley. She summited several smaller peaks over their village and even walked to the glacier that was the source of the river. After she became pregnant, her outings became shorter and shorter, eventually subsiding to a "voyage" up and down the village street. Eventually, in those last months, her restlessness dissolved, and she felt a void filled by stillness. Maya's birth and growth into a young girl became the change she took notice of. With the restlessness of her body leaving came the calmness of her mind. When there was some progression in the village: perhaps a neighbor had a new child, the seasonal festivals arriving, the yearly food preparation for winters, she viewed these small changes with the same enthusiasm that trekking up the mountains once brought to her. She realized that the world was constantly changing, and it wasn't solely determined by her own form of movement. Sometimes the details were so particular and minuscule that she had to concentrate to witness them.

Sitting outside her home, listening to her husband hum while cleaning the kitchen, Sanjana was at peace. Some of those she shared the world with may have been struggling with the change they observed around them, and she wished she could lift the burden off of them all. She wished that they knew the secret it had taken her most of her life to understand. Eventually, she was sure, they would understand.

Breaking away from that reverie, she noticed someone coming down the road to the house. As they grew nearer, she saw it was Khayo again. She raised an arm to wave but withdrew it as his face came into the light of the receding sun. His face was serious, possibly even a little sad.

"Hello, Sanjana. I'm sorry to return like this…"

"What's happened, Khayo?"

"Can you call for Suman, I want to speak to you both."

She did, and Suman appeared quickly, a look of concern growing on his face as well.

"It's Ukali, I'm afraid. There's been an accident."

"…"

"He lost control of his motorcycle past the next village. He drove off the side of the road, into where the river gorge narrows…They are still trying to recover his body…"

"Oh, Ukali…" Suman bowed his head towards the ground. Sanjana stood to hug him. Then they approached their neighbor and embraced him. Tears started to fall softly down Khayo's cheeks.

"He could be such a pain…but I never thought…" Khayo's voice cracked as he tried to speak.

"I know," Suman said. "He had his own struggles, but

he was just a part of our village as anyone…"

Sanjana looked at the mountain above them. The light of the sun started to move up the final ridge of Chatima. The light around them receded and the lamps from the house helped cast shadows across the three souls embraced on the front steps.

"May he find peace in his next journey," Sanjana said.

"May he find peace," Khayo repeated. "I need to return to my family now, I just…I wanted to tell you tonight."

"Thank you, my friend," Suman replies. "We will talk in the morning."

Khayo slowly drifted back to the village. His small figure wove around a line of bushes and disappeared behind the nearest house. Raindrops began to fall on the ground Khayo left and soon found their way to the couple. They started to retreat inside, but Sanjana took Suman's hand. She motioned to the table, which stayed dry under an outstretched roof.

"Sit with me?" She asked.

"Of course."

XXII

Jiang sat in his swivel chair and inadvertently noticed the clock confirming his on-time arrival to the tower. He leaned back. He knew that he could easily sit there, lost in the deepest corners of his head, but he also worried that he might emerge in the morning completely deranged. He set about filling the coffee machine with fresh grounds and refilled the small reservoir on the back with water from a plastic jug he had carried in. The books on the table and the television both beckoned him into a more passive use of the evening, but the tiny room felt stuffy. He needed some air.

He walked a circle around the tower outside, before stopping to lean against the railing. The air was brisk and still. It was wet outside, and the moisture made its coldness even more present to the touch. It had rained earlier in the evening, during his dinner in the cafeteria trailer. He didn't believe that he was the cause of it, although the staff sitting around him had blamed him.

At dinner, Jiang asked if it ever rained this time of year. First, someone berated him for posing the question, saying it was bad luck, and that the mountains would hear and gather the clouds. Then they told him about the monsoon season, week-long downpours that completely soaked someone in an instant. They said it was impossible to stay dry, even indoors, and the trailers all smelled moldy with wet clothes and damp linens.

Just then, outside, it began to rain. Someone said, "Thanks a lot, kid."

High above the pump house, Jiang stood outside for a couple of hours, listening to the turbine's never-changing tune, straining to hear a chord from the river or anything more natural sounding. Just motors, gears, and spinning fan blades replied up to him.

Then he started to hear rocks shifting. *Landslide?* He wondered. He looked around in the darkness. No, it was coming from below, near the lower fences of the compound. More rocks, deep depressions in the scree, evenly spaced apart. *Someone is walking.* But no one should be out walking around at this time of night. Only two other guards were on duty, one above and one below at the second gate. Maybe the lower guard was looking for something.

He listened for the footsteps again, but they had stopped. He thought about using the tower's searchlight to inspect the sound more, but he waited and listened instead. After several minutes, still nothing. He remembered from his research on the area, that there could be wild animals around. Perhaps a mountain goat. Or even a yak that was separated from its herd. To be sure, he waited a little longer, listening to the darkness. He finally decided to turn on his searchlight and aim it toward where he last heard the sound. Its beam lit up a boulder and the scree around it, he moved it around the vicinity slowly, expecting any moment for an animal to burst through the light. But nothing happened. He left the light on, thinking that it alone would scare away whatever may have been there.

After some time, he began to shiver a bit, feeling the cold air seep through his thin uniform. *Maybe I'm hearing things…* He made a mental note to switch off the light in ten minutes or so.

Jiang returned to his box in the watchtower. The warm air welcomed him immediately. Eventually, his mind left the strange sound for the village Devas to deal with, and his thoughts drifted towards his own village. He always admired his father for sitting in the road on the day the police came to remove them from the farm. He admired Li Jie and that new group of friends for standing up for something they believed in. But what did he believe in? He knew his place in the lonely tower was serving someone important to him. He felt he really was helping his family, but the larger implications of the dam riddled his mind with anxiety. *Am I part of the suffering of that village down there? Could my participation be hurting Suman's friend who was troubled by the dam?* The electricity of the dam would surely serve many people, perhaps hundreds of thousands. Was it worth the cost of one man's suffering?

Jiang considered that this question was impossible to answer. Perhaps Sanjana was correct that this battle was too large for Jiang to face. His mind wandered to his future and what would happen to him after his contract expired. What about Li Jie and his struggle? Surely his government was too big for some young people to take on alone. It would take so many of them. Jiang wondered if his place was among those ready to fight, but the answer seemed as far away as his city did at that moment. *The only thing I need to worry about is surviving one more night in this damn box.*

☼☼☼

The downpour of rain was over quickly. Sanjana and Suman were about to retreat back into the warmth of their home. It was about time to usher Maya into her bed. They held each other as the last drops of rain rolled off their roof and onto the ground just beyond the wooden table. Suman lifted his arm over Sanjana's head, while simultaneously kissing her on the forehead.

"Wait, Suman…"

"Ok, let me see those lips."

"No, look…" Sanjana pointed at the street. There was another figure coming towards their house. It was moving quickly and was too tall to be Khayo. They both realize that it was Tauko's wife. Sanjana moved with Suman and they walked to the front gate.

"I'm sorry, my dear friends. I know it's late…"

Suman wished deeply to not hear more news of tragedy.

He couldn't take anymore after finally letting go of the image of Ukali crashing into the gorge.

"It's Tauko. He didn't come home tonight. Have you seen him?"

"We haven't, but we've been here most of the day," Sanjana replied.

A bell in Suman's head rings. He had wanted to check on Tauko after lunch.

"I think I know where he is," Suman said, seeing Sanjana looking at him through the corner of her eyes. "I'll go look for him."

When Suman reached the fence that borders the dam site, he didn't see anything suspicious. He remained out of the front light and watched as the guard in the small house sat in the glow of a small television. The guard seemed to be speaking to someone. As he inched closer, he saw the man talking into a cell phone calmly. There didn't seem to be any stress in the man's voice. *Maybe Tauko didn't come to the dam after all. Maybe he had heard about Ukali and was simply on a walk.*

As he turned to leave, he noticed something strange up the hill. The bottom of the fence was shining peculiarly bright in one place. When he started up the incline, he realized that part of the fence had been cut and pulled back. A torso-sized hole was crudely cut out of the fence. *Oh, Tauko…*

Suman carefully stepped through the hole in the fence, one foot at a time. A cut piece of the fence's mesh snagged his sleeve after his head was through and nearly made him lose his balance. Shifting his weight back towards the hole, he picked his sleeve off the metal with his other hand. The fence rattled slightly, emitting just enough noise that someone uphill might have heard it. He crouched and listened. He wasn't sure how crouching would help and Suman felt like a startled animal; maybe a dog who was caught digging around in someone's trash bin.

After a long minute of listening, he figured the sound of the fence hadn't been loud enough to travel very far. The ground by the fence was covered in loose rock, a man-made scree pile. It was difficult to walk smoothly on, and more than once, Suman's feet sunk into the rock. He made slow progress up the hill but took the time to survey his surroundings, hoping to find a clue about Tauko's direction.

He spotted a small depression in the loose rock that could have been a shoe, but then the spacing of it didn't appear to be an ordinary stride.

After several minutes he crested the top of the scree hill. He could see flood lights towards the top of the dam, but down below were only several smaller lights, indicating metal walkways and doors. Down the line of the fence, he could see the security kiosk by the front gate, and deeper into the complex, he spotted a small tower with a lit-up room on top. *Where are you Tauko?*

In front of him was an open space. It was at least fifty meters until the first object he would be able to hide behind. Keeping in a low, crouched position, Suman scurried quickly across to a box-like, metal object. His shoulder bumped against the metal silently and he could hear an electrical humming inside the box. He glanced down to the kiosk and then up towards the floodlights. Seeing no new movement or signs of alarm, Suman released a small sigh.

He peered towards the metal walkways. He guessed that Tauko, trying to remain undetected, would opt for the lower walkways and doors, rather than head straight for the larger lights. Suman checked behind towards the kiosk again, then made his move downhill to the walkways. Knowing that the metal would surely make a loud noise if walked on, he stopped just before the first step down. Grasping a cold railing above the step, he carefully put his sandals on the metal. Sure enough, a deep metallic sound reverberated slightly at the touch. Suman took another step down, glancing up and around him for any signs of life. As he moved at a painstakingly slow speed, he surveyed the paths after the few sets of stairs.

The walkway split towards the dam every twenty meters or so. His eyes followed each path towards the dam, which from his perspective, was just a giant wall that disappeared in the darkness above him. He couldn't even see the reinforcing rebar at the top of the unfinished wall.

He waited for a long time at the first junction, unsure how to proceed. His eyes darted from walkway, to walkway, and to several doors along the lower wall. He felt each moment that passed was too precious to be wasted with his wandering, so he started down the first walkway on his right. He remembered to keep his feet moving silently, which meant he had to almost drag his sandal along the metal surface. He grasped the handle of the door and tried to twist it. Nothing. He pulled it toward himself, then pushed his shoulder into it. It was locked from the inside. He immediately spun around and shuffled quickly back up the walkway and down to the next junction. He started to pivot his feet when a gleaming object caught his peripheral vision.

There was hardly much light on the walkway and it seemed to just end in a black void farther along, but now he noticed that there was no dead end. Instead, the walkway bent around the corner of the wall. About halfway up the wall, he spotted the corner of a staircase peeking out from where it was bolted above the last door. Suman paused. He stared at the nearest door on his right. It was almost as identical as the last, and if locked, he'd need to check three others down the length of the walkway. Tauko, whatever his mission was, wouldn't want to move this slowly. In his gut, Suman felt an urge to climb the stairs. He sensed his friend's past self, standing at the same junction, considering the same move. Suman slid his hand down the railing, feeling small bumps from the connecting bolts along its otherwise smooth surface. He shuffled his feet forward, then began to take long, cat-like strides. He used the railings to hoist some of his weight off the metal floor, making his moves faster but still stealthy enough.

His eyes shifted occasionally to the doors that he passed, but he maintained the course, understanding that he should trust his instincts. At the last corner, he lifted his body off the floor and swung his feet around, in front of his hands. He came down on the walkway more aggressively than intended. He was moving too fast, but there wasn't anything he could do against the inertia. His sandalled feet connected with the floor, which spit out a deep, metallic grunt. He froze for a second, then dropped to his stomach. Once prone, he touched the metal planks with his hands. They were wet and cold. He strained his ear towards the air behind him, thinking that his ill-managed jump must have echoed throughout the work site. But he heard nothing. The air was completely silent. The moisture of the walkway seeped through the front of his clothes, sending a shiver from his chest to his fingertips. He waited until he was satisfied that the unfortunate sound wasn't recognized.

He rose carefully to his feet and finished the short distance to the foot of the staircase. Wasting no more time, he took high strides upwards, skipping two or three steps at a time. There were no lights on this side of the wall, but he now understood that the wall was actually an enormous block-shaped building. His eyes caught sight of a second building above the rooftop. The edges of the rooftop were illuminated by a faint light that grew brighter with each bound he took upwards. He couldn't be close to the top of the floodlights, and he imagined he must be far enough away to be seen.

When he neared the top of the staircase, the light became so intense that he suddenly thought it must be a searchlight, waiting for a trespasser to show himself. But as he peered over the edge, he saw a searchlight, hanging below a tower, pointed down towards the front gate, but its powerful beam still able to flood the entire rooftop. It was bright enough that it hurt Suman's eyes when he tried to see through it. He squatted just below the light and waited. He waited and listened.

He heard the hum of the dam for the first time. Large, muffled motors mixed with a droning sound from some electric wires above him. The tower by the dam was even larger close up. Inside the building, it rested on, impossible alien-like noises cranked and turned into themselves. It was like a giant, rock beast, and the sounds reminded Suman of heavy breathing. *A giant, sleeping beast*, he thought. *Let's not wake this thing, Tauko.*

After what felt like several minutes, the light finally shut off. Suman pulled his head over the edge a bit more. He could see a lit guard tower that was hidden by the light. A shadow crossed the room inside the tower. Suman could only see the top side of someone's head. The guard was facing away from the stairway, towards the lower gate. Suman scanned the rooftop, looking for any sign of Tauko. His eyes were readjusting slowly from the searchlight's temporary blinding. The rooftop was empty except for several air vents. If Tauko did make it this far, what would be his next move? Suman glanced around the corner, back down to the first metal walkways, wondering if he should have tried all the doors.

Then, out of the left corner of his eye, he noticed a shadow move briefly in the direction of the guard tower. When he swiveled his head, he didn't catch the movement again. Either he just missed something or his eyes were playing with him. *It must be getting late in the evening by now.* Suman checked his pulse with two fingers under his neck. He hadn't felt his heart race that fast in a long time. Feeling defeated, Suman decided to watch the rooftop a bit longer before turning back. Maybe the futility of doing something to stop the construction of the dam dawned on Tauko while he was here. Maybe his friend cooled off and ran off after the light turned on.

"YAAAAAH! HEY!"

A voice pierced through the silence above Suman. He ducked quickly, waiting for a light to come searching for him. Instead, he heard a high-pitched scream start, and then suddenly muffled by something. Sounds of metal banging on a floor erupted up above, in the guard tower. Suman peeked his head over the edge again. There were more shadows inside the windows of the tower. Through the open door, he heard two people struggling.

Tauko!

Suman hoisted himself over the edge and pushed himself to his feet, which had already started to run towards the noise. He scaled the ladder at the base of the tower in seconds, pulling his body in a swinging motion onto the landing, just outside the door. His feet slid to a stop inside the room, halting his torso, like somebody threw a heavy rock at his waist.

Inside the room, Tauko had a young man pinned to the floor, one hand covering the man's mouth and the other wielding a knife, which was held to the man's throat. A thin stream of blood glimmered in the overhead lamp and pooled slightly at the man's collarbone. It took an instant for Suman to recognize Jiang's face, terror pushing through his eyes.

332

"Tauko! Stop!"

Tauko's teeth were clenched tight and with each slight wiggle of Jiang's arms, Tauko's body pushed him down harder. Suman recognized the anger on Tauko's face but there was something else there as well.

"We have to stop them all, Suman. I can't take it anymore."

Jiang moaned behind Tauko's cupped hand.

"Tauko, he is just a kid. He has nothing to do with building this thing."

"He's one of them. The only way to destroy the wall is to force them to do it, or stop them from going any further."

Suman could feel his heart trying to push itself out of his coat. His legs felt heavy, stuck in place above his feet. He tried to breathe through the noise of his heartbeats.

"Tauko, I know you're angry. But hurting him is only going to make things worse for you. For us."

The moment in the tiny room expanded. Tauko glanced at Suman, then down to the ruffled hair on Jiang's head. Suman was staying still, waiting. He breathed deeply, letting the sound of his expressed breath pass through the tense air in the room. He locked his eye on Tauko's face, holding a look of steadfast compassion.

"I understand, dear Tauko. I feel you, my friend. I love you."

Tears started to form at the edges of Tauko's eyes, pulling themselves out slowly.

"Suman, I…"

Before Tauko could finish, the room started moving. The corners of the little box seemed to lift and teeter. Suman stumbled forward, losing his balance, moving one buckled knee in front of the other.

Tauko fell backward as a small box television slid off a counter and crashed to the floor, spilling several cassettes around it. His hands released Jiang's twisted face, and Jiang slumped forward, next to the cassettes. The room lifted again and rocked to the side, pushing each of them closer to the ground. The lamp overhead swung violently back and forth, illuminating each side of the room with a flickering of light. Tauko's knife slid across the floor and a loose book collided with it.

"Suman! What's happening?"

Tauko pulled his knees to his chest with one arm and covered his head with the other. Jiang crawled away from his attacker and huddled under a desk. Suman moved across the floor, bracing himself with outstretched arms. He made it next to Jiang and pulled him into his arms.

Tauko scooted himself away from the other two, backing himself up until he was under the door frame.

Then the door slammed itself shut, as the tilting of the tower gained momentum.

"Earthquake, Tauko! Get under the desk!" Suman's voice felt detached from himself as he heard himself yell across the sounds of metal breaking beneath the tower.

Bolts above them pried loose from a thin metal bar and bounced on the floor of the room. They heard the searchlight come loose outside and its glass shattered on a catwalk somewhere below. Before Tauko could reach his friend, the metal bar swung over his head and connected with Suman's forehead.

Darkness flooded Suman's vision. He felt himself lying on his back. His neck strained itself over Jiang's shoulder as someone's scream started in his ear and then faded away slowly. He felt something grabbing his arm as he lost consciousness, seconds stretched into a timeless void, as he slipped away from the noise. He was weightless above the rocking movement of the room, like his body was being lifted away from the chaos. Then, he felt nothing.

XXIII

The 7.8 magnitude earthquake was the largest and most destructive earthquake in the area in over 80 years, long before Suman was born in his village. In his valley, and the site of the dam, three people died from the violence it caused. Farther down the river, in the larger cities to the south, thousands more lost their lives. Entire neighborhoods were reduced to rubble. Ancient structures that watched generations live in their shadows now sat in a pile of broken bricks and cracked wood.

When Suman opened his eyes again, he was being pulled out of the wreckage of the twisted and mutilated watchtower. A man he didn't recognize yanked on his arm, which hung loose from his shoulder. The man pushed pieces of metal and concrete debris off of Suman's chest, slid an arm under Suman's torso, and lifted him up. There was a soft-pitched ringing sound in his ears and his eyes blinked through a morning ray of light that found his face amid the dust and movement around him.

He tried to speak, but his throat was dry and his tongue felt trapped within his mouth. He closed his eyes, opening them again to see his surroundings had changed again. He was lying on his back, hard plastic held his body in place, and someone wearing a blue helmet fasted a strap around his waist. An engine roared to life, and from his horizontal position, he saw a metal door bang shut. The Jeep he was in bounced down rocky terrain. *Tauko...* Suman tried to lift his head to peer out of the windows of the jeep, but his forehead ached and he let his head fall back onto the plastic stretcher he was held in. *Jiang...*

The Jeep came to a sudden stop, and the rear door was thrust open to reveal more men in blue helmets. He tried again to speak, but his mouth wouldn't obey him. The blue helmets lifted his stretcher and carried him across a gravel lot. Everywhere he looked, there were other people racing around, some yelling orders, some standing still, with their helmets in their hands. Suman was hauled swiftly into a white-walled tent, unstrapped from the stretcher, lifted, and carefully placed on a green cot. His head felt like it was burning under the aches.

He looked to his side and saw someone with their head completely bandaged up with white gauze. Hints of faded blood stuck to the side of the person's head. He turned to face the other side to see a familiar face.

Jiang was sitting upright in the cot next to him. His hand bandage up but otherwise he looked unharmed. His clothes were covered in gray dust, and when he met Suman's face, he smiled.

"Hi, Suman. I'm happy to see you."

Suman tried to speak, but his dry mouth stopped him again. His shaking arm lifted from the bed and he pointed towards the door. He mouthed the name of his friend, as his eyebrows turned down questioningly.

"Nurse!" Jiang called out. "He needs water!" Jiang then looked back to Suman. "I saw them taking your friend away to a hospital. His leg was hurt badly, but that's all I know."

Suman breathed out heavily, shaking his head. A woman in a nurse's uniform came between them, offering Suman a bottle of water with a straw. Suman blinked and tried to thank her with a soundless movement of his mouth. She smiled, spun around, and walked briskly deeper into the tent.

"Two workers died." Jiang was speaking. "I'm sorry, I heard some of your village was damaged too."

Suman released his lips from the straw, emitting a gasp of air. Life was returning to his dry mouth. He swallowed the remaining water over his tongue and released a long breath. He tried to move his head from the pillow it rested on, but it was heavy, and a film of exhaustion and distortion crept across his vision. His head was pounding. He shut his eyes for a moment, trying to steady his throbbing mind, wanting to calm everything around him. But before he could open his eyes again, a deep sleep found him first.

When he finally awoke, Jiang was gone. Only an empty cot stared back at him, and to the other side, he saw the nurse standing over him again. Her eyes were shining with compassion and what he recognized as pity. Her skin was dark like his, and when she spoke, he finally recognized that her accent came from the capital city.

"I'm going to take you home, sir."

A navy blue Jeep dropped off Suman at the entrance of his village. He steadied himself with a firm grip on the door of the Jeep as he swung heavy legs onto the ground outside. The earth below his feet was still wet, and a thin layer of mud rose to the top edge of the new sandals the nurse gave him after his discharge from the medic's tent. He looked back inside the Jeep and the young army private behind the wheel gave him a nod. Suman shut the door, stepping back as the vehicle lurched forward, heading downhill through the village. Suman's field of vision moved slowly into the scene around him. His heart sank.

The houses immediately around him had almost completely been flattened by the earthquake. Bits of mud bricks were piled up crudely with broken beams of wood and dismembered roof thatch topping the mess. Several rooms in the nearest house were still standing upright, with the walls minimally damaged, but most of the home was in ruin. Suman's headache returned and he shifted his vision down the road. Most of the village houses were in a similar state, and the only piece of the village that seemed to be unharmed was the long line of prayer wheels at the entrance.

He shuffled his tired feet down the road, soon reaching the prayer wheels, and stopped to spin the first wheel. Opening his mouth, he hoarsely muttered the sacred mantra as he spun each wheel. *Om mani padme hum, om mani padme hum.*

When he approached the next line of houses, he found some villagers picking through the rubble. He approached them slowly, waiting just outside by a crumbled garden wall until an elderly man recognized him. They locked eyes while the old man softly shook his head, then reached down to pull a broken chair out from a pile of bricks. Suman decided to press on, leaving the old neighbor to his toil with a deep bow.

With every house he passed, he noticed that while most of the village sustained significant damage the night before, some houses were lucky. Outside of the undamaged homes, small groups of people huddled together as the owners of the house stood in their doorways, handing out steaming bowls of food. Outside Khayo's house, his son was pouring cups of tea for younger children. Suman didn't see Khayo, but his thoughts instead turned to his own family. Quickly, his shuffling pace picked up, and his sandals snapped at his heels as he rounded a corner towards his own home. When the house finally came into view, his feet slid to a stop on the moist stone path. He reached out to a nearby tree at his right to steady his body upright. His heart seemed to skip several beats when he began breathing heavily, his worry and anxiety catching up and overwhelming his lungs.

In front of him, he saw his house apparently untouched from the destruction around him. His nearest neighbor's homes were also less damaged. The only thing he noticed that took some of the weight of the quake was the front roof, which had broken mid-beam and crushed his wooden table by the front door. He reached to wipe tears from his cheeks, just noticing that his face was wet. He saw Sanjana and

Maya standing with Khayo and several others to the side of the house. Maya transferred bowls of rice from Sanjana's hands to the outstretched hands of their neighbors. After she handed off the last bowl, Maya saw him.

"Dad!" She shrieked and started off in a full sprint towards him. Sanjana looked up from the pot she was scooping rice from and a grin started to radiate her face. Suman watched her hand the spoon to Khayo just as Maya collided with his legs. He lifted her off the ground and swung her into the air. His tears fell freely as Maya squirmed and giggled in his arms. He hugged her tight, squeezing her tiny body in his arms.

"Dad! Where were you?"

Suman sniffled in the air between them and cleared his throat. His voice came out between a few choked-down sobs.

"I was...just out for...a walk."

"I was so scared, Dad. Everything was moving so much."

"How do you feel now?" He asked.

"Better," she replied. "Now, much better!"

Sanjana arrived next to them, taking Suman by the arm. She looked deep into his eyes, her whole face glowing, tears passing over her smiling mouth. She moved in front of him, hugging their little girl between them.

Suman could feel his heart beating through his jacket, through Maya, and reflecting off the beats of Sanjana's own heart. His throbbing headache evaporated and his head shed the burdens of anxiety and worry.

"You're crushing me!" Maya exclaimed, her tiny voice muffled in his chest.

They stepped apart and set her down on the road. Sanjana hadn't attempted to cease staring into Suman's eyes. The strength of such a look seeped through his skin and found its way to his heart and into every vein of his body. For Suman, everything stood still and time seemed to lose its hold on their moment, fading away into irrelevance.

"Come on, Dad!" Maya broke their silence again. "Mom cooked for everyone." With that, she bounded back down the path to the house, scooting in next to Khayo, who looked up, beaming from ear to ear.

"I wasn't worried, you know," Sanjana said.

Suman looked back at her, his ears patiently waiting.

"I felt you were ok," she continued. "I knew you were coming back to us."

"How are you, my love?" He asked.

"We are fine. There was enough time to get out of the house. We stood on the streets until dawn with everyone…" Sanjana's gaze found the ground between them.

"What is it?" Suman searched her face.

"Someone didn't make it…the woman, the one you told me no longer sat on the chair outside her house…near the land…she was inside when her house collapsed."

Suman breathed out deeply, looking up to the sky above them. Overhead two birds chased each other, darting upwards then spiraling down towards the village, then back up again. Behind them, branches from the top of a tree rustled in a gentle breeze. In the distance, a yak bellowed.

"We will hold a ceremony for her…" Suman spoke, finding his words slightly hollow, but couldn't find any other words for the woman he had last seen through a window. "…for her, and for Ukali."

Sanjana's hand had found his own as he spoke, and at the last word, she squeezed his hand delicately.

"Tauko…" he began.

"I know, we saw the jeep that took him down the valley. He'll be ok, Suman."

Suman nodded. His mind flashed to the night before. The knife in Tauko's hands. The tears building in his friend's eyes before everything around them shook. He swallowed the vision. What transpired in that watchtower was the act of a desperate man, pushed to the edge of a force that he could not control. But Suman also knew how quickly change could come. He

343

had silently learned from watching Sanjana over the years. He held onto an image of Tauko's face, smiling, gazing over their valley from his plot of land. Somewhere deep in Suman, he knew that Tauko was still that man smiling above his crops, he knew the cycles of the change that could come for them all, and he knew all he had to do in that brief moment was wait to see that smile again.

"What do we do now?" Sanjana's voice brought Suman out of his contemplation. Her eyes were holding steadily, watching his own. In her eyes, he felt steady too. He kept his eyes fixed on hers, noticing the beauty within them radiating throughout her whole face. Her face was still the most beautiful thing he had ever seen, and with one glance, she could still make him blush like a teenager in love. Beyond her face, the gentle soul that illuminated the vivid colors of her eyes gave him the deepest sense of the beauty that the whole world could hold.

"We do what we can. We rebuild. Everything." He said.

"We can fit a family or two in our house," Sanjana added, gesturing with her head back to the group standing around Khayo and Maya.

"I love you."

XXIV

Jiang was standing just behind the faded yellow line at the edge of platform number 4 in the largest train station in the city. It serviced other cities and counties in most directions of the vast country. The platform was full of moving bodies, swarm after swarm in the ebb and flow of arrivals and departures. Every few seconds someone brushed against Jiang's arm, once almost making him lose his stance over the brown suitcase between his legs. Inside the suitcase was pretty much everything Jiang owned, or at least after days of careful consideration, he decided it was everything worth owning.

The train in front of him, a high-speed marvel of engineering, reflected the platform's fluorescent lights easily off its fresh white and blue paint. The train had already blown its first boarding whistle, and before too long, it'd sound the final warning. Jiang wasn't sure how long between the first and last whistles, but now he was wishing the clocks would stop and that interval of time would stretch on for as long as he needed. Suddenly the accumulation of all those last days, no, months, or perhaps his entire life has seemed to have led him to this point of decision-making. His mind flashed through the two clearest choices laid out before him, so clear and so different, each with its own merits and possibilities of disastrous consequences. Jiang was frozen. To the busy human bees buzzing onto and off the platform, he must have looked like some kind of living statue performer, but inside his mind, he was as busy as the world outside. Pulled now from the unknown realm of the future, his mind quickly jumped back into the past, and to everything that had happened since he'd left that little valley and the twisted corpse of a dam.

☼☼☼

When he was discharged from the medical tent, he was brought to the head office of the hydro-power company. Outside the little trailer that held the office was still complete chaos. Rescue workers ran towards the dam, and stretchers carried others from the wreckage. Trucks and Jeeps moved constantly, and voices were carried across the scene by megaphones. Inside the trailer, men in tailored gray and black suits typed furiously on computers and spoke into satellite phones. It was clear to Jiang that while the physical mess and injuries were outside, the financial mess of the natural disaster was at play in front of him.

As Jiang began to understand, he had sustained a form of injury, which seemed to worry the manager he was speaking to quite gravely. The words "compensation" and "sympathetic" were repeated throughout the speech laid out before him. For Jiang, his head still felt like it was lying on the pillow inside the medical tent, soaking in a fog of shock and disbelief. He remembered wondering if he had a concussion.

When he finally did leave the dam site, he was light three fingers on his right hand, but his pockets were heavy with the first round of corporate compensation for injury at his workplace. A representative of the company's legal section explained that two workers had died from their injuries during the earthquake, and several more were injured enough to warrant extra time recovering in a local hospital. Because Jiang's injury, although it was severe and irrecoverable (the lawyer had tried to joke that science still hadn't found a way to grow new human fingers), he did not need extra time to recover locally and would be the first employee to be sent home. In exchange for Jiang's cooperation and for speaking positively about the reactions of his employers in the aftermath of the disaster, he would be well-compensated, more than triple what his annual salary would have been. Jiang remembered trying to laugh to himself during the drive to the airport. Three salaries. One for each finger. He felt numb to the loss in those first hours.

A legal representative from the office joined Jiang on the long journey to the nearest airport. The road was bumpy and hardly ever led them in a straight line. Once outside of the capital city, the tires from the company car were still kicking up dust even though they had been on a paved road for the previous hour. To Jiang, it seemed like the rising urbanization around him had been transplanted directly onto a vast open field. The driver of the car calmly yanked at the steering wheel, swerving around motorcycles, pedestrians, and the odd farm animal. The driver's relaxed demeanor and slackened face were an implausible contrast to the jostling and lurching of the vehicles around him. Jiang held onto the inside railing of the car with his fully functional hand, breathing deeply through each near miss of something or someone on the road. The legal rep, who rode up front, also held on, and Jiang could see his eyes shut quickly on each swerve.

When they neared the airport, they were again reminded of the earthquake. Many of the houses leading up to the fenced airport apron were damaged, and some had completely collapsed. But on the other side of the fence, planes stood, waiting outside of unscathed terminals, as the quake had apparently failed to jump the fence.

"The airport and most other modern structures weren't damaged," reported the man up front, who had turned around to face Jiang. "I called ahead to make sure. They've added some flights to move around emergency personnel," he added.

Jiang kept his eyes out the window. Over a taxiing Dragon Air aircraft, he could see the foothills of the Himalayas in the distance. The clouds above them were thickening, but several strands of sunlight pushed through, acting like slow-motion searchlights from the heavens. Somewhere up there, he thought, Suman and his family were picking up pieces of their broken village. He was feeling a tinge of guilt stuck in his throat. He was being escorted to the airport immediately, paid off handsomely, and could be whisked away from disaster almost instantly. The last 24 hours had brought Jiang village wisdom, an attacker with a knife, a natural disaster, a less useful hand, and a pocket full of cash. He purposefully shook his head from side to side. He couldn't yet begin to process all the events of the last day, then the man up front had begun to talk again.

"...and in case the media meets you on the other end..."

"...we've spoken to your father, he's..."

"...if anyone asks, you sh..."

Jiang only caught quick sections from the rambling man's speech in the front seat. He had kept his eyes glued to the scenery through the window. Now and then, he caught a glimpse of a snowy peak. When silence returned to the inside of the car, Jiang realized that the driver had already parked outside the departure hall.

Jiang had never flown in an airplane before, and although it initially worried him, he doubted that it could be any worse than tectonic plates shifting underneath him. He instead became a little excited about what the world looked like from the sky.

But soon after take-off, his busy mind shut down, the adrenaline of the last day wore off without warning, and Jiang slept through his entire first flight. He was lost somewhere in his dreams when a flight attendant poked him with a bony finger. They had already landed, and the man next to him seemed to be almost growling with annoyance, as Jiang had apparently been blocking his exit from the plane. Jiang managed to wake up his legs and feet, then shuffled, off-balance, through the cabin into the next airport. Like a futuristic portal, Jiang entered the door of one airport and suddenly was walking out the door of another. It was initially difficult to ascertain whether he was still dreaming.

Suddenly he was surrounded by familiar words and the oscillating tones of his language. People around him looked more like his family and less like Suman's. He wasn't sure exactly where he was, but it felt more familiar than where he'd come from. Inside his pocket, next to a stack of bills for travel expenses, he had a detailed list of steps that would take him from the airport to his home. The man from the company insisted, wanting Jiang's journey home to be as smooth as possible. Luckily, there was no media waiting for him in the airport, as he had been warned could happen. No cameras, nobody there to ask him anything.

Two buses later, Jiang stood outside his apartment building. It felt like a lifetime since he was home. An uncomfortable sensation crept over him as he stood on the sidewalk outside. Had he really left at all? Was it all some twisted dream? The corners of the building had the same amount of paint peeled from them, the nets on the basketball hoop rims still hadn't been replaced, and even the bushes that lined the sidewalk looked like they hadn't grown at all. Jiang looked up towards the floor that held their apartment. A slice of sunshine gleamed from around the corner of the structure, forcing Jiang to shield his face with his right hand. The bandages still covered his missing fingers. He wished it had really been a dream.

He pushed open the entrance door with his shoulder and dragged his suitcase in behind him until the little wheels on the bottom of the suitcase became momentarily stuck on the door frame. Every step and tug at his suitcase, through the doors, and up the stairwell, required a stronger effort from his one useful arm and legs. By the time he arrived at the front door, he was ready to collapse.

He figured his father had already been told that he would be coming home. Before he knocked, he wondered whether he should talk about the money or his injury first. The nerves in his hands and stomach tingled with the anticipation of seeing his father. He would at least ask to visit his mother at the hospital as soon as they could.

After knocking three times on the metal door, he heard footsteps and then saw a flash of a shadow cross the peephole in the center of the door. Then, there was a muffled scream from behind the door, but it was a strange sound. He couldn't recognize the voice. It wasn't his father, surely, he'd never heard the man make a sound like that before. When the door swung open and his mother stood in the threshold with her hands on her hips, Jiang burst into tears.

He completely broke down in her arms. He cried and between sobs, told her everything. The terrifying night with his throat almost cut open, the wreckage of the dam and the screams from the workers crying over their dead in the morning, the pain in Suman's eyes in the medical tent, and the devastating loss of his fingers. The loneliness and loss that met him in that distant place. Every word that she tried to soothe him with only made him cry harder. His stomach hurt, his head and disfigured hand throbbed. They held each other in the doorway for so long that Jiang's knees began to feel weak from the outpouring of emotion.

Eventually, he was led inside. When his tears finally dried up and he had spilled out his hurt and heart into his consoling mother's ears, he managed to find out why she was already home in the apartment.

During the last week, while Jiang had contemplated his existence in a tiny watchtower deep in the mountains, his mother was released from the hospital. Her cancer had gone into remission. The treatment was working, and the doctors said that each day looked better than the last. They hoped for a complete recovery and had no doubts, considering Hien's mood was constantly improving at the same time.

"It was your letters!" His mother exclaimed during Jiang's first dinner home.

"The medicine may have helped a bit too, Hien." His father offered, his eyes reading over a letter from his employers that Jiang had produced.

Hien ignored him and continued. "Every time I felt upset, I would read one of your letters you sent from the dam. I didn't expect they would give you so much responsibility, but we were very proud."

Jiang blushed. He thought about the romance novels and lame old movies that kept him sane in that little room.

"I guess they appreciated your work too," his father said. "This compensation package is pretty impressive."

"Well, I did lose three…"

"We're very proud, and so thrilled to see you home safely." Hien moved around the table and squeezed Jiang tightly. In the embrace, she whispered that his father was proud too and really did feel sorry for his loss.

Jiang learned that Li Jie had been released from prison, not too long after he'd left. He had called about Jiang's well-being several times and left an address and phone number. Jiang learned that Li Jie had moved out of his parent's house and into a different district. After his mother offered it to him, Jiang turned the note card with the new address over in his hand. He decided to wait a day or two before trying to contact his old friend. All he really wanted to do that first night home was to fall into a deep sleep, perhaps even a small coma, and just be absolutely sure that he wasn't, in fact, dreaming all along.

When he did finally feel rested enough to venture out of the apartment, he had slept most of the 48 hours he'd been at home. Jiang loaded his old school bag with two water bottles and a handful of snacks. After all the traveling, he decided to walk as much as he could on the way over to Li Jie's new place. He found that he only needed to take one bus if he managed two or so hours on foot. From the city map he had laid across his bed, he found that the most direct route crossed a forested hill and a couple of little parks. Jiang's mind was still in the dam's valley, somewhere between the evergreen trees and the millions of stars overhead. The idea of crossing an enormous city slightly terrified him, but he figured if he could carve the maximum amount of greenery into the route, he might make the journey somewhat pleasant.

As he approached the front door, his father stopped him with a soft hand on his shoulder.

"I want to talk to you about something."

The words held briefly in the air between them. Jiang sensed something serious behind the words. But his momentum was already pushing him through the door and down the first flight of stairs.

"Can we wait until I'm back? I'll be home for dinner."

The eyebrows above his father's eyes shifted slightly, as if they hinted at a thought that crossed his mind, but it was quickly rejected by a muscle twitch. He held Jiang's attention for a moment until finally the muscles behind his cheeks relaxed, and he smiled at his son.

"Sure. I'll be here."

Jiang took to the staircase with a spring in his legs, skipping every other step down each floor. His still bandaged hand trailed somewhat behind, sliding along a metal handrail attached to the plastered wall. At the final flight of stairs, he swung his legs over the last five steps by holding both hands out, pushing against the walls on either side and letting the built-up propulsion carry his weight ahead. It was a practiced move and he was pleased at the realization that he still possessed this youthful burst of energy and it could be summoned when needed.

The enthusiastic pace carried into his walk along the sidewalk outside his building. He felt like the protagonist in an adventure novel, returning home, still full of adrenaline from the voyage. Sure, he was slightly maimed during a crusade, as were most heroes in the novels he'd read, but he had matured and by journeying through an adventure as he had, was full of new, cultured wisdom about the greater world. The one thing he needed now was to relate the details of an adventure with the protagonist's best friend.

His mind wound itself through fragments of the events that he'd been through since he'd last seen Li Jie, his thoughts pouring through information, seemingly without much cognitive assistance from himself. It was just a natural flow of introspection that he was getting used to. His walk through a forested park, down several long avenues, twisting through crowds of people all blurred into the smallest sliver of pages in the book of this adventurous hero's journey. Jiang was riding the thrill of having survived an ordeal as he had and writing his own book simultaneously. His mind was nearly separated completely from his earthly self when suddenly he found himself at the entrance of Li Jie's building.

He pulled out a piece of paper with the address written on it, noted the apartment number, and reached the line of buttons next to the entrance door. After a couple of seconds, the entrance buzzed and unlocked. Jiang, now feeling more present and emerging from his hazy, dream-like walk, pulled at the door and slipped inside.

When he pressed the doorbell button next to Li Jie's door, he could hear his friend shuffling around, steps coming closer and closer. The door opened and the familiar face appeared, Jiang couldn't help but laugh at the high-pitched sound that sprung out from the shock in Li Jie's voice.

"Eeek! Jiang! What the hell! I thought you were the pizza guy!"

They embraced in the hallway, and Jiang was quickly ushered inside.

"Come, come in, man. Holy shit, I didn't expect that, wow." Li Jie kicked a few pieces of clothing that were left on the floor, clearing the path into a studio apartment. "Sorry, I'm a slob. I never noticed really until I lived on my own."

Jiang found space on a sofa in the corner of the room and Li Jie hopped onto the edge of his bed, brushing a few books to the floor as he sat.

"Tell me everything, man," Jiang began. "I left so soon after the protest, that I lost out on everything that happened afterwards."

"Wow, what a thing, right? I figured I was done for. When they put me in the back of that police wagon, I thought that was it. I'd be disappeared to some far corner of the country and never see my family again."

Li Jie shifted his legs around as he spoke, eventually settling into a cross-legged position.

"And Steven? The others?" Jiang asked.

"Steven's out. You know, he was in the hospital longer than he was in with the police. He had a broken nose, and concussion, and lost a few teeth. Pretty rough, but now that everyone is free again, I think I can speak for most, we're feeling more determined. More than ever. But we have to be more careful too. We have plans, Jiang. Right now, we're totally being watched closely. Steve figures that since we're first timers, like first time being arrested, they let us go and are watching our every move. My phone's tapped for sure, and I have to be careful what I write online and all that. Me and the others, we only talk in person now. I moved over here because I think they probably wired my parent's house. As well, I don't want them to get into trouble or anything."

Jiang was taking it all in. He had to blink his eyes a few times to help process everything. "What's your plan?" He managed to ask. Before Li Jie could speak, the doorbell rang out. Li Jie returned to the front door and tapped a small button near the light switch.

"There's the pizza," he said, from across the room. "Nice timing, man. I got a big one. But wait, I don't want to say anything more, until you tell me what the heck happened to you. I mean, I heard a bit from your mom, yeah, but tell me, man."

Jiang blushed a little, he tried to hold his thoughts from straying back into his adventure novel role-playing world.

"And first," Li Jie said, thumbing through a wallet and removing a few paper notes. "Tell me why your hand is all bandaged up like that."

Between mouthfuls of a mushroom and sausage pizza, Jiang divulged his entire saga, starting with the abnormally concise job interview for the security firm. He relayed his first impressions of the Himalayan valley after the long drive, and how he eventually found himself starting to know the villagers and their lives more intimately. He told Li Jie everything he learned about how dams create electricity and what the crew of the dam was like. When he eventually came to the night of the knife attack and earthquake, he had Li Jie nearly sliding off the edge of his bed with anticipation. His friend had stopped eating his half of the pizza a while before and was holding his hand over his mouth for some time. Then Jiang held up his hand.

"Three fingers man, and I did everything with this hand."

Li Jie shook his head and clicked his tongue. "How do you feel, coming back here?"

Jiang breathed in deeply, taking his time to answer. He had been musing over his understanding of the past events, ever since that first morning in the medical tent and was just beginning to find words to piece his reflections together.

"At first, I think I was in shock. The earthquake, almost

getting cut with that knife…I was a little angry as well. I thought, why me? How did I end up in that situation? So far from here, all some bizarre build-up of possibilities for how my life would turn out. But then, when I passed through the village for the last time, something became clear. I was meant to be there. I had to be there. Instead of being arrested with you guys, I was meant to run away from that protest, because I had to end up in that village. It was such a reflection of our old village, your dad's rice fields, and the old house my grandfather built."

Li Jie silently chewed another slice of pizza, keeping his eyes fixed on Jiang.

"I think I lost a piece of me when we all moved here. I lost this interest in simplicity. Everything in the city here is about stimulation, one hundred percent of the time. Our phones, movies, those video games we used to play. Kids in that village were still happy just chasing each other. It was so…well, refreshing to see. Now we are here, trying to fight against this invisible force of control that we call the government. Something that is so complex when I try to dissect it. Meanwhile, we are using so much energy, electricity, that tiny little villages like ours, are being sucked up in the process. When those people, Suman and the rest, told me that people were changing because they never had power before, I thought about my dad. How depressed he became when we left the farm. How strange I felt at first….It's like my teachers told me, that we need to modernize. But I'm not sure anymore. I don't know if what we are doing here is better than what those people are doing, down there, in those mountains…"

"I get you, Jiang," Li Jie said, wiping his hands off on his trousers. "The way the world is structured is totally out of balance. Little people shouldn't have to be screwed for other people to live. There should be a way for everyone to benefit and everyone to be able to pursue the life they want. Which is why we need to fight. The police, these politicians, they don't give a damn about your picturesque little countryside world. The machine world, the industrial world you're in is the king, and they want profits and the little people can go to hell!"

Li Jie was standing on his bed, holding a finger to the ceiling to punctuate his last sentence. He looked down at Jiang, holding up his digit, shaking it up and down.

"We need to fight, Jiang. It's that, or close your eyes and roll over."

"But what if we opt out instead. If people chose a simple life. If they gave more value to growing food, to walking through a forest, there's less need for this industrial world. Less participation and less energy it needs. We can go our separate ways..."

Li Jie was shaking his head.

"...and, let me finish, when people live in simplicity, they will realize it's better."

"Oh, Jiang, my poor romantic friend. I know you said you were watching those cheesy old films in your watchtower, but damn man." Li Jie held his stomach as he laughed. "Cities already won. Since they began,

360

people rushed to move into cities. Do you think they really want to change video games for a shovel and back-breaking farm work?"

Jiang now shook his head to the side. While his friend's wisdom usually swayed him easily, everything Li Jie now spoke about began to be rejected by his own strengthening beliefs. Jiang had a simmering feeling when he first landed back in his own country, that he wasn't the same person that had left.

Jiang let loose thoughts that had been swimming around his mind. "But what have cities really won? What is the end goal for them? For all of us? From our early days here, I've been led to believe that our society is working towards some sort of progress. I hear that word constantly. An agricultural society is progressing into an industrial one. Comfort and standard of living are progressing…and so on. But what if progress is just an illusion?"

"Maybe. But believe me, Jiang," Li Jie said. "I would love to have stayed where we grew up. Pop out some kids and teach them to dive into the river. But that wasn't our fate. Like you said, you were meant to travel where you did. Something led you to work at that dam, meet those people…"

"If I was meant to, it wasn't to end up in a specific destination or state of being. Humans act as if there is some final goal to strive towards. Some finish line. The way I see it, there are only two facts of life. First, things change over time. Nothing is ever constant. Second, that we are all only guaranteed one destination: death. That's the only place we can progress towards.

Everything else is just noise. Little stories people make up along the way. We only have this one body to live, then at the end, we die. Human's constantly step on each other for their own gains, trying to live better than the others around them. But everyone is on the same path. We come into the world with nothing, and leave with nothing. So, what is progress really? Because we cannot alter our final goal. No matter what we change, the ending is the same."

Li Jie nodded, seeming to understand more than Jiang imagined he would. "For me, I feel the calling to change something during my lifetime. I cannot just relax and go about my life forgetting all the evil in the world. I was meant to be here, in this body. I'm not a kid anymore, and this is my city. So, I'll have to fight to make it better. You should think about that too. How you want to spend your time before death. I wanted to tell you that we're going underground soon. The whole group, and several more that we met since then. From next week, I'll be very difficult to find."

Jiang chewed over the words for a moment before he spoke. "Man, I hear you, I do. Part of me feels that way too, but I don't know if I feel it like you do. You got the passion, for sure, but I feel all mixed up…"

"You had a crazy adventure, man!" Li Jie interrupted. "Hey, I'm not judging you or anything. But I remembered seeing you at the protest. You were great with that camera. I'm sure you haven't seen, but your photos were published. A few newspapers in Europe and the U.S. used them. You did good, man. I'm telling you all this now, because your timing is absolutely amazing."

"Like how I planned to come over once I knew you ordered a pizza?" Jiang joked.

"Exactly!" Li Jie smiled. "How you came back home just in time to go underground with us. To continue the fight. To give regular people, like you and your farmers a voice in this country. The government's idea of progress is a total lie. Our progress would be real. It would help everyone."

The room stayed silent. Jiang was deep in his thoughts again. He kept hearing his own words over and over again. *Progress is an illusion.* He wished that he could say more. To explain better. Maybe his friend was right, or maybe he was just as lost as Jiang. Either way, Jiang felt there wasn't much left to say. He needed more time to think.

☼☼☼

When Jiang opened the door to his parent's apartment later that evening, his friend's words were still reverberating inside his skull. His anxious mind could hardly take more information to process and he imagined the recent additions to just be bouncing around his brain but not yet being absorbed. All of a sudden, he wanted to be back in his security guard uniform. He wanted to hold onto that ice-cold railing and look up at the stars. He wanted to be lonely in that little room again. With nothing to do but stay awake.

But his desires evaporated with another strong-armed hug from his mother. She'd noticed him daydreaming under the door frame and pulled him in as close as was humanly possible. He pulled away before the tears that were building up in his eyes could make a break for his cheeks.

"Hey Mom, I missed you too."

"Come to the kitchen and join us," she said, leaning in to whisper. "Your father is very excited to speak to you."

Before Jiang could surmise the nature of his parent's excitement, a chair was pulled out for him, and he found himself seated at the opposite end of the table with his family, as if he was about to be interrogated for something. A foreboding and confusing feeling of dread crept up his spine. *What did I do?*

"Jiang." His father spoke first. "Since we first came to this city, I know we haven't exactly lived as well as some of your friends do."

Jiang tilted his head to the side, not understanding.

"We know you didn't bring other kids over often, because, well, our apartment is old and we never bought you exciting toys." His mother added.

Jiang still looked on without responding.

"It's fine, Jiang," his father continued. "It's just time to explain. We've been saving. Every paycheck. Every government stipend, we put some away." Both of Jiang's parents had their hands interlocked on the top of the table.

"We were saving up to buy another piece of land. To get out of this city, to move somewhere else, to be surrounded by animals and farmland again. To hear the sounds of a wild creek, instead of all these damn car horns. We have been saving and saving, and well, you know, your mother's medical bills set us all back quite a bit. I mean…it did also cost you three fingers…"

His mother nodded. "We are so proud of you, Jiang," she affirmed. "You really helped our family so much. We know what it took for you to get all the money your company is paying you…"

"We want to ask you again for help, son. Your mother and I have nearly enough to resettle in the countryside again. If we can use, I don't know, probably a good portion of your compensation package, we can do it! We can leave this old, depressing apartment forever and plant a garden again. We know the place too. Some of our old neighbors went there years ago. It'll be great, Jiang. You can come, obviously. But we spoke too, and if you want to stay in the city, we can figure out something. This place is already rented through the year, and…"

Jiang didn't realize it at first, but he had stood up from his chair. Both of his hands were covering his mouth. Some loose strands of his bandaged hand were tickling the front of his neck. His parents became quiet, they kept their eyes on his own, and in an instant, this soundless void that was enveloping them all sucked every consideration out of his mind. He looked at them, and they watched him in return. The room remained completely still, and he realized that it was the most static point in time Jiang had ever experienced. It was a juncture of nothing and everything at once, like a point of reference that pointed to itself. In the same moment, Jiang felt soft, flexible, as if he was a pillow for his own head. He knew the money mattered the least of all. Of course, he would free his parents from the misery of the apartment they endured to build upon their dream. For his own decision, he chose not to decide in that silent, comfortable moment, but instead to remain in the luxurious moment of new-found clarity and of the success of his parent's dream.

☼☼☼

The second whistle for the train boarding on platform number 4 sounded louder than the first. It began to break the ice that was forming around Jiang's indecisive mind. He tipped his feet up on their toes over the faded yellow line, then rested them back down on his heels. He looked down toward his hands. Now uncovered, he watched as he made his disfigured right hand form a pinching movement. He missed the bandages and felt the path to being accustomed to his crab-like hand was going to be longer than he could imagine.

He stuck his hand in his pocket and looked back up. In

the doorway of the train, his parents were both watching him. He'd packed his bag soon after he told them they could have every cent that he earned from the dam. But he never said any confirmation that he would be joining them in the countryside. It was because he still was deciding.

A week, Li Jie had said. One week and they'll be underground, and perhaps unreachable until Jiang would read about them on the news. Jiang felt so small when he stood on that massive dam in the mountains. That enormous feat of human engineering sandwiched between a tiny valley among the tallest mountains in the world. When he survived the earthquake, he had felt he'd grown a little bit. He had felt powerful. He'd lived an adventure that he could not have imagined he'd ever experience. But when he came back to the city, he felt excruciatingly small again. His friend's fight against the system, against the state, felt insurmountable. The train and the countryside beckoned. He could nearly smell the dirt that he would shake off his clothes before coming indoors. The chickens talking in the morning, and the sucking sound of boots lifting out of a muddy field. Then again, would passing his days, watching hens peck the ground, be an adventure that would make him feel powerful again?

The accumulation of all those last months, or perhaps his entire life seemed to have led him to this point of decision making. His mind reviewed the two choices laid out before him, so distinct and so...

The final whistle blew across the platform and cut right through Jiang's thoughts. It was time to decide.

XXV

Maya cradled a heavy mud brick in her arms like it was a precious toy. She stepped carefully over the tools that lay on the ground in the shadow of a broken wall. She retraced the steps she had just taken when she moved the previous brick away from the congestion of adult bodies. When she reached the growing pile of bricks, resting safely on the cobbled street outside, she placed the brick she held carefully on top of the pile. She looked down at her dirty hands, then calmly brushed them off on the lower part of her dress. Then she wiped a small bead of sweat that had just begun to cross her forehead. From the street, she could see her father, who was carrying a large wooden post with one of her uncles. When he set the post down, he noticed her staring at him. His mouth formed a broad smile and he motioned her over to him.

"How many bricks, so far?" He asked.

She used her thumb to count on the fingers of her other hand.

"Fifty-two. No, wait, Fifty-three!" She answered, putting her hands on her hips and puffing out her chest.

"Excellent! And how many until we can call it a day?"

Maya rolled her eyes at her father and kicked a little at the air between them.

"You know!" She giggled. "I have at least…at least a thousand to go! We can't stop until everybody's house is fixed!"

"That's my girl," Suman smiled and bent down next to her. "But, if we can take a break, today, let's say after twenty or so more bricks, there's something I really want to show you."

Maya stroked imaginary hair on her chin, trying to suppress a smile by pressing her lips together. "Ok…but I should get back to work." She snorted a little laugh through her nose as she bounded back to the ruin of a house. Suman smiled and saluted her with one hand as she went.

When his eyes moved from the wreckage and group of neighbors, hustling to remove and organize the pile of debris before them, he saw a small figure in the distance. One man was walking up the road, just entering the village from the lower end. Suman recognized the jacket the man was wearing instantly, but the man was walking with a limp he didn't recognize. Suman started a slow jog over to meet him.

Tauko stopped and leaned on the nearest stone wall as he watched Suman coming towards him. He reached into his pocket to fish out a small box of matches. He pulled a bent cigarette from his shirt pocket, straightened it, and lit it with a match. Then he blew a small stream of smoke at the ground and raised his head to find Suman's eyes already on him.

"I'm going to stop the smoking soon," Tauko said. "I already promised my family."

"I didn't say anything." Suman smiled at him, then stepped forward to hug Tauko. He held his friend for a few long seconds before releasing him.

Tauko wiped at the corner of his eye with a sleeve. "It's good to see you, Suman."

"You as well. How are you? You've been away for quite a while."

Tauko smiled and looked down at his leg and lifted up part of his pants. Under the pants, he showed Suman a long scar on his leg. He tapped his leg with his knuckles.

"They had to rebuild part of my leg. They put pieces of metal where my bones should be." Tauko saw Suman's face start to distort with worry, his friend's forehead crinkled with deep lines. "Don't worry, I'm fine. I'm getting used to walking with it already. It's a small price to pay for everything I've done…"

"Tauko, it's fine…"

"No, Suman." Tauko raised up a hand. "I was

completely taken over by my anger. I was angry at the dam, at Ukali, and I'm ashamed to admit but at you for not helping me try to destroy everything. I've had plenty of time to think. You saved me in the end, Suman. If you didn't show up when you did, I don't know what would have happened. If that earthquake came and that boy got more hurt..." Tauko wiped at his eyes again.

"It's fine, Tauko. I know that you were struggling, I..."

"You've always been there, Suman. I just...Well, I lost myself for a while. I went crazy and now I've come out of the other side. And I want to make it right. Anything, you say it, and you have my hands to help you."

Suman placed his hand on his friend's shoulder, then looked back at the crowd shifting the pieces of their devastated homes around. His eyes followed the procession of houses along the street, just barely making out the top of his thatched roof.

"Right now, Tauko, all we have to do is rebuild. Rebuild everything for our friends and our neighbors." He paused and began to smile wide at Tauko. "I'm really glad you have two legs, my friend, because this will be a lot of work."

The two men walked up the street towards the rest of the village, with one arm around Tauko's back, Suman took a little weight off the injured leg. When they reached the ruined house, Tauko moved through the crowd, greeting the villagers, one by one. Suman stood back and watched for a moment, taking the whole scene in. They lost a couple of the members of their tiny valley to the disaster, and their homes had seen some destruction that none of them considered possible. The force that caused the damage, to their village, to the dam, and to what he'd heard happened to parts of the city, felt so powerful that Suman questioned whether the force had really come from the earth itself.

When he looked around him, he did see the tragedy that fell over some of them, but he also saw the incredible fortune they now held as well. Many more could have died, of course, but without thinking too deeply about it, he did realize that his family was very lucky. But more than their luck, he recognized a force more vigorous than the earthquake. His village was different than it'd been before the disaster. The addition of electricity and technology into their world had begun to isolate them from each other, even making some of them lose the reigns of their own mental peace. It drove his closest friend mad with vengeance and frustration. But the disaster, this violent shaking of the earth, of their world, shook away the alienation that was beginning to plague the village. He could barely remember a time when he saw the entire community working together so closely. Instead of crying over the destruction, he watched as his neighbors laughed and chatted through the cumbersome and difficult work ahead.

The common struggle that awaited them, for as long as it was going to take, was indeed a force that was uniting them again. Not long ago, his mind was constantly at odds with the ripples of problems he saw building up across their valley. Now, he felt calm. The space between his ears was at peace.

Something pulled at the sleeve of his coat. He looked down to see his daughter looking up at him, one hand on his coat and the other picking her nose.

"You wanted to tell me something?" She pulled at his sleeve again.

Suman reached into his pocket and pulled something small out. He kissed Maya's head and slowly got down on his knee to look her in the eyes.

"I want to give you something, my magic girl." She watched him carefully.

Suman held out his hand to reveal the heart-shaped rock she had given him over a year before. She noticed the new writing on her rock and traced the letters with one finger.

"That's me!" She exclaimed, looking up at him. He saw a few smears of mud on her forehead and smiling cheeks. "How did you do that?" Suman smiled back at her.

"It's a family secret, and I'll tell you. But you have to promise to listen carefully." Maya nodded, a serious, concentrated look hardening in her eyes.

"I'll listen," she said softly, almost whispering.

"Alright, but first, I need to show you where we carve these stones. It's a little walk up that hillside." He pointed through the village, towards his favorite perch above the gardens and orchards.

"Ok, I've finished carrying bricks for today, I think." Maya patted her hands together in front of her, slapping off traces of dust.

They left the movement and sounds of construction behind them and wound around the first corner of the street. There, as if she was waiting for them, Sanjana was leaning against a wall.

"Where are you two going?" She inquired.

"It's a family secret!" Maya let out, then quickly shut her mouth. She skipped over to her mother and leaned in closely. "It's a family secret," she whispered. Sanjana arched an eyebrow, moved to face Suman, then winked.

"Really?" She turned back to Maya. "Then who am I to you?"

Maya slapped her cheek lightly and let out a quick breath. "You're right!" Spinning around, she motioned to Suman to come closer. "We need to tell Mom too," she declared. "She is family, you know…"

Suman laughed and put his arm around Sanjana, who patted him on the chest with her hand and reached down to grab Maya's hand with the other. When Suman found her eyes, she started to laugh too, throwing her head back.

"Let's go!"

The valley before them folded open, clusters of trees converging upwards, as the three of them merged into the cradle of the mountains. The peaks above them rose with every step forward. Thin wisps of clouds meandered in the dark blue void of sky above. Although they couldn't see through the thick forest growth below them, where the river was hiding, during the brief pauses between their footsteps, it reminded them of its presence, sending surges of sound up the hillside. Water collided with stone, a constant pumping of the mountain's veins over the rough landscape. Behind them, the sun drifted cautiously towards the land below it. As his family climbed upwards, about to reach the first hill outside of the village, Suman sensed the sunlight touch his back. He took his eyes from his feet and lifted them towards Chatima. He saw its rock-covered ridge glowing gold.

☼☼☼